For Lisa, Alice and Will - as everything is
For Kath and Eli Middleton
For Keith and Barbara
For Lee Beddow and the team at AbbeySound Audio

I'D LIKE TO ACKNOWLEDGE THE SUPPORT OF THESE READERS

Ben Peyton, Xavier Hodencq, Sara, Summer, and Tommy Feeny-Marks, Phillip Greig, Bev Kingscote-Davies and Evie, Sally Orchard, Lynda Brown, Phil Jones, Leah Alvarado, Katina Zaninovich Reich, Pauline Beattie, Dawn, Skye and Hayden Hills, Douglas Sims, Sheelagh Rogers, Stacy Parr, Sarah, Michael and Madison Murphy, Carol Day, Wendi Morris, Joshua Dawson, Carol Ardeeser, Pauline Beattie, Mary Atkinson, Mike Eldred, Gayle Migliorini Hillman, Dave and Emily Boyden, Anneliese Neu, Freya Cushley, Angela Baker, Elouise Pedler

1

AMELIA

The Pacific Ocean. 2 July 1937

Amelia Earhart stared anxiously out of the plane's cockpit. Overcast and gloomy, the many clouds cast dark shadows on the sprawling ocean below, making them resemble tiny islands.

How she wished they were. Then she could've made an emergency landing.

At least they would've stood a chance.

Instead, they were a hundred miles from Howland Island and running out of fuel fast. Furthermore, the broken radio receiver meant they couldn't contact the U.S. Coast Guard's ship, *Itasca*, who were monitoring their navigation at this stage of the expedition.

And what an expedition it should have been.

She would've been the first female pilot to circumnavigate the globe.

But that wouldn't happen now. She and Fred Noonan, her navigator, were in serious trouble... as serious as could be.

Amelia closed her eyes for a second and made a silent

prayer. The hum of the twin-engines scratched at her ears. Ordinarily, it was her favourite sound in the world, but today it resembled the drone of a funeral dirge.

'We're in trouble, Amelia,' Fred said from the seat on her left. 'You know it, and I know it.'

'Now, Fred,' Amelia replied in her usual midwestern twang. 'I've had my fair share of airborne hitches before, and I'm still flying.' She hoped to sound more optimistic than she felt.

Fred wasn't convinced. 'We're going down, Amelia, and we're not coming back up.'

'Geez Louise, Fred,' Amelia replied. 'That's the pessimist in you talking. Besides, it's been a testing trip so far. I think we're owed a miracle.'

'Then you'd best hope it arrives in the next half hour, because that's how long until we crash into the sea.'

Amelia was about to reply when she saw something in the distance. 'I'll be a son of a biscuit!' she gasped.

A few miles ahead, a glittering green fog thickened the air.

'What the heck is that?' Fred said, equally amazed.

'I don't know,' Amelia replied. 'I ain't witnessed its like before.'

'Maybe it's that miracle you think we're owed.'

'Perhaps,' Amelia replied. 'Either way, for good or ill, there's no avoiding it.'

A short while later, the Lockheed Electra 10-E airplane vanished into the mist.

As GREENNESS ENVELOPED THE COCKPIT, Amelia felt her throat tighten. In her seventeen years as a pilot, she'd flown in all conditions - blizzards, fog, thunderstorms, heavy snow - but had seen nothing like this. She glanced at Fred, but could tell from his expression he felt the same.

Their passage through the vapour lasted less than a minute, but then, gradually, it thinned out, and the plane emerged on the other side to a different vista entirely.

'Oh – my – word!' Amelia gulped.

It was like they'd opened a door to another world.

A fierce sun dominated a cloudless azure sky, shedding a golden light on a vast tropical island on the horizon.

Dazed, Fred looked at Amelia and laughed. 'I'll be a monkey's uncle. You got your miracle.'

'I told you, Fred,' Amelia said, relief flooding her. 'Sometimes you've just gotta have faith.'

Steering them toward the island, Amelia saw thick jungle, long sandy beaches, high cliffs, and perhaps most strikingly an extinct volcano, which rose from the island's centre like a cooling tower.

'But I don't understand,' Fred said, confused. 'There's no island close to this size in this area. In fact, there's no island in this stretch of the Pacific... period.'

'Then we must not be where we think,' Amelia replied.

'I know exactly where we are.' Fred held up his time-worn map. 'And that is why I know this island should not *exist!* This ain't my first rodeo, Amelia.'

'Bless your heart, Fred, but I'm happy to trust my eyes,' Amelia said, beaming. 'Now keep a look-out for some place flat and firm, so we can land this bird and fix that dang radio. We'll be in touch with *Itasca* in two shakes of a lamb's tail.'

Amelia pulled back the throttle and manoeuvred the wheel to begin their descent.

It was then something terrifying happened.

A colossal flying creature appeared from nowhere. Its giant wings clipped the cockpit, cracking the window, before its torso spiralled into the wing, smashing into the right-side propeller.

BOOM –

– The propeller shattered. The fuel stored in the wing detonated and it exploded into flames.

'WHAT THE!' Fred yelled.

Amelia stared open-mouthed at the raging fire. Nothing could be done now.

They were going down.

Just then, the crack in the glass extended, and with a thunderous roar of incoming wind, the cabin window shattered.

Glass showered Amelia's face, slicing her skin. Air pounded her with the force of a boxer.

The plane nosedived like a missile.

Wrestling in vain with the controls, Amelia watched the ocean approach rapidly. Levelling the plane as best she could, there was no way to prevent what would happen next.

They hit the water hard.

Amelia's head snapped forward, missing the wheel by an inch. Her seatbelt sliced into her shoulders like cheese wire.

Water exploded all around, drenching the cockpit.

The plane bounced twice on the water's surface, then struck the beach at an angle.

The left wing snapped off. The plane spun wildly like a top, before its momentum decreased and it came to a slow, steady halt.

Barely conscious, Amelia tasted blood in her mouth. Through blurred eyes, she turned to her navigator. 'Fred... Fred!' she rasped.

There was no reply.

Amelia's vision sharpened, and a wave of horror swept through her.

Fred Noonan's eyes were wide open; blood pooled in the crook of his mouth. His head was twisted at an abnormal angle, his expression frozen in a chilling death mask.

'Oh, Fred... I am sorry,' Amelia breathed, tears filling her eyes.

Promptly, her survival instincts kicked in. The plane was a ticking time bomb - she had to get out... *and quick!*

Unclipping her seatbelt, she pulled herself through the window frame and onto the plane's nose. Lowering herself onto the sand, she limped away as fast as she could, trying to put as much distance between her and the plane as possible.

She'd taken about twenty steps when –

– *BOOM!*

The plane exploded in a ball of fire, blasting her off her feet.

Landing face first on the soft sand, she turned and stared at the burning wreckage, her ears ringing with a penetrating whine.

She gulped. In a matter of minutes, she'd lost everything – her friend, her plane, her radio, her expedition, her reputation. *Everything.*

Amelia stared into the jungle that lined the beach's edge. Just where was she? Was the island inhabited – and if so, by whom?

The one thing she knew for certain was she had nothing - no food, no water, no shelter, no weapons, and no way to contact the outside world.

As a thousand other questions filled her mind, she spied something on the beach a few hundred metres away, something large.

At first, she thought it was a broken section of her plane, but then another idea formed: Was it the carcass of the bird that caused the crash?

Intrigued, she pushed herself to her feet, ignoring the pain that filled her body, and stumbled toward it. As the creature came into view, however, she froze with astonishment.

It wasn't a bird at all. It was a reptile.

With giant wings, the creature had a furry torso, a stubby tail, an enormous head with a long, toothless beak, and a pointed crest to the rear of its skull.

And in her deep, paralysing shock, she was a thirteen-year-old girl again, standing beside her father, Samuel Earhart, at the American Museum of Natural History in New York. It was then she'd seen this very creature as a fossilised exhibit, and it captured her imagination like no other.

In fact, she'd often said afterwards the exhibit prompted her obsession with flight.

Still, she'd never expected to see a creature like this in the twentieth century, and certainly not in the wild. After all, its species had become extinct seventy million years ago.

Amelia Earhart was staring at a dead Pteranodon.

2

PERIL ON PERCY ISLAND

Percy Island, Australia. 1510AD

Inhaling the salted air, Jacob Schmidt sipped his Earl Grey tea and stared out at the Coral Sea. He'd never had tea before arriving in the twenty-first century as a guest of Percy Halifax, but now he'd become something of an addict.

He looked over at the building he and his wife, Maria, had occupied for the last week. A smile curled on his mouth. After all, how many people could say they'd stayed in a two-storey ski-lodge on a desert island seventy miles off the Australian coast? Even fewer could say they'd done it in the sixteenth century, two hundred and sixty years before Captain James Cook discovered the island.

He chuckled to himself.

Time travel was truly remarkable.

And what a week it had been. Despite their reasons for coming – being kidnapped, terrorised, and used as pawns in a wicked game called *The Empedoclean Trials* – he and Maria had spent a wonderful time together. They had laughed, talked, eaten good food, and enjoyed long, leisurely walks, exploring every inch of the island.

But for Jacob, the most astonishing thing occurred the previous night.

He and Maria had just finished their evening meal, and retired outside to view the sunset, when a blue whale appeared a hundred metres offshore, dipping in and out of the water's surface, singing its shrill song as if serenading the dusk.

In his seventy-six years, it was the most humbling thing he'd ever seen.

As Jacob took another sip, an image of his granddaughter, Celia, formed in his head, smiling and carefree. Guilt flooded him. She was his pride, his joy... his world. She was also brutally murdered by the Nazis in nineteen thirty-eight.

How he wished Celia could've seen the whale.

He would've happily given his own life for that.

A tear formed in his eye.

At that moment, a *SNAP* echoed from behind the lodge, bringing him back to reality. It was an arriving portravella – he knew that. Had Percy Halifax come to visit? If that were the case, had Becky and Joe Mellor made the trip, too? He hoped so. He adored them both.

Jacob climbed from his chair to greet the visitor.

Instantly, his blood turned to ice. *A stranger was approaching.*

In his mid-forties, the man wore a double-breasted tweed suit, shirt and tie, and a grey Homberg hat. He was short, slender, with gaunt features and penetrating eyes. Reaching Jacob, he spoke with a heavy German accent. 'Good morning, Herr Schmidt.'

It was then Jacob noticed the Walther P38 pistol in the man's left hand. He didn't reply.

'Do you not wish to speak with me?' the man said.

'What would you want me to say?'

'A simple *hello* would suffice,' the man replied. 'Perhaps you'd prefer we speak in German?'

Jacob ignored him. 'Who are you? What do you want?'

'It does not matter who I am,' the man replied. 'As for what I want – well, I want many things, but for now I shall make do with you and your wife.'

'What do you mean?' Jacob asked, masking the fear in his voice.

'Your holiday is at an end,' the man said. 'You will come with me at once. *The Wraith* wishes to see you.'

At hearing that name, Jacob felt nauseous. 'I will not be a player in one of his games again. I would rather die than that.'

'There is no game this time,' the man replied coldly.

'Then what does he want with us?'

'All that matters to you should be that he has no intention of harming you or your wife, providing you comply with his wishes, of course.'

Unconsciously, Jacob's eyes found the gun. He knew he had no choice but to obey. 'Then just take me,' he pleaded. 'Leave Maria here.' His lips tightened into a line. 'She cannot cope with more of this evil. It will kill her. Please... just take me.'

The man shook his head. 'I shall take you both.'

Jacob stared into the man's eyes, and recognition filled him. '*I - I know you.*'

'Perhaps you do,' the man replied. 'Perhaps you do not.'

Jacob felt a rage building within, sweeping his body like a fire. 'You are Heinrich Müller,' he said through gritted teeth. 'They called you Gestapo Müller. You were the head of the secret police. You escaped capture after the war and avoided the hangman's noose. Many believed you dead, but they never found a body.'

Müller gave an ugly smile. 'I am glad you've heard of me, because now you know I'm a serious man, and should be taken seriously.'

'I know exactly what kind of man you are,' Jacob said. 'You represent the very worst of mankind, the very filth of humanity.'

Müller cocked the pistol and pointed it at Jacob's head. 'Be careful what you say, old man. I can leave your corpse here and just take your wife. The Wraith only needs one of you.'

'Shoot me then,' Jacob replied. 'I am too old to be afraid, and I have seen too much. But I have waited for many years to say these words to someone like you. I care not about the consequences.'

'Oh, but you should care,' Müller spat.

'And yet I don't,' Jacob replied coolly. 'I saw your kind instil a cancer into my beautiful country many years ago, and I saw that cancer spread... infect... poison. Like so many others, I sat back and watched that rot set in, hoping, praying it would not take hold... and yet it did. I am and will always feel ashamed of that.'

Jacob's confidence grew with every word.

'But it is nothing compared to the shame you should feel. And what pleases me most is you failed. For all your regime's brainwashing, your bluster, your bullying - you failed.'

He sucked in a deep breath.

'And that is your legacy: *failure*. Your regime is but a cautionary tale in a history book. And as for you, Herr Müller, you are a pimple on the face of humankind. Always remember that... you are a *pimple!*' Then he spat on Müller's shoe, coating it with saliva.

Müller's face blazed with fury. His knuckles whitened on the gun's grip. His hand trembled, but he still didn't fire.

'And yet you can't shoot me?' Jacob said defiantly. 'Are you so scared of the Wraith to pull that little trigger? So, now we have learnt something else about you – you're a *feigling*... a coward. *A coward and a pimple.*'

'SHUT UP, OLD MAN!' Müller screamed.

'But I won't... I can't,' Jacob said, satisfaction in his voice. 'I speak for the many millions who are not here to speak for themselves, those that were butchered at your hands. Now take that toy and shoot me... *pimple!*' He grabbed Müller's gun and pressed the barrel to his forehead. 'Come on, *coward... feigling.* SHOOOOT ME!'

Maria was happily making gingerbread in the kitchen, listening to her music at full volume.

She didn't hear a thing.

Even when Heinrich Müller shot her husband.

3

SHOPLIFTERS OF ADDLEBURY UNITE

Present Day

A raised voice echoed off the classroom walls. '*BECKY MELLOR!*'

Becky snapped from her daze. 'Yes, sir.' She looked up at her history teacher, Mr. Hegarty, a short, squat man in a navy-blue suit two sizes too small and two decades out of date.

'Ah, you are awake then? That's nice to know,' Mr. Hegarty said smugly.

Mister Hegarty had an annoying knack of using sarcasm to compensate for his poor life choices.

'Yes, sir,' Becky replied.

'Smashing,' Mr. Hegarty replied. 'Because I wouldn't want you to miss something that might – I don't know – come up on your GCSE exam next summer. You wouldn't want that, would you?'

'No, sir.'

'Then perhaps you should concentrate on my class, instead of daydreaming about TikTok, or your next selfie.'

Mr. Hegarty's subsequent chuckle resembled the croak of a frog.

At that moment, Becky felt tempted to use her telekinesis to throw him through the window. Instead, she restrained herself and said, 'Yes, sir. Sorry, sir.'

In all fairness, Becky always found it hard to concentrate in Mr. Hegarty's class. Not only was it her last class on Friday afternoon, but as teachers went, he was both patronising and as dull as a kidney bean. Moreover, he'd been waffling on about the Dark Ages for an hour, and almost everything he'd said was plain wrong. Of course, she couldn't tell him how she knew that, how she'd visited the era a dozen times and seen first-hand the impact of Roman withdrawal on Anglo-Saxon Britain, but knowing what she knew meant his class was as useful as a blocked drain.

As Mr. Hegarty continued his lesson, Becky's thoughts returned to the previous weekend.

What a fantastic time she'd had.

After returning from their recent time hunt to get the Odin Horn, she'd spent time with the minotaurs, Edgar, Vilja, and their newborn cub, Darrian, walking the grounds of Bowen Hall, swimming in the lake, and exploring the forest. That was, until the minotaurs left to continue their journey to Caradan, an island somewhere off the coast of Sierra Leone.

When she wasn't with Edgar, she practised swordplay with her brother, Joe.

To her surprise, Joe was an excellent teacher, and after countless hours of hard work, she felt confident handling a sword against an opponent of reasonable skill.

Becky also spent time with Tusk, the legendary Viking, Ragnar Lothbrok, transformed into a squirrel by the magical snake, Jörmungandr.

She couldn't believe how well Tusk had adapted to life in the twenty-first century. He'd learned to ride a bicycle, become addicted to television soap operas, and had developed a fondness for salt and vinegar crisps, pork pies, and Ed Sheeran.

The only person Becky had seen little of was Uncle Percy. It seemed to her if he wasn't working alone in his laboratory, he was on a time trip with his new girlfriend, Felicity Butterworth. Indeed, they'd recently been on their first official date to the premiere of Gilbert and Sullivan's operetta, H.M.S. Pinafore, at the Opera Comique in London on May 25th 1878.

Becky couldn't be happier for the two of them.

One thing, however, marred her general feeling of positivity. The summer holidays had ended, and she'd returned to Coppenhill High School for her final year.

The timing couldn't have been worse. Her mother and father were still frozen in stone because of a curse by the gorgon, Medusa, and she couldn't fully concentrate on school until that situation had been reversed.

Still, she knew Uncle Percy, Felicity and the rest of GITT (the Global Institute of Time Travel) were working hard to find The Isle of the Blessed, a mythical island with an enchanted pool of water that could restore her parents to their normal selves. She had every confidence that would happen... *and happen soon.*

At that moment a distant bell rang the end of the school day.

'OKAY, EVERYONE!' Mr. Hegarty yelled over the uproar of children scrambling to pack away as quickly as they could. 'YOU MAY GO NOW!'

Not a single child listened to him. Many were already at the door.

Swiftly, Becky slid her books into her bag, threw it over her shoulder, and joined the mass of pupils desperate to get as far away from Mr. Hegarty as they could.

Becky entered the packed corridor and weaved her way to

the staircase. It was then she heard a female voice shout her name.

'*BECKS! GET OVER HERE!*'

Becky glanced over at a group of females gathered around a mobile phone, laughing hysterically.

Her friend, Emily Kumar, was holding the phone. 'COME ON, BECKS!' she yelled. 'YOU'VE GOTTA SEE THIS.'

Intrigued, Becky walked over. 'See what?'

'You know Addlebury, don't you?' Emily said. 'Isn't that where your uncle lives?'

Becky couldn't believe her ears. Emily had mentioned Addlebury – the small village a few miles from Bowen Hall. 'Yeah – well, near there... why?'

'Look!' Emily angled the phone screen toward Becky.

Becky saw the familiar *YouTube* logo and a headline in bold: '*SQUIRREL MAN OF ADDLEBURY – REAL OR FAKE?*'

Becky's jaw nearly hit the floor.

'Watch!' Emily said, hitting the play button. A video of night-time footage appeared on the screen.

Becky knew the location immediately: *Addlebury High Street*. The shot cut to a particular building, which she recognised as the local convenience store, *The One Stop Shop*. Suddenly, a second-storey window opened, and a squirrel wearing jeans and a t-shirt appeared. Walking upright, he climbed out onto the ledge, carrying a bulging sack over his shoulder.

The breath snagged in Becky's throat. She watched in disbelief as Tusk sprang onto the roof of a parked car before leaping to the ground. Then he scurried up the high street, and was lost to the night.

From every direction, laughter pounded Becky's ears.

'T-that's a real squirrel!' a girl giggled.

'Nah,' another girl said. 'It's gotta be a bloke in a squirrel suit.'

'No way,' a third girl said. 'It's too small to be a man. Plus, no human being can jump like that. It's definitely a squirrel... a squirrel in jeans. That is so weird!'

Becky was speechless.

'It's ace, isn't it, Becks?' Emily said, beaming.

'Err, yeah, it's hilarious,' Becky replied unconvincingly.

'It's got over a million hits, and it was only uploaded yesterday.'

'Er, cool.'

'Do you know the shop?' Emily asked.

'No, err, yeah. Maybe. Not sure.' Becky pretended to look at her phone. 'Oh, Joe's waiting for me in the concourse. I've got to go. See you next week.' And with that, she sprinted off. As she charged down the stairs, her head spiralled.

What was Tusk thinking?

Reaching the ground floor, she dashed into the concourse and saw Joe standing beneath a large clock, which had just turned three. She raced over to him, her face beetroot-red.

'We've got to go,' Becky panted. 'Quickly.'

Staring at Becky, concern flashed on Joe's face. 'What is it? Is everything okay?'

'Not really.' Becky pulled out her mobile phone and keyed in a search. 'Here... watch this!'

Joe watched the clip. As he did, his eyes ballooned. 'What's Tusk doing?'

'He's doing what he did in that Viking town, *Sandvik*,' Becky replied. 'He's waiting until nightfall and then popping into town to steal anything and everything he wants. He's lost his marbles.'

'How many hits has it got?' Joe asked.

'Over a million, and it was only uploaded last night.'

Joe grinned. 'Tusky's gone viral, then.'

'Yeah,' Becky replied. 'And it's not funny.'

'It's a bit funny,' Joe said.

'It's really not.'

'A little bit.'

'No.'

'Just a tad bit funny.'

'Not at all,' Becky replied. 'Uncle Percy won't be happy about this at all.'

'He'll go nuts,' Joe replied. 'And when I say nuts, I don't mean the kind squirrels eat when they're not out on the rob.' He laughed.

Becky didn't think that was funny, either.

A SHORT WHILE LATER, Becky and Joe were standing in the lounge of the family house at Lyndon Crescent. Even though the Mellors had moved into Bowen Hall now, the Manchester house was kept as a base for Becky and Joe to arrive and depart when attending school. Uncle Percy had sound-proofed the building to ensure the neighbours wouldn't hear the regular blasts from the portravellas embedded within their mobile phones.

One time hop and twenty minutes later, they were in the morning room at Bowen Hall, watching Uncle Percy glare at Tusk, who was sitting casually on the velvet chaise lounge.

'ARE YOU INSANE?' Uncle Percy shouted. 'I MEAN... GENUINELY INSANE?'

Tusk gave a dismissive wave of his paw. 'What is the basis of your rage, Englander?' he asked. 'I have done nothing wrong.'

'NOTHING WRONG? YOU'VE BEEN CAUGHT ON CAMERA STEALING ALCOHOL.'

'And crisps,' Tusk added. 'I stole many bags of salt and vinegar crisps, too. Crisps are a delicacy fit for Odin himself.'

Uncle Percy was stuck for words. 'But you can't just go around stealing things!'

Tusk looked confused. 'But I did. It was easy. I have the spoils to prove it.'

'What I mean is you shouldn't go around stealing things,' Uncle Percy clarified.

'Why not?' Tusk replied. 'I explored the land. I amassed spoils. That is the Viking way... that is *my* way.'

Uncle Percy was getting flustered now. 'They are not *spoils!*' he fired back. 'Until purchased in the correct manner, they are somebody else's property. This is the twenty-first century. You don't just steal from innocent shopkeepers. Plus, there are cameras sited everywhere.'

'I do not understand these *c-amm-eraas*,' Tusk replied. 'They seem unholy.'

'Well, they're not,' Uncle Percy said. 'But they are omnipresent, and if they record you – as they have done – well, there's no other way to put this, but you're a squirrel, and stealing cans of lager and crunchy snacks is not what squirrels do.'

'But it is what I do. Remember, I am Viking.'

'That's as may be.' Uncle Percy sighed. 'But you've left me no choice but to prohibit you from leaving the grounds.'

'Prohibit?'

'Ban you.'

Tusk looked shocked. 'You cannot ban me, Englander.'

'Just watch me.'

'Ragnar Lothbrok – Chief of the Norsemen, Leader of the Viking Horde – will not be banned from roaming where he wishes.'

'Maybe,' Uncle Percy replied. His voice rose to a yell. 'BUT RAGNAR LOTHBROK, KING OF THE SHOPLIFTING SQUIRRELS CAN!'

Tusk's tiny fist clenched into a ball. 'You watch your tongue, else you shall lose it.'

'Don't threaten me!'

'I shall threaten who I choose.'

'Then I'll strap a portravella to your tail and send you back to the last Ice Age. See how you like that!'

But Becky had heard enough. 'That's enough now, you two!' she snapped. 'Stop this before one of you says something you'll regret.' She turned to Tusk. Her voice softened. 'Uncle Percy's right. You can't leave Bowen Hall again. Lots of people will scour Addlebury and surrounding areas looking for you now. If you're found - well, we're all in massive trouble. You don't want that, do you?'

Tusk thought about this. 'No,' he replied. 'I would never wish you to suffer because of me.' He fell silent. 'I am sorry, Becky Mellor. I did not consider the cost of my actions.'

'That's alright,' Becky said. 'You weren't to know about the cameras.'

'Truly, I did not.'

Uncle Percy gave a remorseful smile. 'And that's my fault, Tusk,' he said sincerely. 'I'm sorry. I should've explained. I also apologise for raising my voice.'

'And I am sorry I threatened to remove your tongue,' Tusk replied.

'I doubt you're the first person to propose that.'

'I just wanted to see outside the compound,' Tusk said. 'This is an exciting new world for me and exploration is in my blood.'

'I understand that,' Uncle Percy replied. 'And I don't want you to think of Bowen Hall as a prison. You've spent enough time in one of those.'

'I have.'

'I'll tell you what I'll do,' Uncle Percy said. 'I can fix an invisiblator to you, and -' The *BOOM* of an arriving time machine somewhere nearby interrupted his words. 'I wonder who that can be?' he said. Approaching the window, he saw a small brown car had materialised on the front lawn. 'That's Helena Bradshaw's mini clubman.'

Becky joined Uncle Percy at the window and watched an elderly woman exit the car. Dressed in a long linen gown and sleeveless tunic, the woman's grey hair was covered with a wimple.

Becky recognised her immediately from the recent GITT meeting in the marquee.

Uncle Percy's eyes narrowed to slits. 'Something's wrong,' he said.

Unsteady on her feet, Helena Bradshaw stumbled toward the Hall.

In a flash, Uncle Percy sprinted out of the morning room and into the entrance hall, Becky and Joe following. Emerging into brilliant sunlight, they raced over to Helena, who was trembling.

'P-Percy?' Helena panted.

'What is it, Helena?'

'Something awful has happened.'

'What? Is Eric okay?'

'It's not Eric. It's Ben.'

Immediately, Becky recalled Helena's nephew, a teenage boy she'd met just after the GITT meeting had concluded.

'What's the matter with Ben?' Uncle Percy asked.

'He's been captured,' Helena replied. 'Oh, this is terrible.'

'Calm down, Helena,' Uncle Percy said. 'I've been captured myself a number of times.' He smiled. 'And I'm still here. Now where is he?'

'He's in medieval Yorkshire in the late-twelfth century,' Helena said. 'I wanted to show him Bowland Forest, but he was caught by the local Lord's men, who thought he was a deer poacher.'

'Then we'll contact Tracker division, and they'll rescue him. They're good at that.'

'No, Percy,' Helena said. Her voice turned fragile. 'I'm embarrassed about this, but I don't want anyone else at GITT to know. I didn't log the trip, you see. I took a new teenage time traveller on an illegal time trip. I should be locked up.'

'Don't be silly, Helena,' Uncle Percy said. 'That's barely a misdemeanour.'

'Please, Percy,' Helena said. 'You've got experience with this sort of thing. Would you get him back for me?'

Uncle Percy looked hesitant. 'I... I –'

'Percy, I beg you,' Helena said, desperation in her voice. 'I trust you. I know you can do it.'

Before Uncle Percy could respond, however, Joe spoke up. 'No sweat,' he said. 'We'll go right now. He'll be back before you know it.'

'You will?' Helena said.

'Sure,' Joe replied. 'We've got no plans today, anyway. It'll be fun.'

'Hang on, Joe,' Uncle Percy said. 'You don't get to make that decision.' His gaze returned to Helena. 'Please, let me contact the Trackers and –'

'– But we can be there before them,' Joe cut in. 'And we're good at rescuing people. Remember, we saved you from being hanged in the same time period. Come on, Unc. We'll be back by tea-time.'

Conflicted, Uncle Percy stared at Helena's reddened eyes, and his resolve melted. He gave a defeated sigh. 'Very well.'

Helena looked beside herself. 'You'll do it?'

'We will.'

'Oh, thank you, Percy.' Helena flung herself into his arms. 'I'm so sorry to even ask, but I've got no choice.'

'That's okay.'

Helena looked hesitant to deliver her next sentence. 'But there's one thing you should know about the local Lord... the one who captured Ben.' She paused. 'He might have a connection to your past.'

Uncle Percy looked stunned. 'My past?'

'More precisely, Will Shakelock's past,' Helena replied. 'Like Will, he, too, is considered a significant character in the Robin Hood mythology.'

Joe's face changed. 'What? What about Will? What significant character?'

'The Lord's name is Sir Guy Cavendish,' Helena replied. 'But most refer to him as *Sir Guy of Gisbourne*.'

4

MONEY, MONET, MANET... MUST BE FUNNY

Becky watched Joe's body stiffen. She recalled Will Shakelock mentioning Guy of Gisbourne in the tree-house at Bowen Hall. She remembered his words as if they were yesterday:

"But it was Guy of Gisbourne who was evil incarnate. One of my regrets is leaving my time without dealing him the brutal justice he had dispensed to so many others."

Becky glanced at Uncle Percy, but his expression remained blank.

'How did you escape when Ben didn't?' Uncle Percy asked.

'I was studying a patch of Great Butterfly Orchids when Ben disappeared into the forest,' Helena replied. 'Suddenly, I heard horses and followed him in to see a group of men surround him. He was dressed like a peasant, so of course they assumed he was a poacher. Anyway, I hid behind a tree and watched as he was taken away.' Her lip trembled. 'Oh, Percy, it was horrible. I didn't know what to do, or who had taken him, so I went to a nearby village, and the villagers told me the forest is under the protection of Sir Guy Cavendish.'

'What did the villagers say about him?' Joe asked coolly.

Helena fell silent. 'They said he's a dangerous man, a cruel man,' she replied. 'They said Ben will be imprisoned in the castle dungeons, tortured... and almost certainly killed.'

'Then it's a good job we're going,' Joe replied. 'And if Guy of Gisbourne is dealt some *brutal justice,* then that's no bad thing.'

Uncle Percy looked sternly at Joe. 'If you carry on like that, young man, you won't be going at all. We're going there to rescue Ben, and that's the extent of our business with Sir Guy Cavendish.'

'Will regretted not killing him,' Joe said. 'He told us that. Didn't he, Becks?'

'That's not exactly what he said,' Becky replied.

'It's close enough.'

'I couldn't care less what Will did or didn't say,' Uncle Percy replied sharply.

'I care,' Joe replied, a terseness in his voice.

Sensing tempers were rising. Becky thought it best to steer the conversation in a different direction. 'How do you intend to get Ben back?'

'We'll offer Gisbourne some money,' Uncle Percy replied. 'In my experience, there's no motivator like greed for these mindless brutes.'

'What sort of money?' Joe asked. 'I doubt he'll take Bitcoin.'

'GITT have a special fund for ransoms and such-like,' Uncle Percy replied. 'He'll get a bag of period coins, jewellery and gold from GITT's fiscal stores.'

'There's a ransom fund?' Becky asked, surprised.

'Of sorts,' Uncle Percy replied. 'It's not accessed often, but it's there for occasions like this.'

'Should we really be giving Guy of Gisbourne cash?' Joe said. 'Will said that –'

'– But Will is not here, Joe,' Uncle Percy cut in. 'And I wish you'd stop trying to emulate him.'

'I'm not.'

'You could've fooled me,' Uncle Percy said. 'Anyway, you have your wish - we're going to get Ben instead of sending a Tracker team, so you should be happy with that.'

'I am,' Joe replied. 'When are we going?'

'Just give me an hour,' Uncle Percy replied, 'and I'll pop to GITT HQ and get the ransom. I'll also arrange for period specific clothes to be placed in your rooms.'

'And weapons?' Joe said.

'Yes, weapons, too - swords only on this occasion.'

'Then you'll need one for Becky,' Joe said. 'She's good with a sword now.'

Becky shook her head. 'I don't want one. I'm not ready for that.'

'You are, Becks,' Joe replied. 'I promise you.'

'If she says she's not ready, Joe, don't push it,' Uncle Percy said. 'Personally, if I had my way, neither of you would take any weapons.'

Joe gave a sarcastic smile. 'And yet my using weapons has saved your life loads of times.'

Fully aware that Joe made a good point, Uncle Percy blew a raspberry. 'You have an answer for everything, don't you, young man?'

Joe didn't have to reply for everyone to know he'd won that argument.

AFTER THAT, Uncle Percy took Helena Bradshaw home, before heading to GITT headquarters to get the ransom.

Becky and Joe got something to eat before returning to their rooms to prepare for the trip.

Becky entered her bedroom to see an outfit hanging from her wardrobe door. A quick glance revealed an ankle-length dress, richly embroidered and colourful, a surcoat, and polished leather shoes. A gold bracelet and necklace had been placed on her dressing table.

Instantly, she knew Uncle Percy's intention was for them to appear affluent and well-heeled, cementing the idea that handing over a substantial ransom was a trivial matter to them.

As she changed, Becky found herself filled with doubt. Was this really a good idea? Should, as Uncle Percy said, GITT's Tracker Division be coordinating Ben's rescue? The one thing she knew was that if Guy of Gisbourne was as dangerous as Will Shakelock said, this could all go very wrong quickly.

Becky met Joe outside the Time Room, and they entered to see Uncle Percy, looking resplendent in a dazzlingly coloured silk tunic, breeches, leather boots, and a fur-lined cloak pinned at the neck by a shimmering golden brooch.

'Good evening,' Uncle Percy said brightly.

'Love the bling!' Becky said.

'We must give Gisbourne the impression we're people of substance,' Uncle Percy replied.

Joe approached a table set upon which were a raw-hide bag, a range of swords, and a pair of leather scabbards. 'Is one of these swords for me?'

'Yes,' Uncle Percy replied.

Joe picked one up and turned it in his hand. 'What type of sword is it?'

'It's a *knightly* sword,' Uncle Percy replied. 'It's lighter and shorter than the more famous broadsword, which wasn't exactly practical for day-to-day use.'

'I like it,' Joe said, admiring the blade.

'Don't get any ideas. These swords will not be leaving their scabbards on this trip. They're merely for decoration.'

'That's up to Gisbourne,' Joe replied darkly.

Uncle Percy frowned. 'Is it now?'

'And should I take a Joe-bow, too?'

'I don't think that's necessary,' Uncle Percy replied. 'Now, are we ready to depart?'

Joe slipped the sword into the scabbard and fastened it to his waist. 'Deffo.'

'Yes,' Becky said. 'Are we going by portravella?'

'We are,' Uncle Percy replied, pulling back his tunic sleeve to reveal a device strapped to his wrist.

Joe nodded at the bag on the table. 'And is that the dosh?'

'It is.'

'Can I have a look?' Joe said.

'Be my guest.'

Joe walked over and unzipped the bag. Peering inside, he marvelled at the mass of coins, gold and silver within. 'That is a serious stash of cash.'

'It is, indeed.'

'How much is there?'

'I don't know,' Uncle Percy said. 'A small fortune for the late twelfth century, that's for sure.'

'And how are you going to explain paying it?' Becky said.

'What do you mean?'

'Well, if Ben is a peasant, why would you, as a nobleman, give over that kind of money for his release?'

'That's a good point, Becky, and I don't know,' Uncle Percy replied. 'Hopefully, Sir Guy Cavendish will be too preoccupied with his newly gained wealth to ask the question.'

'So let me get this straight,' Joe said. 'GITT has treasure rooms filled with cash for ransoms and payoffs and stuff like that?'

'Not rooms, as such,' Uncle Percy replied. 'But time-specific funds are available if necessary.'

'What do you mean time-specific?' Becky asked.

'It's pointless trying to give Guy of Gisbourne a million pounds in twenty-first century currency. He'd laugh in our face. Therefore, any ransom raised must be collated from capital applicable to the time it's needed - in this case, the medieval era. Hence, there are plenty of precious stones, gold coins, silver adornments and suchlike.'

'I understand,' Becky said.

Then something occurred to Joe. 'I bet every time traveller is minted, aren't they? I mean, like, *stinkin' rich*!'

Uncle Percy looked surprised. 'Why would you say that?'

'Well, old stuff – antiques, I mean – can be worth a fortune, can't they? I mean not only in a posh auction house, but on eBay.'

'I suppose.'

'And anything can be an antique if enough time has passed.'

'That's true.'

'Then all a time traveller has to do is go back in time, pick up any load of rubbish – a spoon, a toy doll or a can of coke – and by the time they've returned that item could be worth a fortune.'

'Perhaps,' Uncle Percy said hesitantly. 'But –'

'But *nowt*!' Joe replied animatedly. 'Becks, after we've rescued Ben, we're travelling to the 1990s.'

'We are?' Becky replied.

'Yeah.' Joe couldn't get the words out quick enough. 'We're gonna walk in the first bookshop we see, and buy a shedload of *Harry Potter and the Philosopher's Stone* first editions.' His mouth arched with a wide grin. 'Then we'll come back and sell them. We'll never have to work again.'

'You don't work now,' Becky said.

'Whatever,' Joe replied. 'What do you say? Ain't it the best idea ever?'

'Not really.'

'Course it is.'

'It really isn't.'

'I'm afraid I couldn't let you do it anyway, Joe,' Uncle Percy said.

Joe's face dropped. 'Why not?'

'It's against GITT's rules.'

'What rules?'

'Travellers are not allowed to use time trips for financial gain,' Uncle Percy said.

Joe looked stunned. 'You're kiddin' me!'

'Not at all,' Uncle Percy replied. 'It's actually one of GITT's oldest rules. Obviously, when GITT was first formed it quickly became apparent that this could be a major problem. Subsequently, a stringent set of policies was implemented to ensure this couldn't and wouldn't happen.'

'What kind've policies?'

'All kinds,' Uncle Percy replied. 'But particularly in terms of a traveller gaining anything of potential value during a trip and selling it on their return. For instance, a traveller wouldn't be allowed to pop to nineteenth century Paris, acquire a Manet or Renoir or Monet painting, and then return to sell it at a twenty-first century auction. If a traveller breaks that rule, they're instantly ejected from the organisation.'

'But Bowen Hall is full of antiques,' Joe said. 'Are you telling us you didn't pick any of them up on your trips?'

'Bowen Hall does indeed have many valuable antiques,' Uncle Percy replied. 'But I inherited most of them, and those I didn't I bought at a contemporary auction. I have brought nothing back from a time trip and tried to sell it on for a profit... and I never would.'

'That's nuts.' Joe said. 'I mean, what are the chances of GITT finding out?'

'Well, for one thing, GITT has access to every time traveller's bank accounts,' Uncle Percy said. 'The committee does regular checks on our finances to ensure we abide by these rules. Any sudden influx of funds into our accounts has to be justified and evidenced... an inheritance, for instance.'

'That's all rather invasive, isn't it?' Becky said.

'Arguably, yes,' Uncle Percy replied. 'But there really isn't any other way to ensure corrupt practices don't occur. Most travellers agree this level of transparency is essential to prevent corruption and exploitation.'

'And what if someone doesn't agree to give over their financial details?' Becky asked.

'Then they don't become time travellers,' Uncle Percy replied simply. 'Luckily, most involved in travelling do it for the love of knowledge, erudition, and discovery, and certainly not for any potential profit.'

'Is that why you never let me keep any of the treasure we find?' Joe said.

'Not really,' Uncle Percy replied. 'I just think you already have more than you need. We all do – we're very lucky. Besides, money would change you, Joe, and I don't want you changed. I like you just as you are.'

'I like me just as I am, too,' Joe said. 'But I'd really like me with a few million quid in the bank.'

Uncle Percy chuckled. 'Of course you would.' He lifted a sword, slid it into the remaining scabbard, and attached it to his waist. Then he picked up the ransom bag. 'Anyhow, we have a boy to rescue.' He entered a series of digits into his portravella. 'Hold on tight. Next stop: Medieval Yorkshire.'

Becky and Joe touched Uncle Percy's arm as the portravella flashed green.

As she awaited departure, Becky glanced at Joe, whose expression had suddenly changed. Instantly, a knot formed in her stomach. A dangerous glint tinted his eyes, one that told her this trip might not be a good idea.

In fact, it could be a huge mistake.

5

GISBOURNE

Within moments, a cold autumn wind gripped Becky's skin. They had arrived beside a gnarled oak tree, one of many in a dark, shadowy forest.

'This could be Sherwood Forest,' Joe said.

'It could, but it's not,' Uncle Percy replied. 'However, like Sherwood, Bowland Forest was one of the great Royal Hunting Forests owned by the King.'

'And what year is it?' Joe asked.

'1190AD.'

'The owner would be my birth dad, King Richard I, then?'

A curious look crossed Uncle Percy's face. 'I never thought of that.'

'I guess all of it is actually mine then,' Joe said. 'Do you hear that, Becky? You're trespassing on my property.'

Becky grunted.

'As you've not actually been born yet, you can hardly lay claim to it.' Uncle Percy paused. 'Still, as you have a connection to this period, perhaps we should return to our time and rethink this.'

'What?' Joe said. 'Why?'

Uncle Percy opened his mouth to reply, but no words came.

'Exactly,' Joe continued. 'Now let's rescue Ben.'

Uncle Percy looked conflicted. 'Very well.' He set off, negotiating the countless trees, their leaves veiling the sky, making it impossible to tell if it was day or night.

The further they went, the more the forest thinned, until they emerged onto a landscape of gritstone fells and heather covered peat moorland.

It was then Becky heard a snapping sound from somewhere behind them. Assuming it was a fallen tree, she turned to see a large castle framed against an inky black sky.

'So that's Gisbourne's castle?' Joe said.

'Apparently so,' Uncle Percy replied.

'It's big.'

'He was a wealthy man,' Uncle Percy said. 'And a close associate of Prince John.'

'You mean my Uncle John,' Joe said.

'I suppose I do.'

'What do you know about Gisbourne?'

'Only what Will told me, and that wasn't much,' Uncle Percy said. 'But I believe Prince John employed him from time to time as, shall we say, an enforcer.'

'He's like Otto Kruger then?'

'I didn't say that.'

'Emerson Drake used Kruger as his rent-a-thug. It sounds like Prince John does the same with Gisbourne.'

'There are similarities,' Uncle Percy replied. 'There's certainly no doubt that Sir Guy Cavendish instilled fear into everyone that met him.'

'Not Will Shakelock,' Joe said resolutely.

'No... not Will Shakelock.'

'Personally, I can't wait to meet him,' Joe said.

'I bet you can't,' Uncle Percy muttered under his breath.

Approaching the castle, Becky felt a rising dread. Even

though she'd seen many medieval castles, this was by far the most intimidating. With grey stone walls twelve metres high, its walkways patrolled by countless archers, it had three circular towers and a moat filled with oil-black water.

From behind, Becky heard the drum of hooves; the ground shuddered beneath her feet. Looking back, she saw four horsemen emerge from the forest.

'And so it begins,' Uncle Percy mumbled as the riders approached. 'GOOD MORNING, GENTLEMEN,' he yelled, with a friendly wave.

One rider, a short, stocky man took the lead, and drew his horse to a halt. He had a dishevelled mass of muddy brown, scraggly hair, an unkempt beard, and a scarlet complexion that suggested he ate too much red meat and very little else.

'WHO BE YOU, STRANGER?' the man barked in a tone more like a threat than a question.

'I am Sir Percy of Bowen,' Uncle Percy replied in a haughty voice. 'This is Rebecca and Joe of Wythenshawe. We wish you a merry day.' He gave a broad smile.

The man didn't reciprocate. 'What business 'ave you 'ere?'

'I am here to meet with Sir Guy,' Uncle Percy said.

'And is my liege expecting ye?'

'No, but he will be pleased at my arrival,' Uncle Percy replied. 'I come bearing gifts.'

'Gifts?'

Uncle Percy held up the bag and opened it. 'Yes... *gifts*.'

The man's mouth tumbled open. 'V-very well, Sir Percy.'

'Now, what is your name and role?' Uncle Percy asked.

'I am Gerold of Haworth, and I am the Marshal of Gisbourne castle.'

'Excellent,' Uncle Percy said. 'Then you will take us to your liege, Gerold.'

But there was something on Gerold's mind. 'Where be your horses?'

'We have made camp a few miles from here. We wished to savour the morning air with a stroll.'

Gerold looked confused. 'Why? The weather's as frosty as a gravedigger's arse!'

The other horsemen laughed.

Uncle Percy's face furrowed with anger. 'You shall not utter such words around me,' he barked. 'I am not a lowly stable-boy - I am Sir Percy of Bowen, and you will watch your tongue, or I shall have it removed.'

The grin left Gerold's face. 'Beggin' your clemency, sire.'

Becky doubted the swear word offended Uncle Percy, but his response certainly cemented his story as a nobleman.

'You should,' Uncle Percy said. 'Now take me to Sir Guy, and we shall leave this matter on these moors.'

Gerold nodded dutifully. 'Yes, sire.' He tugged at his horse's reins and steered toward the castle.

As they walked, Uncle Percy looked at Becky and spoke in a whisper. 'The British class system never ceases to astonish me. Even in the twenty-first century, it's amazing how a title, a privileged background, and an arrogant manner can help someone get away with murder.'

'Yeah,' Becky replied. 'That sums up most politicians, doesn't it?'

'Indeed, it does.'

Becky, Joe and Uncle Percy trailed Gerold over a lowered drawbridge, through a raised portcullis into a large court swarming with activity. Peasants and farmers carried animals, birds, fruits and vegetables, and passed them to the castle staff who took them into the kitchens.

Gerold came to a halt. Summoning a stable boy to tend to his horse, he leapt down before walking over to Uncle Percy.

'The castle is busy, Gerold,' Uncle Percy said.

'This night is the feast of Saint Jude,' Gerold replied. 'Two dozen Yorkshire nobles shall be in attendance. The farmers and bordars are giving their offerings to my liege as a tax for his protection and mercy.'

'He doesn't pay them for it?' Uncle Percy asked.

Gerold looked surprised. 'Why would he? He allows them to live, that is payment enough. Now follow me to the Great Hall.' He set off toward the castle's keep.

Becky trailed Uncle Percy and Joe as they followed Gerold through a large wooden door, into a gigantic hall adorned with tapestries, wall hangings, candles, and a stone fireplace, which enclosed a roaring fire. An enormous banner emblazoned with a wolf, its fangs bared, hung above a carved wooden throne, which overlooked a series of lengthy banquet tables and benches.

However, it was when Becky looked right that her blood turned cold. A set of makeshift gallows had been constructed on the north wall; a noose fashioned from thick rope dangled from its crossbeam.

'Wait here,' Gerold said, exiting the room through a side door.

Joe nodded at the gallows. 'It looks like Ben's the entertainment for tonight, then?'

Before Uncle Percy could answer, the side door opened, and a man stood in silhouette, his massive body filling every inch of space.

Becky gulped. *Guy of Gisbourne was huge.*

Dressed in a black tunic, horsehide robe, and boots, Gisbourne was handsome, with short raven-black hair, a muscular torso, and a sculpted goatee beard that tapered to a point. His skin would be considered flawless, if not for the deep scar that traced a line from his right eye to his chin.

Gisbourne emerged from the shadows, followed by Gerold and six armed guards.

'Gerold informs me we have guests,' Gisbourne said, his voice measured and menacing.

'You do, Sir Guy.' Uncle Percy stepped forward. 'I am Sir Percy of Bowen, and these are my wards, Becky and Joe Mellor.'

'You dress as a noble, and yet your name is not familiar to me,' Gisbourne said.

'I am from a borough in Cornwall, sir. It is slight of size, but grand in its beauty.'

Gisbourne walked over to the throne, his gait slow like a prowling tiger, before sitting down. 'And why you are here, Sir Percy?'

'I believe you have a boy in your dungeons,' Uncle Percy replied. 'He is mine and I wish to pay for his release.'

'A boy of yours?'

'A member of my household.'

'And what is this boy's name?'

'Ben.'

Gisbourne paused. 'The poacher?'

'With respect, you are mistaken, sir,' Uncle Percy replied. 'He is no poacher,'

'But he was seized in my forest.'

'We are camped near here,' Uncle Percy said. 'He went for a stroll. He did not know the forest was under your dominion.'

'And is that an excuse for trespass?'

'It is not,' Uncle Percy replied. 'And you have every right to feel aggrieved... but let me sweeten your temper.' He opened the bag, revealing the ransom within.

Gisbourne peered inside. 'Forsooth, tis a tidy sum.'

'And it's all yours in exchange for the boy.'

Gisbourne looked confused. 'But who is this boy that you would pay such a toll?'

'That is of no matter,' Uncle Percy replied. 'Do we have an accord, sir?'

Slowly, Gisbourne stood up, his hand stroking his chin as if in deep thought. 'But you present me with a quandary,' he said. 'The boy's execution was to be the amusement at my feast this very night. If he is not here to swing, what entertainment shall I afford my guests?'

'I'm certain your guests will be more than happy with your company,' Uncle Percy replied.

Gisbourne was about to respond when he glanced at Joe, who was staring at him with a fierce intensity. 'Have I offended thee, boy? Why do I see such rage in your eyes?'

Becky saw Joe's expression and her stomach sank. *What was he doing?*

'I'm certain you don't, sir,' Uncle Percy said quickly. 'Now, shall we complete our deal and leave you to prepare for your special night?'

Gisbourne ignored Uncle Percy, his focus remaining on Joe. 'I know that look, boy. It is the stare delivered when one wishes harm to another. Do you wish me harm, boy?'

'Just take the cash,' Joe replied bluntly. 'And release the boy.'

Gisbourne could scarcely believe his ears. 'You use that tone to address me?'

Joe didn't look remotely intimidated. 'Just get him.'

Gisbourne gave an ugly laugh. He glanced at Gerold. 'This youth is as courageous as David or as dumb as an ass.'

'Aye, sire,' Gerold replied.

Gisbourne's eyes returned to Joe, and then, suddenly, his expression changed. 'Have we met before, boy?'

'No.'

'Your features look familiar. Who is your father?'

'Please, Sir Guy,' Uncle Percy said, suddenly anxious. 'Have our money and let us take Ben.'

Again, Gisbourne ignored him. 'I demand an answer, boy,' he growled. 'Who is your father?'

'That's not important,' Joe said. 'But there is someone we both know – *Will Shakelock*.'

'JOE!' Uncle Percy snapped. 'Leave it alone!'

'You know Will Shakelock?' Gisbourne snarled.

'He was my teacher.' Joe paused. '– And my best friend.'

'Shakelock was an outlaw... a thief... a hedge-born churl.'

Becky was worried now. Things were escalating quickly.

'That's what he said about you,' Joe said. 'Tell me, was it him that gave you that big ugly scar?'

Gisbourne's eyes blazed with rage. In a flash, he threw his right arm around Uncle Percy's neck, pulling him close, choking him, as his other hand jerked a dagger from his belt.

Simultaneously, Joe withdrew his sword. 'Let him go, Gisbourne. This is between me and you.'

Uncle Percy tried to shout at Joe, but Gisbourne's arm blocked his airway.

'WHAT'RE YOU DOING, IDIOT?' Becky shouted at Joe.

'Perchance, Sir Percy would value a scar like mine?' Gisbourne snarled. He pressed the dagger's tip against Uncle Percy's cheek, breaking the skin.

A line of blood leaked down to Uncle Percy's chin.

Becky knew she had to act. Immediately, her eyes found the dagger. She focussed hard, pressure building behind her eyes. Within moments, she knew she had the telekinetic power she needed. Feeling the dagger's contours in her mind, she willed it away from Uncle Percy. She could feel Gisbourne fighting her, trying desperately to regain control of the knife, but she knew her power was stronger than he could ever be.

Confusion lined Gisbourne's face. '*What - is - this - witchcraft?*'

Becky didn't hear him. With a single flick of her head, she wrenched the dagger from Gisbourne's hand, and sent it clattering to the floor.

Neither Gisbourne nor his men could believe their eyes.

At the same time, the main door opened, and a small hooded figure entered.

'IN THE NAME OF ODIN, WHAT IS THIS I SEE?' the figure shouted.

Stunned, Becky looked over, and her heart leapt. Immediately, things made sense. The snapping sound she'd heard as they left the forest was not a falling tree at all - it was a portravella.

A portravella that had brought Tusk to the twelfth century. *Uncle Percy had arranged an escape plan.*

'You shall unhand Percy Halifax,' Tusk said to Gisbourne. 'Although he and I quarrel like Freya and Mimir, he is still my good friend.' He lowered his hood to reveal his squirrel features.

Although astonished at the sight of Tusk, Gisbourne maintained his grip on Uncle Percy.

In the silence that filled the hall, Tusk studied his opponents. 'Men of Gisbourne castle, for countless moons I've longed for combat, and nothing feeds my Viking soul like a hearty brawl. Now, Percy Halifax has given me a strict no slaughter policy, which displeases me, but for that end he has crafted me this fine weapon.'

Tusk pulled a large hammer from beneath his cloak, its oblong head made of thick rubber. He held it high for all to see. 'It may not rival Thor's Mjölnir, but I judge could inflict sufficient pain on you. So, what say you, men of Gisbourne castle... shall we fight?'

Without waiting for a reply, he shouted, 'FOR LAGERTHA...'

6

BREAKING OUT BEN

Tusk sprinted over the floor, his tiny feet barely touching the tiles, before springing high and landing on a guard's shoulder. BAM! He slammed the hammer onto the guard's head.

Before the guard had hit the ground, Tusk had moved to his next victim. BAM! The hammer fell again.

Simultaneously, Joe aimed his sword at Gisbourne, who still gripped Uncle Percy's neck. 'Release him,' he snarled.

'When he is a corpse,' Gisbourne replied, his eyes wild. His forearm tightened on Uncle Percy's windpipe, choking him.

Uncle Percy fought back desperately, but Gisbourne was too strong.

Again, Becky knew she was Uncle Percy's only chance. Immediately, her gaze found the wolf banner. She concentrated hard and swiftly knew it was under her control. Tearing it off the wall, she flung it over Gisbourne's head, its thick material covering his mouth, suffocating him.

Confused and bewildered, Gisbourne clawed at the material, releasing Uncle Percy.

Joe stared at Gisbourne and grinned.

'N – no killing, Joe!' Uncle Percy managed, between coughs and splutters.

'I wasn't gonna kill him,' Joe replied. He took two steps toward Gisbourne, balled his fist, and pulled back his arm like a spring. 'Will Shakelock sends his regards,' he said, before thumping Gisbourne with the force of a professional boxer.

A sickening *crunch* rent the air; Gisbourne crumpled to the ground, unconscious.

Relieved, Becky looked over at Tusk. Guards surrounded him, lashing out with their swords, but he was too fast; dodging the blades, he smashed his hammer into one guard after another until they fell like dominoes. Soon, all of them lay unconscious at Tusk's feet.

Barely out of breath, Tusk said, 'My thirst for combat is quenched.'

Uncle Percy stood up, finally breathing normally. 'I'm glad to hear it.'

Becky noted the blood on Uncle Percy's cheek. 'You're bleeding.'

'It's barely a scratch,' Uncle Percy replied, mopping it with his sleeve.

Joe patted Tusk's shoulder. 'Cheers. Tusky. You really saved our bacon. You swing that hammer like Emma Raducanu swings a tennis racket.'

'I do not know this Raducanu,' Tusk replied. 'But tis a fine weapon.'

'Can I have one?' Joe asked Uncle Percy.

'Absolutely not,' Uncle Percy replied.

Becky stared at the guards. 'Erm, any chance we can rescue Ben before this lot wakes up?'

'Good idea,' Uncle Percy replied.

'Do you know where the dungeons are?' Becky asked.

'I studied the castle's architectural plans before we came,'

Uncle Percy replied. 'Follow me.' He marched toward the right side-door.

Soon, they were walking down a narrow corridor lit by torches. Turning left, they came to another door.

Lifting a torch from the wall, Uncle Percy pushed it open.

Becky tracked the others down a series of stone steps, which plunged to the blackness below. Straightaway, images of the dungeons of Svartalfheim returned to her, and she knew, like those, this was somewhere prisoners came to face torture and death, not an impartial trial. Reaching the bottom, she heard movement, followed by a young man's fearful voice.

'H-hello?'

'Hey, Ben,' Joe said. 'It's Joe Mellor. We've come to rescue you.'

Uncle Percy fanned the torch, shedding orange light on eight filthy cells, which were all empty except for one.

The last time Becky had seen Ben, she thought he possessed the kind of confidence that comes with having good looks, money and status, the exact kind she felt she lacked herself. Now, however, he looked vulnerable, scared, and broken. He had a black bruise on his right cheek, multiple cuts on his face, and dirt and blood knotted his fine blond hair.

Ben's eyes gleamed with gratitude. 'Oh, thank god,' he said. 'I knew Aunty Helena wouldn't let me down.'

'She didn't,' Uncle Percy replied. 'And you're fine now. This ordeal is over for you.'

'Mr. Halifax, thank you so much for coming,' Ben said. 'And Becky, and Joe, and –' His eyes found Tusk, and the words lodged in his throat.

'This is Tusk,' Joe said. 'He's a talking squirrel, but he's well hard, so be nice to him, and don't stare.'

'O-of course,' Ben stammered. 'H-hi Tusk.'

'Hello, boy,' Tusk said.

'Let's get you back home, Ben,' Uncle Percy said.

'The prison guard has the key,' Ben said. 'I don't know where he is.'

'The only key we need is a *Bec-ky*.' Joe grinned. 'See what I did there, Becks?'

'Hilarious,' Becky replied dully. She approached the cell door and cupped the shackle padlock in her hands. She focussed on it, and activated her telekinesis. *CRACKKK* - it shattered.

Ben gasped loudly. 'Wow! I heard you were telekinetic,' he said. 'But it's awesome to see it in reality. I'd give anything to be able to do that.'

'You wouldn't,' Becky said. 'Trust me.'

Ben pushed open the gate, grabbed Becky's hand and shook it. 'Cheers, Becky. You've saved my life. They were going to hang me.'

Looking into Ben's bloodshot eyes, Becky felt a peculiar feeling. Immediately, she recalled the sensation once before when they'd first met – a sensation both recognisable yet unfamiliar, both physical and yet abstract. She couldn't describe it if she tried.

'Thank you all so much,' Ben said.

'No sweat, mate. It's been fun,' Joe said.

'It has?'

'Yeah,' Joe replied. 'I got to deck Guy of Gisbourne. It felt good.'

'You did?' Ben said. 'But he's like a beast of a bloke.'

'Yeah. One punch. He'll be out for a week.'

'Good for you,' Ben said.

'Anyway,' Uncle Percy said. 'I've seen enough dungeons like this to last me a lifetime. Shall we go?'

'Please, Mister Halifax,' Ben agreed.

Uncle Percy raised his sleeve and tapped a key on his portravella. 'Hold on tight everyone.'

Everyone reached over and touched Uncle Percy as the portravella cocooned them in a shimmering white light.

A moment later, they'd vanished.

BECKY FELT relief wash over her. She swallowed a lungful of fresh, clean air and stared out at the Time Room, its spotless white walls in direct contrast to the dark, dank dungeon.

'So, you'd planned for Tusk to come all along,' Joe said to Uncle Percy.

'It was important to have a back-up plan,' Uncle Percy said. 'I didn't really know how Gisbourne was going to react. I also wanted a second portravella present in that time period... just in case.'

'Makes sense,' Joe replied.

Uncle Percy turned to Ben. 'Anyway, young man, I'll take you to your Aunty immediately. She'll be relieved to see you.'

'Okay,' Ben said. 'Listen, I want to get you all something individually – you know, as a thank you. What do you want, Becky?'

Becky shook her head. 'I don't want anything. I'm just glad it's over.'

'But I want to get you something,' Ben replied. 'I would've been dead for sure if it wasn't for you lot. Please, let me do this. I've got plenty of money. Just name it, and it's yours.'

'I'll have a car,' Joe said.

'What kind of car?' Ben replied in all seriousness.

'He does *not* need a car,' Uncle Percy said.

'Spoil sport,' Joe said.

'Then what are you into, Joe?' Ben said.

'I dunno,' Joe replied. 'I support Man City.'

'Okay then,' Ben replied. 'Leave that with me. Seriously, Becky, what about you?'

'There's nothing I want,' Becky replied.

'Well, I'm getting you something,' Ben said. 'If you're not going to tell me, I'll just choose something myself.'

'Give some money to charity then,' Becky said.

'I'll do that, and still get you something,' Ben replied.

Before Becky could reply, Tusk stepped forward. 'I shall accept a tribute of crisps,' he said. 'Lots of crisps.'

'Crisps?' Ben laughed. 'Any particular flavour?'

'Salt and vinegar crisps bring me great joy.'

'Deal,' Ben said. 'And Mr Halifax - what can I get you?'

'There is one thing,' Uncle Percy said. 'A promise you'll try to avoid forests run by medieval sociopaths in the future.'

Ben smiled. 'Then I can promise that right now. But I would like to get you something more.'

'I have all I need, Ben,' Uncle Percy replied. 'Now let me take you to your Aunty Helena. She's worried sick.' He tapped a few keys on his portravella. 'Hold on.'

Ben reached out and held his arm. 'See you soon, everyone, and cheers again.' He cast Becky a wide smile. 'I'll see you soon.'

A moment later, Ben and Uncle Percy vanished.

Joe turned to Becky. 'Do you really think he would've got me a car?'

'He comes across as the loaded type,' Becky said. 'It wouldn't surprise me.'

'He does,' Joe replied. 'He's also got the hots for you.'

Becky scowled. 'Don't be daft.'

'I saw that smile when he was leaving,' Joe said. 'You two have a love connection.'

'Rubbish.'

'It's not,' Joe said. 'Anyway, speaking of being loaded - do you think we should zoom back and pick up all that dosh before Gisbourne wakes up?'

Becky had never heard of anything so ridiculous in her life. 'No. I do not.'

Joe frowned. 'It's just I'm miffed a scumbag like him will get to keep it all.'

'I know what you mean,' Becky replied. 'But it's only money.'

'It's a *lot* of money,' Joe said. 'Still, when I smacked him in the mouth I heard a *crunch*, so hopefully I've smashed his teeth in. For all that cash, there aren't any dentists in Medieval England.'

7

DREAMS NEVER END

Becky and Joe spent the next few hours at the stables with Pegasus and Gump before making some supper and calling it a night.

At ten, Becky entered her bedroom and immediately heard a high-pitched buzz from a black box on the windowsill: a *hologramophone*. She walked over and read the LED display.

INCOMING HOLOGRAMOPHONIC MESSAGE
   Recipient: Becky Mellor
   Sender: Percy Halifax
   Location: Time Room

PRESSING A BLINKING GREEN BUTTON, she watched as three lasers shot out, forming a life-sized three-dimensional image of Uncle Percy, still dressed in his medieval robes.

'Hello, Becky,' he said cheerily.

'Hi,' Becky said. 'Have you only just got back?'

'I have,' Uncle Percy said. 'Oh, Helena was so relieved at Ben's return, she insisted I join her for a fish and chip supper and I couldn't turn her down, could I? Anyhow, I have some news. Whilst I was tucking into my battered cod, Edgar pagidized me. He, Vilja and Darrian have arrived at Caradan.'

'And they're all safe?' Becky asked.

'They are indeed,' Uncle Percy replied. 'He's been there for a few days and become quite at home. Remember, he stated his concerns about her family liking him, because he was, shall we say, less macho than your archetypal minotaur?'

'Yes.'

'It seems he had nothing to worry about – they adore him.'

'I knew they would,' Becky replied.

'As we all did.' Uncle Percy smiled. 'Anyway, as he said he would, he and Vilja have talked to the scholars of Caradan, and apparently, they have some information about the Isle of the Blessed. He didn't go into details, but he wants us to visit him when we can. I thought we'd do it tomorrow.'

'Fantastic,' Becky said eagerly. 'I can't wait.'

'Good,' Uncle Percy said. 'To be honest, I'm rather excited myself. We're going to visit an actual minotaur town – as a unique learning experience it's one of a kind.'

'Is Felicity coming?' Becky asked.

'I'm afraid not,' Uncle Percy replied. 'A close friend of hers has suffered a sudden illness, and she's offered to help with her recuperation.'

'I'm sorry about that,' Becky said.

'As am I,' Uncle Percy said. 'Anyway, we're leaving at 9.00 a.m. from the Time Room, so make sure you dress for hot weather, and I'll contact Joe now to tell him the same. Cheerio.'

Uncle Percy's image vanished.

Becky's heart skipped a beat. The next morning, they were visiting a minotaur town. In truth, she'd only met a handful of minotaurs, and some – Gergo, Gergan, Kraven and Thoth – were considerably scarier than Edgar. However, the idea of seeing a town, a community, with all of its history, architecture, and customs fascinated her, particularly because there was no actual archaeological evidence of minotaurs existing in the first place.

Becky thought excitedly about the impending trip as she cleaned her teeth and changed into her pyjamas. And when she finally climbed into bed, she stared at the ceiling for an age, unable to consider sleep. It was then the setting changed.

She was no longer in her bedroom.

She was no longer in Bowen Hall.

She was no longer in the twenty-first century.

As raindrops fell from thick black cloud, she was standing on the muddy thoroughfare of a village, set in a deep valley and surrounded by mountains. Judging by the surrounding buildings, she thought she was somewhere in Eastern Europe in the sixteenth or seventeenth century. In the distance, a large ash-grey castle with a horseshoe-shaped tower stood on a steep hill lined with broad-leaved trees.

As Becky surveyed the village, however, revulsion gripped her. The dead bodies of villagers - men, women and children - dressed in little more than peasant rags lay all around; their faces were pale, serene, impassive, as if they'd fallen calmly asleep and died on the spot.

Upon closer inspection, however, Becky's horror rocketed.

The villagers' eyes were wide open, their eyeballs scarlet like cherries.

Sickened, Becky couldn't look anymore. Turning away, she saw movement at the far end of the path. Two people wearing contemporary hazmat suits and other protection gear were moving from corpse to corpse, scribbling something on notepads.

Scientists in sixteenth century Europe?

It made no sense.

And then she noticed more movement. From a distance, a short, slender man was walking toward her, dressed formally in a long black coat, hat and suit. Before she could discern any particular features, however, the scene changed again.

Still traumatised by the sight of the dead villagers, Becky was now standing before a three-storey building framed by a cloudless blue sky. Constructed in the collegiate gothic style, the building had leaded glass windows, a slate roof, and was fashioned from red brick and limestone. All around, beech and sycamore trees bordered a large grass courtyard dotted with wooden benches.

Becky watched as a side door opened and a group of young people appeared, talking excitedly to each other. Judging by their accent, haircuts and clothing, she thought she was in North America in the nineteen thirties or forties.

At that moment, she saw an older man sitting on a bench, facing the building, his face hidden from view. He wore a crumpled tweed jacket, charcoal-grey cotton trousers, and his long silver hair fell onto his neck.

Was it Uncle Percy?

It was then she noticed he held a single red rose.

Was it a Stephanie Rose – the flower unique to Bowen Hall?

Her heart pounding, Becky was about to approach him when the scene changed again. She was back in her bedroom once more. She glanced at her bedside clock: **10:23pm**.

Becky waited for her pulse to decelerate. Even now, she couldn't tell if it had been a nightmare or, more terrifyingly, one of her premonitions of future events. It had been so long since she'd had one of her '*turns*', she simply couldn't tell.

As she lay there, fragmented images returned to her again and again: the scientists, the castle, the old man holding a single rose, but most of all the faces of the dead villagers, their calm, peaceful expressions transformed into masks of horror by their lifeless blood-red eyes.

The one thing she knew for sure was any excitement in visiting Caradan, had been replaced by a deep-rooted fear something terrible was just around the corner.

8

DEPARTURE

And do you think it was one of your freaky visions of the future?' Joe asked, the next morning. 'I mean, those dead red-eyed villagers being studied by scientists – you think that might be real? D'you think we might see all that in the future?'

Becky held onto the treehouse's balustrade and stared out over Bowen Forest. 'Yes. No. I don't know.'

'And what about Uncle Percy and that flower?' Joe asked.

'I can't be sure it was Uncle Percy,' Becky replied.

'But you said you thought it was him.'

'It looked like him,' Becky said. 'The long silver hair was identical, but I really don't know. I was a distance away, so I can't be sure.'

Joe thought about this for a moment. 'These future visions of yours are always so *flippin' weird*.'

'That's it - it might not have been a premonition at all,' Becky replied. 'It might just have been a bad dream. Let's face it - we'd just been in a fight with Guy of Gisbourne. I was pretty stressed. Maybe that filled made my head with funny ideas.'

'There's nothin' funny about red-eyed corpses being studied by mad scientists.'

'I know.'

'And it's even less funny it might happen in our future.'

'It might've just been a dream.'

Joe pondered this for a moment. 'Are you going to tell Uncle Percy?'

'I don't know,' Becky replied. 'Do you think I should?'

Joe shrugged. 'That's up to you.'

'Then I don't think I will,' Becky said. 'We all need to stay focussed on finding the Isle of the Blessed, without him fretting over something that might just be a stupid dream.'

'But what if it's not just a stupid dream?'

'Then I guess we'll just have to deal with it when it happens.'

'Fair enough,' Joe said. He pulled out his phone and checked the time. 'Anyway, it's 8.50 a.m. Shall we get going?'

Ten minutes later, they entered the Time Room to see Uncle Percy in his favourite outfit – a cream linen jacket, violet waistcoat, Bermuda shorts, shirt and tie. 'Good morning.'

'Hi,' Becky said.

'Becky's had one of her freaky-deaky future visions,' Joe said bluntly.

'What?' Uncle Percy said, aghast.

Becky looked at Joe with astonishment. 'I thought you said it was up to me if I told him or not?'

'Soz,' Joe replied. 'I forgot.'

'Nevermind that,' Uncle Percy said. 'What about these visions?'

'Don't worry about it,' Becky said. 'I don't know whether or not they were visions. It may have just been a bad dream.'

'What kind of bad dream? Tell me everything.'

'I was in a village,' Becky said. 'I think it was an Eastern European village.'

'Why do you think that?' Uncle Percy asked.

'It reminded me of that time we visited Bran Castle in Transylvania in the sixteenth century.'

'I remember that,' Joe said. 'Dracula's Castle.'

'Allegedly the inspiration for Dracula's Castle,' Uncle Percy clarified. 'Continue, Becky.'

'The village in my dream was like the one we saw near Bran Castle,' Becky said. 'What was that village called again?'

'*Sohodol*,' Uncle Percy replied.

'Yeah. It was like Sohodol in terms of size and architecture,' Becky replied.

'Was it Sohodol?' Joe asked.

'I don't think so,' Becky replied. 'There was a castle nearby, though, but it looked really different from Bran Castle.'

'And what happened in the village?' Uncle Percy asked.

'Not much,' Becky replied. 'Everyone was dead.'

Uncle Percy's brow creased. 'Dead?'

'Yes - the villagers... all of them were just lying dead in the street. It was weird. It looked like they'd been going about their day and just collapsed dead on the spot. I mean, there was no sign of a massacre or anything, no arrows sticking out of anyone or anything like that.'

'And tell him the weirdest thing about the corpses,' Joe said.

'Their eyes were open,' Becky said. 'And their eyeballs were red... *blood red.*'

'Blood red?' Uncle Percy replied.

'Yes,' Becky replied. 'And there was something else. There were scientists there... modern scientists.'

'Scientists?' Uncle Percy said. 'What kind of scientists?'

'I don't know,' Becky said. 'They were wearing full PPE. They looked like astronauts.'

Uncle Percy's eyes tapered to slits. 'So, you think you were in a contemporary setting?'

'No,' Becky said. 'I've seen enough period costumes to know the real deal when I see it. This was the fifteenth or sixteenth century. I'm certain of it.'

Uncle Percy fell silent.

'What're you thinking?' Becky asked.

'I don't know what to think, Becky.'

'And tell him about his being in it?' Joe said.

Uncle Percy looked shocked.

'Oh, yeah,' Becky said. 'I think I saw you.'

'I was in the village?' Uncle Percy said.

'No,' Becky replied. 'I had a second vision, dream, whatever - a different one. You were sitting on a bench with a flower in your hand. At least I think it was you. I couldn't see your face, but there was this older man with the same shoulder-length silver hair as you.'

'And what was the setting?' Uncle Percy asked.

'I think it was a university campus or a college in America,' Becky said. 'There were lots of young people carrying books and looking studenty. I heard some of them talking, which is why I think it was the States. And it was definitely a long time ago - all the males were wearing ties and tank tops, and their hair was short and really old-fashioned. The females all wore really boring dresses and cardigans. If I was going to guess a decade, I'd say the nineteen thirties or forties.'

'And what was I doing there?'

'Nothing,' Becky replied simply. 'You were just sitting there, as if waiting for someone... with your flower.'

'What kind of flower was it?'

'I think it was a Stephanie Rose.'

Uncle Percy raised his eyebrow. 'Really?'

'I was a distance away,' Becky said. 'That's a guess. Maybe it was just a plain rose.'

'And was there anything else?'

'No,' Becky replied. 'That's when I woke up... or at least, came out of whatever it was.'

Uncle Percy thought about this for a moment. 'And did it feel like when you've had premonitions in the past?'

'I really can't say,' Becky said. 'I was tired. I was stressed. It'd been a tough day.'

'I understand,' Uncle Percy replied.

'I mean, it's probably nothing,' Becky said. 'It probably is just a dream.'

'Probably,' Uncle Percy said. 'Either way, there's no point in lingering on it. We'll just have to see what happens in the future. We can't let it influence all we have to do now.'

Becky nodded. 'I agree.'

'Then shall we depart for Caradan?' Uncle Percy said.

'Deffo,' Joe replied. 'Who doesn't want to see a minotaur town?'

'I am intrigued,' Uncle Percy replied. 'It's amazing to think I didn't believe in mythical creatures until a few years ago.'

'Yetis, aside,' Joe said.

Uncle Percy chuckled. 'Ah, yes. Yetis aside.'

'Now let's get serious,' Joe said. 'What weapons are we taking - you know, just in case?'

Uncle Percy shook his head. 'Not this time, Joe,' he replied. 'I refuse to believe we need to be armed to the teeth every time we embark on a time trip.'

'They sound like famous last words to me,' Joe said.

'We'll be under the protection of a town filled with the most powerful warriors to have ever graced the earth.'

'And what if an army of Spartans are attacking the town, trying to get a minotaur cub or two?' Joe said. 'Let's face it - it's happened before.'

Uncle Percy opened his mouth to say something, but no words emerged. Eventually, he gave his two-word reply in a strong, emphatic tone. 'No... Weapons!'

'Suit yourself,' Joe replied. 'But don't say I didn't warn you.'

'I won't be saying that, because there won't be a hint of trouble.'

Becky could tell from his expression he wasn't quite as confident as his words implied.

9

MEET THE PARENTS

A few moments later, Becky was standing on coarse sand, facing a dense wall of banana, mango, and breadfruit trees. To her a left, a spectacular green ocean lapped lightly onto a golden shore.

'Wow,' Joe said. 'The minotaurs picked a cool island to shack up on. Where exactly is it?'

'Just off the coast of West Africa,' Uncle Percy replied. 'And it truly is an island paradise, isn't it?'

Just then, a friendly shout filled the air.

'YOO-HOOOOO!'

Becky turned to see Edgar, Vilja and Darrian surface from the trees. Staring at Edgar, she couldn't help but laugh at the long grass skirt that covered his knees.

'What are you wearing, Eddie?' Joe shouted.

Beaming, Edgar did a twirl. 'It's a *Lithula* skirt – it's traditional Caradarian dress. Isn't it stylish?'

'It's awesome,' Joe said sarcastically.

'I'll acquire one for you, Joe.'

'Don't worry, Eddie,' Joe said. 'I'm good.'

'You look very smart, Edgar,' Uncle Percy said.

'Thank you, Perce, my most excellent friend,' Edgar said. 'Oh, I have so much to tell you all. So much has happened since I last saw you at Bowen Hall.'

'And we're very keen to hear it,' Uncle Percy said. 'Good morning, Vilja. It's delightful to see you again.'

'And you, Percy,' Vilja said. She held up Darrian, who was asleep in her arms. 'Darrian welcomes you to Caradan.'

'Thank you, Darrian,' Uncle Percy said.

'Hi, Vilja,' Becky and Joe said at the same time.

Becky approached Darrian. 'He's growing quickly.'

'He is, Becky Mellor,' Vilja replied proudly. 'He'll be standing before the season has passed.'

'He's a belter,' Joe said.

Vilja looked confused. 'A belter?' she said. 'As in he, err, will punch well?'

Joe laughed. 'It means he's good looking.'

'Ah.' Vilja smiled. 'Then you have my gratitude.'

'Anyhoo,' Edgar said. 'We have a smashing day planned for you. The Caradians are most eager to meet you all.'

'They are?' Uncle Percy asked, surprised.

'Oh, Lordy, yes,' Edgar replied. 'You are considered celebrities.'

'Celebrities?' Joe said.

'Of course,' Vilja replied. 'I said I would tell them of your adventures, and I have. Ever since they were Calfans, they have heard tales of the Battle of the Henge, how Thoth vanquished the traitor, Kraven. I have told them of your ability to journey through time, and about your saving the creatures of Atlantis in Egypt.' She gave a broad smile. 'Truly, they are overjoyed at meeting you.'

'Indeedy,' Edgar said. 'And they've arranged a marvellous feast in your honour, and after that you have an invitation to the inner sanctum to meet the Caradian scholars, for they have information about the Isle of the Blessed.'

'They do?' Becky said.

Edgar's ebony eyes shone as they found Becky's. 'Lordy, yes.'

'That's ace,' Becky said. 'What information?'

'I know not,' Edgar said. 'But the scholars will tell you everything. Now, is everyone hungry?'

'We've just had breakfast,' Becky said.

'Then you may have to loosen your belts somewhat,' Edgar replied. 'They've made a meal fit for Thoth himself. And with that feast in mind, I'm pleased to see Tusk isn't with you.'

'Why's that?' Uncle Percy asked.

Edgar looked awkward. 'Somehow squirrels were intro-duced to the island many years ago, and it seems Caradian minotaurs consider them quite the delicacy. Amongst many other unconventional dishes, they've made *Ohioritas*.'

'And what are Ohioritas?' Uncle Percy asked.

Edgar hesitated. 'Squirrel kebabs.'

'Squirrel kebabs?' Joe said, repulsed.

'Many Caradians say they're delicious,' Edgar said. 'Being a vegetarian, I wouldn't know.'

Uncle Percy pondered this for a moment. 'Then I think for the purposes of this trip, and out of deference for our good friend, we may become vegetarians, too. What do you think, Becky, Joe?'

Becky and Joe replied quickly and bluntly.

'Definitely!' Becky said.

Joe nodded. 'I'm all about the veggies.'

BECKY, Joe and Uncle Percy followed Edgar, Vilja and Darrian into the jungle, where almost immediately they heard a low, rhythmic thumping sound from some distance away.

'What's that?' Joe asked.

'The *drums of Caradan* are sounded for you,' Edgar replied. 'I'm told it's quite the honour.'

'How kind of them,' Uncle Percy replied.

As they advanced through the jungle, the drums grew louder.

After about ten minutes, the undergrowth thinned to reveal a line of high timber posts, whittled to a point, which rose from the ground like totem poles, and stretched into the distance.

'And here we are,' Edgar said. 'The town of *Caradan*.' He turned toward a vast open gate, its pillars nearly touching the sky.

As the drums filled her ears, Becky entered Caradan feeling like Gulliver in the Land of the Giants. Immediately, her head spiralled. She'd seen many amazing things in her life, and witnessed some of the most extraordinary architecture, but this was unlike anything she'd seen before.

A huge town spread before her, peppered with countless high wooden huts, three times as high as any normal house. At the far end of the compound, she saw a warren of streets and boulevards, with elegant buildings fashioned from limestone blocks, quite out of place in a jungle setting. There were several large statues of distinguished-looking minotaurs and mino-tauras, a Doric peripteral temple, a fresh-water well, and an amphitheatre.

Her astonishment, however, was compounded by the dozens of minotaurs, minotauras and calfans lining the town's perimeter walls, some striking gigantic kettle drums with batons the size of baseball bats, others pounding spears on the ground, in a deafening gesture of welcome. Many calfans leapt up and down excitedly, clapping their hands and waving in the hope they might attract the attention of their new visitors.

With a final earth-shattering *bang*, silence replaced sound, and the minotaurs fell still. The door of a building opened and a minotaur and minotaura appeared, a four-legged creature at their side.

As the minotaur and minotaura walked toward them, Becky saw they were both dressed identically in elegant scarlet robes edged with silver fur; each wore a gleaming orange metal chain around their neck that Becky recognised as being crafted from the Atlantean metal, *Orichalcum*.

However, her greatest surprise came when she spied the animal that accompanied them. At first, she thought it was a gigantic dog, but then she saw the feathered head of an eagle capped its powerful canine torso. Furthermore, she'd seen this same species before, locked in an iron cage in the hellhole that was *The Sanctuary* in Ancient Egypt.

It was a Griffon.

As the minotaur and minotaura approached, Vilja turned to Becky, Joe, and Uncle Percy. 'Everyone,' she said. 'May I present my parents – Gordoth and Perigalla - the chieftain and chieftainess of Caradan.'

Gordoth stopped, and a warm smile formed on his mouth. His sapphire blue eyes sparkled. 'Percy Halifax, Becky and Joe Mellor,' he said in a deep baritone voice as smooth as honey. 'It is a true honour you bestow upon Caradan by visiting us today.'

Uncle Percy stared up at the enormous minotaur. 'The honour is ours, Gordoth. And may we thank you and the rest of the town for this spectacular welcome.'

'I echo Gordoth's words,' Perigalla said. 'The minotaurs and minotauras of Caradan welcome you with the warmest of hearts.'

'We are delighted to be here, Perigalla,' Uncle Percy said. 'Aren't we, Becky, Joe?'

'Absolutely,' Becky said.

'Deffo,' Joe said. 'Those drums are so cool, and your town looks ace.'

'Thank you, Joe,' Perigalla said. 'You are free to wander as you may. No door is closed to you.'

'Cheers,' Joe replied.

Gordoth leant down and patted the griffon's head. 'This is the griffon, *Triaca*. She understands who you are and what you did for her kind - how it was you that saved the children of Atlantis from the human beast, Aribert Heim. It was Triaca's distant ancestor, *Portania*, that you set free from her cage in the Sanctuary.'

'I see,' Becky said, surprised.

Triaca clicked her beak twice and gave a deep bow.

'That is Triaca stating her gratitude,' Gordoth said.

Becky was astonished. 'You are welcome, Triaca.'

'There are many other creatures on Caradan that only exist because of your actions that day.'

'I'm glad,' Becky said.

'We also know of your exploits within the Chamber of the Ancients, about your meeting the legendary Thoth, defeating the traitor, Kraven, and the victory at the great Battle of the Henge. We consider the three of you heroes of your kind.'

Becky felt awkward at the compliment. 'Err, thank you.'

'And there is more to thank you for,' Perigalla said. 'Percy Halifax, I hear because of your swift actions at his birth our grandcalfan, Darrian, was brought safely to this realm and without harm to our beloved daughter, Vilja. For that, we cannot thank you enough.'

'It was my pleasure,' Uncle Percy said. 'Darrian is a fine cub. You must be very proud.'

'We are indeed, Percy Halifax,' Gordoth said. 'It is also important you know how much we value our new son, Edgar the Valiant. We hear he was nervous at our meeting, but he did not need to be. We consider him as much a part of our family as we would a son of our own blood.'

'Edgar's a remarkable minotaur,' Uncle Percy said. 'We think of him as part of our family, too.' He smiled at Edgar. 'Don't we, kids?'

'Too right we do,' Joe said. 'Eddie rocks.'

'He's the best,' Becky added.

Edgar tried to hide his moistening eyes. 'Tush and frapple-potts,' he said. 'You must all stop now, or I'll weep like a calfan.'

Gordoth slapped Edgar's back with pride. 'There is no shame in the shedding of tears, Edgar. They reveal a gentle heart and fine character.' He turned back to Uncle Percy. 'Now we know you are here for a reason, that you are searching for the Isle of the Blessed. I also know we can help you. After we have feasted, the Caradian scholars invite you to the inner sanctum of the Hall of Knowledge, where they will impart information no son of man has received before.'

'Thank you, Gordoth,' Uncle Percy said.

'That's brilliant,' Becky said.

'But first, would you join us in a feast?' Perigalla said. 'We have some of the finest cooks preparing the most delicious recipes of our motherland.'

'We'd enjoy that very much,' Uncle Percy said.

'I forgot to mention, Gordoth,' Edgar said. 'But my friends have recently become vegetarian.'

'We hope that doesn't put you out too much,' Uncle Percy said.

'Not at all. Perigalla and Vilja are both vegetarians,' Gordoth replied. 'It matters not upon what we feast, but that we feast together, as one, an alliance of man and bull, united in friendship and harmony. Now, please, join me, my wife and our clan in the Great Hall.'

Soon, Becky, Joe and Uncle Percy trailed Gordoth, Perigalla and Triaca across the town.

Absorbing the remarkable sights and sounds of Caradan, Becky's mind whirled. There was something new and fascinating around every corner, and she was keen to learn all she could about minotaur culture and customs. However, none of it made her feel any hungrier.

The image of Tusk impaled on a skewer had put a stop to that.

10

THE TALE OF HERATHON

Becky, Joe and Uncle Percy were led to the largest building in the compound, its mouldings adorned with unusual symbols, many of them abstract forms and shapes, others depicting imagery from minotaurean history.

As Gordoth pushed open the front door, Becky's nostrils were assaulted with the smells of delicious food, some familiar, others unlike anything she'd smelt before.

'Welcome to the Great Hall of Caradan,' Gordoth said, gesturing for them to enter.

Stepping inside, Becky's head spun. The hall was crowded with oversized tables and chairs, taller than any human, which were laden with both hot and cold food. The walls were covered with tapestries and hangings in styles she'd never seen before, alongside paintings of warriors, clerics, scholars, and other distinguished minotaurs and minotauras.

'You will sit at the high table,' Gordoth said. 'The legs have been shortened to accommodate your size.'

'It's a low, high table then,' Uncle Percy said with a smile.

Gordoth chuckled. 'That is true, Percy Halifax.'

'And our chairs?' Uncle Percy asked. 'Can we assume they're not your average minotaurean chairs?'

'They are calfan chairs from our infant school.'

Joe laughed. 'We're on baby chairs, then?'

Gordoth looked awkward before saying, 'Is that acceptable for you?'

'Of course, Gordoth,' Uncle Percy said. 'A chair is a chair.'

Perigalla led them to a smaller table at the far end of the hall and gestured for them to sit down.

As they did, the front door opened and minotaurs, minotauras and calfans streamed in.

As far as Becky was concerned, the next hour passed in a blur. Whereas, she assumed the minotaurs would be serious, solemn and intense, the levity and laughter that filled the room surprised her.

Infused with unusual herbs and spices, the food itself was like nothing she'd ever had before. There were countless dishes on offer, and she tried many of them, both out of politeness and genuine interest. These included *Raskatoth* – an aubergine, fig and broccoli pie; Chocha bread; Paka spiced mushrooms baked in a Klani (a clay oven); black-bean and tomato stew; leaf wrapped Agidi in a palaver sauce; banana akrash, and cinnamon cake. It was all surprisingly delicious. Moreover, she avoided seeing anything that resembled a skewered squirrel.

Between each course, a succession of minotaurs, minotauras and calfans came over to pay their respects, ask questions about Thoth and the Battle of the Henge, and to offer their fealty and admiration.

With all the constant attention, Becky felt relieved when the feast and subsequent speeches ended, and the minotaurs left the hall and returned to their homes.

As the tables were cleared, Gordoth and Perigalla approached Becky Joe and Uncle Percy.

'We hope you enjoyed your meal,' Perigalla said.

Uncle Percy tapped his swollen belly. 'Elegance sufficience,' he replied. 'And I may have to ask you for some of those recipes.'

'Why?' Joe said. 'You can't cook for toffee.'

'I might make more of an effort with food that can taste that good.'

'We are pleased it was to your liking,' Gordoth said. 'And you can have any recipe you desire, Percy Halifax, but for now it is time for you to meet with the Caradian scholars.'

Uncle Percy's eyes scanned the hall. 'Are they here?'

'They did not feast with us,' Perigalla replied. 'They are of age and felt the commotion would be too much. They are waiting to greet you in the Hall of Knowledge.'

'Excellent,' Uncle Percy replied. 'Then, please, lead the way...'

A few moments later, they were walking down a tapered road to a building concealed behind the hanging leaves of iron-wood trees. Two giant statues of minotaurs, coated in moss and weathered with age, stood on either side of a wooden door, above which were words etched into the limestone.

Perigalla stopped at the door. 'This is The Hall of Knowledge. It is the most prized, cherished edifice in all of Caradan. You will be the first humans to ever step inside.'

'We are highly honoured,' Uncle Percy replied.

Gordoth opened the door. 'Please... follow me.'

The mournful call of a Namaqua dove met Becky's ears as she entered a massive room. Sunlight streamed through a skylight onto countless shelves, set upon which were books, parchments, silk scrolls, clay tablets, and copper plates, along-side thousands of other Atlantean artifacts.

'My word!' Uncle Percy exhaled. 'This is magnificent.'

Gordoth smiled. 'We knew you would appreciate it. Edgar told us how you are the greatest mind of your age, perhaps of any age.'

'I'm really not,' Uncle Percy replied modestly. 'Where did you get it all?'

'Much of it was rescued from Atlantis during the great exodus,' Gordoth replied. 'Even before the Isle of the Ancients sank, my kind collected and preserved learning, not only from our own antiquity, but from all the great manfolk civilisations – Sumerian, Mesopotamian, Egyptian, Persian. As minotaurs, we value knowledge a great deal.'

'As does every advanced civilisation,' Uncle Percy replied.

'You speak the truth, Percy Halifax,' Gordoth replied. 'And if you would ever be keen to return to study the manuscripts you would be most welcome.'

Uncle Percy's eyes ignited. 'Really? Oh, I'd like that. I'd like that very much.'

'Then you must,' Gordoth said. 'Now, please, follow me.'

Gordoth and Perigalla led Becky, Joe and Uncle Percy down a small corridor, at the end of which was a double door.

'We are here,' Perigalla said. 'Gordoth and myself cannot enter the inner sanctum,' she said. 'Only those invited within by the scholars can hear what they have to say.'

'Then we thank you both for bringing us,' Uncle Percy said.

'Yeah, thanks,' Becky said, her anticipation building.

'Cheers,' Joe added.

'It is our privilege and our pleasure,' Gordoth said. 'We hope you find the answers you seek.' He pushed open the door. 'And one last thing – if you ever need the aid of the minotaurs of Caradan, you need only ask. You, and your kin, are held with such regard that our strength, our hearts, and our spears are yours should you ever need us.'

'Thank you, Gordoth,' Uncle Percy said. 'We'll keep that in mind.'

Becky followed Uncle Percy and Joe into the inner sanctum.

Immediately, Becky found herself in a circular room, lit by flaming torches on all sides, which brightened a circular table in the room's centre. Sitting at the table were three minotaurs and three minotauras.

A minotaura stood up. At around twelve feet in height, she had a sandy-brown head with a long, curly fringe, her long horns curved outward in a flat arc. She wore a floor-length silk dress and held a walking cane as tall as a tree. She hobbled slowly over to them.

'You must be Percy Halifax,' the minotaura said in a voice that still contained a hint of the vivacious minotaura she'd once been. 'We welcome you to the inner sanctum. I am Erikka, the chief curator of *The Hall of Knowledge*.'

'Thank you for seeing us, Erikka,' Uncle Percy said. 'Please, call me Percy.'

'The honour is mine, Percy,' Erikka said. She smiled at Becky and Joe. 'And Becky and Joe Mellor. We have read about your exploits in the *Chronicles of Thermon*, and find it astonishing you stand before us now.'

'Hello, Erikka,' Becky said.

'Hi,' Joe added.

Erikka turned to the other minotaurs, who remained seated. 'This is Brangon, Jarafan, Thombillia, Pengiar, and Hervania.' As she delivered each name, the respective minotaur or minotaura bowed their head in respect of their guests. 'Together, we are known as *The Keepers of the Sacred Word,* and we hear you wish to know of the Isle of the Blessed. It will be our privilege to share all we know with you.'

'Thank you so much,' Uncle Percy replied sincerely.

'But first, Percy Halifax, we would ask for you to return to this sanctum in the future.'

'You would?' Uncle Percy replied.

'Very much so,' Erikka replied. 'Edgar has informed us of your journey to another realm, to the Dwarf kingdom of Svartalfheim. He tells us you believe there may be a connection with our forefathers and this realm. He also tells us you have seen a Suman Stone mine.'

Uncle Percy nodded. 'It's true.'

Erikka's eyes widened with wonder. 'We would very much like to hear your theories on this if you would care to return to us one day and share your thoughts.'

'I'd love to return,' Uncle Percy replied.

'It is agreed then,' Erikka said, smiling. Her demeanour changed. 'Anyway, would you all sit down? We have a tale to tell of a legendary voyage countless years ago, in another age, another time, not long after the fall of Atlantis.' She pointed at three small seats.

Becky, Uncle Percy and Joe sat down as they waited for Erikka to return to her seat.

Becky's heart thumped as Erikka cleared her throat.

'Countless years ago,' Erikka said, 'there was a minotaur named *Herathon*. He was the greatest sailor of our kind, the greatest sailor the world had ever seen. He navigated every ocean from the Icelands of the North, to the Sandlands of the West, and all in between.'

She swallowed a breath.

'He was a courageous minotaur, a true warrior of the sea. However, of all the immeasurable places he visited, he claimed there was only one that filled him with both wonderment and fear in equal measure – an island of such uniqueness he'd never seen its like before. He called it *The Isle of the Blessed*, and amongst other things he found was an enchanted lake, with water that could heal illness, lift magical curses, and give unnaturally long life to anyone that drank from it.'

'And did he drink it?'

'A minotaur's time on this earth is around two hundred and fifty years. I, myself, am one hundred and seventy years of age. Herathon lived for five hundred and eighty years. He kept drinking the water until he chose to die, otherwise I believe he would still be alive to this day.'

'And can you tell us where it is?' Uncle Percy asked.

Erikka gave a single shake of her head. 'I cannot,' she said. 'But Herathon said it was in the open seas to the south of a land filled with *Puuzans*, one of which he said was the largest snow-tipped *Puuzan* he'd ever seen. He said it was so large it stretched from the earth to the heavens.'

'What's a *Puuzan?*' Uncle Percy asked.

'It is an Atlantean word,' Erikka replied. 'In your tongue, it means *fire mountain*.'

Uncle Percy processed this. 'Fire mountain – you mean a volcano? It was a large snow-tipped volcano?' Something occurred to him. 'There's a Japanese island called Honshu, with over forty active volcanoes. One of those is the most famous volcano in the world - *Mount Fuji*.'

'I do not know these names,' Erikka replied.

'Very well,' Uncle Percy said. 'Please, continue.'

'It was while he was on the land of the Puuzan he heard the legend of the Isle of the Blessed, a magical island, with rare flora, strange and amazing wildlife, and an enchanted pool that offered immortality to those that drank from it. And so, with a burning desire to learn more, Herathon set off to find the island. He sailed for countless days, until, one stormy day, he journeyed through an emerald fog, the shade of a Suman Stone, before emerging to find a vast island, one unlike any he'd seen before. Anyway, he moored his ship in the shallows and set off to explore. He declared it the most beautiful, and yet dangerous place he had ever visited.'

'Why dangerous?'

'He said there were creatures there unlike any other in this realm, dangerous creatures that would frighten even the strongest minotaur.'

'What sort of creatures?' Joe asked.

'He said the island was alive with *Dragons*,' Erikka said.

'Dragons?' Uncle Percy said, surprised.

'Yes.' Erikka struggled to her feet and shuffled into the shadows, from which she emerged a moment later carrying a huge object mounted on a wooden plinth. She returned to the table and placed it down for all to see. 'He even slew one of these *dragons*.'

Becky's eyes nearly exploded in their sockets. She was staring at a snow-white skull marked by with two horns, a long snout peppered with spikes and frills, and jaws that were lined with huge, curved teeth.

'Crikey,' Uncle Percy said, as Joe swore loudly.

Becky had no words.

Erikka studied their expressions. 'Can I assume you've not seen a dragon's skull before?'

11

ENTER THE DRAGON

Becky's head spun like a top. Was it really a dragon's skull? A few years earlier, she would've thought the idea preposterous, but after all the things she'd seen since it was more than possible.

'Do you mind if I take a closer inspection, Erikka?' Uncle Percy asked.

'Be my guest,' Erikka replied.

Uncle Percy approached the skull before taking a good, hard look, studying its every contour. 'How remarkable,' he said.

'Herathon thought so,' Erikka said. 'He said this species and others roamed the Isle of the Blessed, making it a beautiful but deadly place.'

'I imagine so,' Uncle Percy said. 'He was lucky to escape with his life.'

'I believe so,' Erikka said. 'But he said the biggest threat to his life came not from any dragon, but from the traitor in his midst.'

'A traitor?'

'A member of his crew, *Kallibane*, a young minotaur he

believed a brother and ally, tried to steal Herathon's ship, and the treasures he'd acquired on the journey. Kallibane attempted to murder Herathon as he slept, but he failed. As was his right under our maritime law, Herathon could either execute Kallibane or inflict another punishment. He chose to maroon Kallibane and leave him at the island's mercy. It is said the tears fell from his eyes like rainfall as he sailed away.'

'And then Herathon returned to Caradan?'

'He did, and never took to the seas again,' Erikka said. 'And that is the extent of our knowledge of the Isle of the Blessed. I hope it was of worth to you.'

'It was,' Uncle Percy replied. 'Very much so.'

'Then our time is at an end,' Erikka said.

'It is,' Uncle Percy said. 'And we thank you for your time.'

Becky, Joe and Uncle Percy left the scholars with a promise that Uncle Percy would return and share his theories on Atlantis, minotaur migration, and their possible connection with another world. After finding Edgar, Vilja, and Darrian, to say their goodbyes, Uncle Percy set his portravella to return to the twenty-first century.

To Becky's surprise, they materialised in Bowen Hall library.

'The library?' Joe said. 'What're we doing here?'

'You'll see,' Uncle Percy replied mysteriously. 'Take a seat, please. There are a few things we need to discuss, and I'd rather do that whilst certain images are still fresh in our thoughts.' He walked over to a shelf and scanned the books.

Becky and Joe took a seat at the table in the middle of the room.

Joe glanced at Becky. 'So, d'you reckon that was a real dragon head?'

'I don't know... maybe. It certainly looked... err, dragonish.'

'It did, didn't it?' Joe said. 'I mean, I thought we'd come up against dragons at some point - let's face it, we've fought everything else - but I dunno, it was still a shock, wasn't it?'

'Yeah,' Becky replied.

Uncle Percy joined them at the table, holding a book, its cover face down on the table; quite unlike most of the books in the library, which were ancient and tatty with age, this one looked relatively new and in pristine condition.

'You think the Isle of the Blessed is near Japan, then?' Joe asked Uncle Percy.

'It's possible,' Uncle Percy replied. 'Mount Fuji certainly matches Herathon's description. Plus, there are other factors that may mark that geographical area as a point of interest for us.'

'What other factors?' Becky asked.

'There's a stretch of ocean near to Southern Japan that is somewhat notorious.'

'Notorious - why?' Becky asked.

'Well, do you recall visiting a part of the Atlantic Ocean known as *The Bermuda Triangle*?'

'Sure,' Joe replied. 'Zombie sharks, sea serpents, and bonkers weather - we had a fab time!'

'That's open to debate,' Uncle Percy replied. 'As you know, the Bermuda Triangle is notable for ships and planes vanishing, and other strange anomalies. Anyway, it just so happens there's an expanse of ocean in the Pacific in which many similar things have happened.' He paused. 'Furthermore, its name seems relevant to the current conversation.'

'What's it called?' Joe asked.

'*The Dragon's Triangle.*'

'Dragons again, eh?' Joe said.

'Indeed,' Uncle Percy replied. 'I'm sure you can see why it's of interest.'

'Why's it called that?' Becky asked.

'There's an ancient Chinese myth that claims dragons lived in that part of the Pacific Ocean, attacking ships and pulling them down to the watery depths. The legend was compounded a thousand years ago, when Kublai Khan, the Grandson of the infamous Mongol leader, Genghis Khan, sent an army of warriors across the sea to invade Japan, and many of that army disappeared without a trace.'

'And what happened to them?'

'I don't know,' Uncle Percy replied. 'Still, that is all the stuff of myth and legend. The one thing I'm confident of is we didn't actually see a dragon's skull in Caradan.'

Becky looked shocked. 'What?'

'You don't think it was a dragon?' Joe asked.

'No,' Uncle Percy replied. 'At least, not in any traditional mythological sense.'

'Then what was it?' Joe asked.

'I think it was one of these.' Uncle Percy opened the book and spread it over the table.

A shiver scaled Becky's spine. The right-hand page displayed the photograph of a skull, almost identical to the one they'd seen an hour earlier, the only difference being the tiny, flat teeth rooted in its jaw, instead of the long, curved ones of the Caradan skull. Beside the photograph was a painted illustration of the actual creature standing in a woodland glade.

'That's a book about *dinosaurs*?' Joe said. 'You think Herathon's dragon was actually a dinosaur?'

'I do. They're almost impossible to tell apart, aren't they?'

'Except for the teeth,' Becky said. 'The other skull's teeth were huge.'

'I know,' Uncle Percy said, nodding at the book. 'This dinosaur was a herbivore. The skull we saw in Caradan belonged to a carnivore, I've no doubt about that.' He swallowed a breath. 'And that's one reason why I'm confused to say the least.'

'What kind of dinosaur is it?' Joe asked.

'It's the new-to-science kind,' Uncle Percy replied. 'It was first discovered in 2004 in South Dakota and presented to the Children's Museum in Indianapolis. It wasn't officially given a scientific name until two years later, when Bob Bakker, the renowned palaeontologist, gave it a name he thought would ignite the imagination of children everywhere.'

'What did he call it?' Becky asked.

'*Dracorex Hogwartsia.*'

Surprise and astonishment crossed Becky's face. 'Hogwarts? Draco?'

'Yes.' Uncle Percy grinned. 'It's an absolutely *wizard* name, don't you agree?'

12

RETURN OF THE MASK

'Are you takin' the mick?' Joe asked.

'Not at all,' Uncle Percy replied.

'There's a dinosaur actually named after Draco Malfoy in Harry Potter?'

'Well, *Draco* is Latin for dragon,' Uncle Percy replied, 'and *Rex* is Latin for king. So Dracorex actually means *Dragon King*, which is clearly fitting, as its skull resembles a dragon, at least the popular visualisation of one.'

'And Hogwartsia?' Joe asked.

'I think Mister Bakker was just having a bit of fun,' Uncle Percy replied. 'Perhaps in an attempt to make palaeontology more accessible for youngsters. Anyway, from what I hear a certain Ms. Rowling was delighted by the name. Who wouldn't be?'

But something occurred to Becky. 'I'm confused,' she said. 'If it's a dinosaur – I mean, a real dinosaur – then how would it exist in Herathon's time? Surely, that's about four or five thousand years ago, isn't it?'

'And that's precisely what puzzles me,' Uncle Percy said. 'The reality is Dracorex walked the earth over sixty-five million years ago, and would've been wiped out like all the other dinosaurs by the asteroid. Yes, something is most definitely very peculiar about all this.'

At that moment, a penetrating bleep echoed from the Hologramophone in the room's corner.

Uncle Percy walked over to it and read the display.

INCOMING HOLOGRAMOPHONIC MESSAGE:
   Recipient: Percy Halifax
   Sender: Maria
   Location: Unknown

'OH, HOW NICE... IT'S MARIA,' Uncle Percy said. Then his brow furrowed. 'That's unusual.'

'What is?' Joe asked.

'She and Jacob are staying at the lodge on Percy Island,' Uncle Percy replied. 'Yet it says *location unknown*. I set up that Hologramophone myself, so unless it's faulty, it should show that very location.' He reached over and pressed a button.

Three lasers shot out of the box, converging about six feet away and forming a three-dimensional image of Maria's face.

Becky's delight soon turned to horror.

Maria's eyes leaked tears, her cheeks red raw. Behind her was a tapestry depicting a dragon chasing its own tail, and below that an ornamental stone fireplace, which encased a roaring fire.

It was definitely not the ski lodge on Percy Island.

'Maria?' Uncle Percy gasped. 'What's the matter?'

'T-they have sh-shot him, sir,' Maria spluttered, her body quivering.

'Shot who?'

'My Jacob... they h-have shot my Jacob.'

Uncle Percy's face drained of colour. 'Is he alive?'

At that moment, the image changed as the camera was repositioned. It came to a halt on a different figure entirely. Dressed in an elegant white suit, shirt and tie, the Wraith's golden mask gleamed in the firelight.

Bile welled in Becky's throat.

'Yes,' the Wraith replied in a voice both sinister and yet matter-of-factly. 'For the moment.'

'Where are Maria and Jacob?' Uncle Percy said, struggling to maintain his composure.

'I suppose you could say they are at my true *home*.' The Wraith gave a sour chuckle. 'It's certainly more of a home to me than Bowen Hall ever was.'

Uncle Percy didn't rise to the bait. 'Bring Maria and Jacob to me,' he said. 'Any grudge you have against me shouldn't involve them.'

'True.'

'THEN BRING THEM HERE!' Uncle Percy shouted. 'JACOB NEEDS TO SEE A DOCTOR!'

'He has seen a doctor,' the Wraith replied calmly. 'He was shot in the leg, and the bullet has been removed. He's quite healthy for the moment, I assure you... whether he remains that way is up to you.'

'How could you shoot an old man like that?'

'I didn't shoot him,' the Wraith replied. 'And from what I hear, Heinrich Müller was provoked. He does have a famously short temper.'

Uncle Percy's fists balled. 'Then you can tell Müller he'll rue the day his temper got the better of him.'

The Wraith gave an ugly chuckle. 'Oh, Percy, such *toxic masculinity*. I'd never expect it from you!'

Uncle Percy ignored him. 'What will it take for us to get Maria and Jacob back?'

'I know you've attained the Odin Horn. I also know you're searching for *The Pool of Life.*'

Uncle Percy's eyes narrowed. 'How do you know?'

'Please, Percy,' the Wraith replied scornfully. 'There's not a move you make I do not know about. Now, based on your past successes, I have every faith you'll find it. With that in mind, I wish you to bring me a bottle of its water, and then you'll give me the Odin Horn. Only then can you can have your friends back. It's a fair deal, wouldn't you say?'

'That's not happening,' Becky said resolutely.

'Not so fast, Becky,' the Wraith replied. 'I shall allow you to use the Odin Horn to douse your parents in the water. It is only after that I will take the water and the Odin Horn. That is my price for the return of Maria and Jacob. Now, do you agree with my terms?'

In the background, Becky could hear Maria sobbing. Her blood boiling, she looked at Uncle Percy and knew they had no choice.

Uncle Percy nodded. 'Yes.'

'Good,' the Wraith replied.

'But I swear to you,' Uncle Percy said. 'If you harm Maria and Jacob further, I'll not rest until I hunt you down and –'

'– ENOUGH OF YOUR PETTY THREATS!' the Wraith roared. His tone softened to a hiss. 'Judgement Day is coming for us all, Percy. I assure you of that. *Save your threats for that day, for it is then you shall hear mine!*' And with that, his image vanished.

Silence cloaked the library.

'I'm gonna kill that guy one day,' Joe said.

'Don't say that, Joe,' Uncle Percy said firmly. 'Not now. Not ever.'

'But –'

'No, buts,' Uncle Percy said. 'He'll answer for his crimes one day.'

'Do you think Maria and Jacob will be okay?' Becky said quietly.

'I'm certain of it,' Uncle Percy replied confidently. 'Whatever his gripe, it's with me. And in this case, it seems he's using them as leverage. He wants something, and if he hurts them further, he won't get it. It's as simple as that.'

Becky felt satisfied Uncle Percy was right. 'Why do you think he wants the water and horn?'

'It's obvious,' Joe replied. 'He wants to be immortal.'

'Perhaps,' Uncle Percy said. 'The one thing I know is this plan was hatched some time ago.'

'What do you mean?' Becky asked.

Uncle Percy's face turned grave. 'I think he ensured Medusa froze your parents because he knew we'd go after the Odin Horn and the water. I think that's what he had planned all along.'

'Why?' Joe asked.

'Only time will tell.'

Becky was about to say something when another loud bleep pierced the air. Her eyes found the Hologramophone in the far corner of the room and a chill surged through her.

What did the Wraith want now?

Hesitantly, Uncle Percy approached the box. However, as he stared at the display panel, his face changed from concern to surprise.

INCOMING HOLOGRAMOPHONIC MESSAGE:
Recipient: Percy Halifax
Sender: Alwyn Thomas
Location: Swiss Alps, Bernese Oberland, Switzerland

'IS IT THE WRAITH AGAIN?' Joe asked.

'No,' Uncle Percy replied. 'It's Alwyn Thomas. A Welsh time traveller. A nice man.'

Uncle Percy hit a button and again another image formed before their eyes.

About sixty years of age, Alwyn Thomas's thick silver hair, parted on the right, crowned a pale, wrinkly face, its warm smile revealing brown teeth stained from years of smoking pipe tobacco. He wore a heavy parka coat with a hood lined with thick fur, over a corduroy suit and tie. He appeared to be standing in a glittering landscape of snow-coated mountains.

'Alrigh', Perce?' Thomas said, his breath forming clouds.

'Hello, Alwyn,' Uncle Percy replied. 'I am indeed.'

'Ah, it's crackin' good to have caught you,' Thomas replied.

'It's good to have been caught,' Uncle Percy replied. 'What are you doing in the Swiss Alps?'

'Nobblin' my scallops off,' Thomas replied. 'Listen, boyo, I've got some tidy news... very excitin' stuff.'

'What sort of news?'

'The word on the street is you're lookin' for *The Blessed Isle*?' Thomas said. 'Is that true?'

'We've always known it as the Isle of the Blessed, but yes – yes it's true,' Uncle Percy replied.

'Good,' Thomas said. 'Because I reckon I can help ya with that.'

'You can?'

'Yeah. I Ain't gonna lie to ya,' Thomas said. 'I've got a tale for you that'll char your Crempogs.'

'What kind of tale?'

'I've met a fella that's been there... to the Blessed Isle, I mean.'

Becky's ears pricked up.

'You have?' Uncle Percy asked, stunned.

'Yeah,' Thomas replied. 'But that ain't the mad thing. You wanna know what is?'

'Er, yes,' Uncle Percy replied.

'This fella went there over two thousand three hundred years ago.'

Uncle Percy looked puzzled. 'What do you mean - he's a time traveller?'

'Nah,' Thomas replied. 'He went there as a young man.'

'But that would mean –'

'– Yeah,' Thomas interrupted. 'On his last birthday he was two thousand three hundred and seventy something years old.'

13

HEATH PINEOS

'That's incredible,' Uncle Percy said.

'But true,' Thomas replied. 'I double-checked and treble-checked, and he's the real deal. The truth is he visited the Blessed Isle in 322BC, and has been drinking water from its magic pool ever since.'

'Who is he?' Uncle Percy asked.

Thomas grinned. 'That's the thing – you'll know him,' he said. 'He's a well-known fella in his field, a real bigwig. Now, d'you wanna meet him? He's available now if you do.'

Becky didn't wait for Uncle Percy's reply. 'Yes, please,' she said. 'We can come immediately.'

Thomas flashed Becky a smile. 'Good... because he's chompin' at the bit to meet you lot.'

'He is? Why?' Uncle Percy asked.

'Because I've told him about time travel,' Thomas said. 'I had no choice, and when you hear the full story, you'll understand why. More importantly, I've told him all 'bout yer adventures, about John and Cathy's situation, and how you're all experts at trackin' down rare, mythological stuff.' He paused.

'The thing is, he wants your help. In fact, I would say he's desperate for it.'

'What kind of help?' Uncle Percy said.

'I'll let him explain that to ya,' Thomas replied. 'Anyway, I'm standin' in the grounds of one of his properties now, and he's here, so we can make this happen pronto if you're up for it.'

'He lives in the Swiss Alps?' Uncle Percy asked.

'Sometimes,' Thomas replied. 'Anyway, the spatial coordinates are 22-87-09, and you'll need to dress up warm. It might look lush, but it's as cold as a Swansea Sunday.'

'That's fine,' Uncle Percy said. 'We'll be there in two ticks and half a jiffy.'

'Tidy. See you then.' And with that, Thomas was gone.

Becky's heart swelled. Promptly, the Wraith vanished from her mind, replaced by the thought they would soon meet someone who'd visited the Isle of the Blessed.

Joe looked at Uncle Percy. 'A bloke exists that's been alive for over two thousand years?'

'So he claims,' Uncle Percy replied.

'That's insane.'

'It is, rather.'

'Let's go and meet him,' Becky said.

'Indeed,' Uncle Percy said. 'Put on your extreme winter wear and I'll meet you in the Time Room in fifteen minutes.'

Wasting no time, Becky raced to her room and found the clothing she last wore to the Himalayas a few years earlier - a honey-coloured padded coat, a fleece, trousers, socks and boots. She got dressed before waddling over to the Time Room, sweating profusely all the way.

Joe was already there when she arrived. Together, they entered the Time Room to see a gleaming pink car in the middle of the room.

Immediately, Becky recalled Uncle Percy's pink Cadillac,

Betty, a time machine that was both a traditional car and a snowmobile fixed with retractable skis.

Dressed in a thick black coat and white hood, Uncle Percy was keying digits into a workstation. 'Are we ready, then?'

'Definitely.' Joe nodded at the Cadillac. 'And it's good to see we're taking a proper time machine this time. It's not as much fun when we use portravellas.'

'Betty certainly came in useful evading that avalanche on Mount Everest,' Uncle Percy replied. He opened the driver's door. 'Now, shall we meet a man allegedly older than Jesus Christ?'

These words made Becky freeze on the spot.

Joe noticed. 'Are you okay, sis?'

'Yeah... it's just... err.'

'It's just this whole thing is proper barmy, ain't it?'

'Something like that,' Becky replied.

Becky and Joe climbed onto the rear seat.

Joe looked at Uncle Percy, and his mouth curled in a mischievous grin. 'So... have you ever travelled back to see him? I bet you have.'

'Who?'

'The Big Boss. The gaffer. The top banana. *Jesus*,' Joe said.

Uncle Percy looked affronted. 'Absolutely not.'

'Really?'

'Really.'

'Why? I mean, he's - I dunno - the most famous person ever,' Joe said. 'Even more famous than Ronaldo.'

Uncle Percy exhaled. 'I have complex feelings about this, Joe. Yes, I could travel in time and see him, even investigate further and authenticate which parts of the bible are true or false. However, I prefer not to know. I have my own thoughts on religion and those are personal to me. I don't judge others on their beliefs, and I don't expect to be judged on mine. Ultimately, I believe in goodness, decency, and compassion, and as most world religions also endorse these things, I support the individual's right to believe in what they choose, without fear of prejudice, maltreatment or persecution.'

'Calm down,' Joe replied. 'I only asked if you'd met Jesus.'

'Then, no. I haven't.'

'You don't half waffle on sometimes.'

'I'm a waffler, what can I say?' Uncle Percy keyed six digits into the chronalometer. A moment later, a white vapour poured from the dashboard, as a low groan echoed from the car's undercarriage.

BOOM!

The Cadillac vanished.

MATERIALISING IN A NEW LOCATION, Becky saw a misty mountain range that stretched all around, set against a back-drop of a clear blue sky. Despite her layers of clothing, the drop in temperature seized her spine. It was when she glanced left, however, that she saw something unlike anything she'd seen before. A huge modernist building made of steel and glass was set on a mountaintop in a vast complex bordered by an electri-fied fence with a guard tower in each corner. Three large black helicopters were sited on helipads, and a dozen men in hooded snowsuits and carrying rifles patrolled the grounds.

'What is this place?' Joe gasped.

'It looks like a prison,' Becky replied.

'I agree, Becky,' Uncle Percy said.

They exited the car.

Just then, Alwyn Thomas appeared. 'Alrigh', gang. Welcome ter Switzerland.'

'Ah, hello, Alwyn,' Uncle Percy said. 'And thank you. It's breath-taking.' He turned to Becky and Joe. 'Alwyn Thomas... have you met Becky and Joe Mellor?'

'Course I 'ave,' Thomas replied. 'You won't remember me, kids, but we first met at the Enchantment Beneath the Sea Dance, just before that mega-shark ruined a perfectly fine knees-up.'

Becky remembered the GITT Christmas party only too well. 'Hello,' she said.

'Hi, mate,' Joe said.

Thomas gestured at the building. 'What d'ya think of that, then? Fancy, eh?'

'It's impressive,' Uncle Percy said.

'It might be one of the few houses on the planet more imposin' than Bowen Hall.'

'It's certainly more fortified.'

'Well, its owner has to be careful,' Thomas said. 'He's a very powerful, important man... not to mention he has a fair few quid, and that's an understatement.'

'I imagine so,' Uncle Percy said. 'And why, may I ask, is it protected by a small army? We're in the Alps... is petty burglary such a big problem?'

'You'll have to ask the gaffer,' Thomas replied. 'I s'pose you get paranoid when you're as wealthy as he is.'

'I see.'

'So, d'ya wanna know his name? He is kinda well known.'

'Do tell.'

Thomas grinned. 'Heath Pineos.'

Uncle Percy's face dropped. '*The* Heath Pineos.'

'Who's Heath Pineos?' Joe asked.

'He's a bloke that makes Bill Gates look like Pauper Pete,' Thomas said.

'Pineos is a businessman, an investor and a philanthropist,' Uncle Percy said. 'His family has been fabulously wealthy for centuries.'

'And that's the crazy thing,' Thomas said. 'He ain't inherited a Glamorgan sausage. He made his own money and grown the pot over the last two thousand years.'

'That is astonishing,' Uncle Percy said.

'Yeah,' Thomas replied. 'But true.'

'How did you find out about him?' Uncle Percy asked.

'I won't lie to ya, through both fluke and some crackin' detective work,' Thomas said. 'A few months ago, I visited Renaissance Florence in 1410AD, and met the Italian landowner, Gianni Pineos. I thought he was the spittin' image of a photo I'd seen Heath Pineos I'd seen that mornin' in The Sun, that mornin'. For a lark, I investigated his family tree throughout history. I visited Rome in 30BC and saw the senator, Ligarius Pineos – again, he looked identical to Heath. I visited eighteenth century Paris to see his ancestor, François Pineos. Again, he was the spit of Heath. Then I went to Victorian London to see the industrialist, Henry Pineos - another dead ringer for our Heath. I did a few more trips and kept seeing what I became increasingly convinced was the same fella. However, it was only when I heard you were searchin' for magical water that made the drinker immortal, that I put two and two together. Anyway, I contacted him – I wanted to put my theory to him face to face – and he agreed to meet me.'

'That must've been quite a meeting,' Uncle Percy said.

'It was,' Thomas replied. 'Of course, I had no choice to tell him about my bein' a time traveller, but after he had got his head 'round that nugget, he confirmed it was actually him I'd seen on all those different trips. Apparently, he'd visited the Blessed Isle – that's what he calls it – as a young man and has been drinking from its water ever since.'

'How did he react to you being a time traveller?' Uncle Percy asked.

'He's seen so much in his life it didn't faze him at all,' Thomas replied. 'The thing is, he's finally run out of water.'

Uncle Percy looked surprised. 'He has?' He paused as something else occurred to him. 'So that would mean... *he's dying*?'

'Yeah... and it's exactly what he wants,' Thomas replied. 'He reckons he's seen enough over the last two thousand years, and he's ready to start another journey, one we all 'ave to undertake in the end.'

Uncle Percy gave a sympathetic nod. 'I see.'

'But the story doesn't end there,' Thomas said. 'He's run out of water – yeah, but he wants some more.'

'More? Why?'

'That's for him to tell you,' Thomas replied. 'He also wants you to get it for him.'

'I don't understand,' Uncle Percy said. 'If he's found the Blessed Isle, then why doesn't he just go back there and get it for himself?'

'Again, that's somethin' else he'll explain to you,' Thomas replied. 'So, are you ready to meet the man himself?'

Uncle Percy glanced at Becky and Joe, who each nodded eagerly. 'I believe we are.'

Thomas nodded at the building. 'Good, because he's waitin' in there for you now... and you don't keep a man like Heath Pineos waitin'.'

'Very well,' Uncle Percy said. 'Then, please, lead the way.'

'Sure,' Thomas replied. He looked at Becky and Joe. 'Oh, kids, and when I said he wasn't short of a few quid – well, I meant it. This very morning, he overtook some French business tycoon to become the richest person on the planet.'

14

THE LOST SHIELD

Joe's face lit like a flare. 'How much would he pay us for gettin' the water, then?'

'Name your price, kiddo.'

'A Ferrari.'

'Why stop at one?' Thomas chuckled. 'This fella could buy you the company.'

'I'll take it,' Joe replied.

'Don't give him any ideas, please, Alwyn,' Uncle Percy said.

'I don't blame the kid,' Thomas said. 'I'm nearly sixty, and been broke most of my life. I'd sell my own mum to have a tenth of the dosh Heath Pineos has got.'

Uncle Percy glanced at the guards. 'But if you need a small army to protect that *dosh*, I'm not sure it's worth it.'

'You live in a stately home, Perce. I ain't sure you know much about the plight of the poor.'

'Point taken,' Uncle Percy said.

Thomas led them across the compound, toward the main building.

All the while, Becky couldn't take her eyes off the armed

guards, who seemed on constant alert as if recently notified of an imminent threat.

'This is like a villain's lair in a James Bond film,' Joe said.

'I thought that when I first came here,' Thomas said. 'The fact is, Heath Pineos is a target. Yeah, he's got lots of friends, but also plenty of enemies. Don't get me wrong, he's a wonderful, generous man – a smart, personable fella, but he's definitely paranoid about his security. I guess it comes with the territory when you're richer than God.'

They approached a high double-door, on the left of which was an electronic keypad and an intercom. Thomas placed his hand on the keypad before leaning into the intercom. 'Alrigh'... it's Alwyn Thomas again. I've brought Percy Halifax to see Mister Pineos as requested.'

A female voice resonated from two speakers. 'Please, Mister Thomas, if you could wait there. Mister Pineos's assistant, Mayara Lenya, will be with you shortly.'

Thomas gave a visible shiver. 'And here's the Bond hench-man, or should I say *henchwoman*,' he said tensely. 'She scares the bejeezus outta me. She may be knockin' on a bit, but there's somethin' 'bout her that sends the collywobbles through me from nose to toe. In my opinion, Pineos don't need all these armed guards. If any thief knew Mayara Lenya were 'ere they'd scarper and go and rob Elon Musk instead.'

The words had barely left Thomas's mouth when the door opened.

It surprised Becky to see a tiny woman of about seventy years of age, her silver hair styled in a chin-length bob. She wore a hand-knitted cardigan, silk blouse, tweed skirt, and a pleasant smile that split a heavily lined face.

'Good evening,' Lenya said with a hint of an Austrian accent long since faded. 'You must be Percy Halifax. I am Mayara Lenya, Mister Pineos's personal assistant.'

'It's a pleasure to meet you, Ms. Lenya,' Uncle Percy said.

'And the same to you,' Lenya replied. She turned to Becky and Joe. 'And you must be Rebecca and Joe Mellor.' She gave a small bow. 'I have heard many things about you both, and it is all most impressive.'

'Er, thanks,' Becky said.

'Cheers,' Joe said.

Mayara Lenya's eyes fell on Alwyn Thomas. 'And Mister Thomas... you have returned, I see.'

This time, Becky detected a chill in her voice that caused Thomas's body to tense like a plank.

'Good evenin', Maraya,' Thomas replied. 'You're lookin' mighty fine today.'

Lenya responded with a low, guttural sound that was somewhere between a grunt and a growl. 'Please, all of you, Mister Pineos will see you now.'

A sweet scent of rose and cedarwood filled Becky's nostrils as they entered a corridor lined with furniture upon which were ornaments, sculptures, and vases from various eras; several paintings Becky recognised from her school art classes hung on the walls. She knew instinctively they were originals and not skilful reproductions.

'This is a beautiful house, Ms. Lenya,' Uncle Percy said. 'And we both know the significance of some of this artwork.'

'We do, Mister Halifax,' Lenya said. 'Mister Pineos is an extraordinary person with exquisite taste, but then I would argue that time is the key component for cultivating that, and that is a luxury he has been fortunate enough to enjoy.'

'May I ask how long you've worked for him?'

'Fifty-two years,' Lenya replied. 'I first met him when I was a girl of seventeen. He saved me from a hideous situation. I considered him remarkable then, and that position has not changed with time. It has been an honour to devote my life to his service.'

'I understand.'

'I'm not sure you do, Mister Halifax,' Lenya said. 'His unqualified goodliness has spanned two millennia and influenced every country in the world. His personal philanthropy and devotion to his fellow man has been unsurpassed in history. Financially, he has donated a dozen times what Jamsetji Tata or George Soros ever gave to their respective causes. And yet, because he has kept his secret for over two thousand years, he has never had recognition for his charity, and humankind does not know what a true friend they have in him.'

'I appreciate that,' Uncle Percy replied.

Lenya approached a wide double-door, which she opened. 'Mister Pineos, your guests are here.'

From over Lenya's shoulder, Becky saw the silhouette of a tall man staring out of a vast window, before hearing his soft, melodious voice.

'Thank you, Mayara.'

'I shall be in my quarters if you need me, sir.' Lenya gestured for everyone to enter the room before leaving.

Heath Pineos walked into the light as he faced the group. 'Good day, all. I'm Heath Pineos, and it is a pleasure to have you at my house.'

Becky was stunned. The very idea of this man being so old was preposterous. Stunningly handsome, he looked no more than thirty, with an unblemished complexion and short, silky dark brown hair styled like a 1930s film star. He wore a stone-grey suit, impeccably tailored, over a cream silk shirt and a thin black tie.

'Good day, Mister Pineos,' Uncle Percy said. 'I'm Percy Halifax, and may I introduce you to Becky and Joe Mellor?'

'Hello, Becky and Joe,' Pineos said. 'It is a delight to meet you both. I have heard a great deal about you from Mister Thomas, and I am astonished by your courage, valour, and empathy.'

'Er, thanks,' Joe said. 'And hiya.'

'Hello, Mister Pineos,' Becky said.

'I've also been told about your parents' situation, and that is why you're searching for the Pool of Life,' Pineos said. 'I hope we can help each other out.'

'I hope so, too,' Becky said.

Pineos returned a killer smile before turning to Uncle Percy. 'As for you, Mister Halifax, I know very well who you are. I've lived a very long time, and you have been on my radar ever since you were at Oxford. Although I'm no scientific expert, I like to keep my eye on the luminaries of the student body and you were certainly that.'

'I was?'

'Please, there is no need to be modest,' Pineos said. 'I even knew one of your teachers, Henry Locket. I first met him when he was a young man just before the second world war.'

Becky recalled the name. Henry Locket was one of Uncle Percy's tutors when he was a student at Oxford University. He also invented the world's first time-machine, *Old Betty*.

'You knew Professor Locket?' Uncle Percy said, surprised.

'I did,' Pineos replied. 'Of course, this was before he invented time travel. He was a hugely gifted scientist, and a lovely human being.'

'He was indeed,' Uncle Percy said.

'As for you,' Pineos said. 'I've followed your career as a scientist and inventor closely. I even bought a thousand of your Gumchumper devices, which I gave to various underprivileged towns in South America, Romania, and Africa. I knew you were a brilliant inventor Percy Halifax, but I never knew you were a time traveller until I met Mister Thomas.'

'I see.'

'Please, all of you, sit down,' Pineos said. 'We have much to discuss.' He ushered them all to sit on a herringbone sofa that stretched from one end of the room to the other. 'Can I get you anything to eat and drink?'

'We're fine, Mister Pineos,' Uncle Percy said.

'Very well,' Pineos replied, sitting down on a leather armchair. 'Now, I'm certain you have a thousand questions for me. Believe it or not, I have an equal number for you, too.'

'I do,' Uncle Percy replied. He was about to continue when his eyes were drawn to a painting above the fireplace. 'Oh, my word!' he gasped.

Pineos gave the hint of a smile. 'You recognise it?'

Becky looked over and saw a circular wooden shield fixed to the wall. For a moment, shock gripped her. A terrifying image of Medusa's severed head adorned the shield, scarlet blood pouring from her neck.

'I've only heard it talked about in legend,' Uncle Percy said. 'I had no idea it had been found.'

'For it to have been found, it would have had to be lost,' Pineos replied. 'And if what I hear from Mister Thomas is true, then it was the three of you that killed the actual creature.'

'Yeah,' Joe said. 'But she was even uglier than that.'

'I'm sure.' Pineos chuckled. 'Truly, your adventures in time have stirred my interest. I thought I had seen astounding things in my long life, but it pales against what you've seen in just a few years.'

'We have seen a lot,' Uncle Percy said. He nodded at the painting. 'Becky, Joe, what you are staring at is one of the most renown lost works of art in history. It's called *The Medusa Shield*, and it was an early painting by Leonardo da Vinci.'

'This is true,' Pineos said. 'But as I said before it was never lost. It was always with me. I met the young Leonardo in 1470AD and I commissioned it to be painted. Ever since my childhood in Ancient Greece, I had heard the legend of the monster, Medusa, and it had fascinated me. I thought it would be an excellent subject matter for this young genius I had met. Anyway, he painted it for me and it has never left my care in over five hundred and fifty years.'

'It's remarkable,' Uncle Percy said.

'As was Leonardo,' Pineos replied. 'Now, I must ask you about some of the things you've seen. I hear from Alwyn Thomas that you have met a minotaur... is this true?'

'We have,' Uncle Percy replied. 'Many of them.'

'How fascinating,' Pineos said. 'As a Greek, the fabled creatures of my old country often inspire a childlike passion in me. Can I ask - are they as terrifying as legends suggest?'

'Not at all,' Uncle Percy replied. 'Minotaurs are a remarkable species - they're noble, decent, caring, and intelligent. Myth has been unkind to them, and particularly the one that was immortalised in legend, the one that lived beneath the city of Knossos.'

'Ah, that is the minotaur named Edgar.'

'Yes,' Uncle Percy replied.

Pineos paused for a few seconds. 'And is it true they're almost indestructible?' he asked, 'that only a weapon made from orichalcum can kill them?'

Uncle Percy looked surprised by the question. 'I don't know,' he said. 'I do know some minotaurs were killed with bullets made from orichalcum, but I really can't say.'

'And that killing was orchestrated by the evil time traveller, Emerson Drake?'

'That is correct.'

Pineos stared wistfully out of the window as if accessing a memory. 'I met him once a few decades ago at a molecular science conference in Monaco. I didn't like him at all. It seems my instincts were correct.'

'They were,' Uncle Percy replied. 'Now, may I ask you a question?'

'Of course.'

'Alwyn told us you had run out of water and were ready to die.'

Pineos took a moment to answer. 'Yes,' he said. 'I have lived countless lives, but my time on this earth is ending now. Immortality seems such a glorious idea, until you realise every child you have, every lover you adored, every friend you made... all will die before you. The pain these losses bring time and time again chips away at your very soul. I have lost too many loved ones over the centuries, and I cannot witness that anymore.' He gave a sad smile. 'So, yes, it is time for me to continue the journey so many before me have already taken.'

'I understand,' Uncle Percy replied. 'But then if you are ready to leave this life, if I may ask, why do you want us to get water for you?'

Pineos exhaled a heavy sigh. He walked over to a set of drawers and picked up a small photograph before returning to the group and angling it for them to see.

The photograph depicted a young girl of no more than eight years of age, with crystal blue eyes, a button nose, and long black hair that tumbled down her back in spirals.

'This is Marietta Pineos, my granddaughter,' Pineos said. 'She is a remarkable child, gifted in so many ways. She is also dying of an incurable illness that, for all my billions, I cannot cure. She has but six months to live.' He lowered the photograph. 'I can travel to outer space in my own spacecraft, and I can go to the ocean's furthest depths, but for all my wealth I cannot help her live.' His voice cracked. 'You must help me, Percy Halifax. I would give everything I have, everything I am, for this perfect child to live.' His eyes shimmered with tears. 'I beg you to help me make that happen.'

15

LAST MAN STANDING

Becky didn't know what to say. She stared at Pineos and her heart melted.

'Of course, we'll help,' Uncle Percy said. 'We'll do everything we can.'

'Thank you. That means more than I can say.'

'But I have another question,' Uncle Percy said. 'Why do you need anyone else to go to the Blessed Isle for you? You've been there, you must know where it is. Why don't you just go back?'

'It's the obvious question to ask,' Pineos replied. 'The fact is, I don't know where it is. I know it to be in the Pacific Ocean, but that is by far the largest ocean in the world. The truth of the matter is, I have spent a fortune, and a thousand years trying to find it again. This is not a typical island that's been documented using reliable sources. As I'm sure you know, Mister Halifax, there are many *phantom* islands throughout history – like Saxemberg Island, or Frisland or Ganges Island. Islands thought to exist based on folklore, or indeed ones that have appeared on navigational charts either as mistakes or for other reasons. But you will not find the Blessed Isle on any map or globe or chart.

It is a mystical, preternatural place, and will either be found by accident or by using a certain ancient artifact.'

Uncle Percy's brow furrowed. 'Artifact? What artifact?'

'*The Dahlia Compass*,' Pineos replied simply. He stood up. 'Now, I believe it is time I told you precisely who I am.'

'Please do,' Uncle Percy replied.

'I was born in Pella, in the Kingdom of Macedonia in 356BC,' Pineos said. 'I was the son of Cleitus of Athens. I was raised in the court of King Philip II, and that was where I met Philip's heir and the man who would become the most prominent, most illustrious figure in the ancient world.'

Uncle Percy reflected on this for a second as a name formed in his head. 'You mean *Alexander the Great*?'

Pineos nodded. 'To me, I just mean my friend, Alexander,' he replied. 'We studied at Mieza together, under the tutelage of Aristotle, who, as you can imagine, was an excellent teacher. Over the years, I became Alexander's best friend, his closest confidant. We did everything together. At fifteen, we sailed to Pisa in Italy together on a makeshift boat. We had very good times.'

A name formed in Uncle Percy's mind. 'You're *Hephaestion*, aren't you? Alexander the Great's dearest friend, his most trusted diplomat, and his most acclaimed general.'

Pineos smiled. 'I like to think that was all true. I certainly considered myself Alexander's brother. We trained together, we fought together, we loved together, and we became men together. I was on the Danube campaign, I was at the Battle of Chaeronea, I helped defeat the Thracians. We took the whole known world – Persia, Syria, Pakistan, Egypt, Gaza, Mesopotamia, and in our fifteen years of conquest we never lost a battle.'

'You achieved extraordinary things,' Uncle Percy said.

'We achieved extraordinary things at a *terrible* cost,' Pineos replied. 'You know it, and I know it. Terror and violence lie at the very heart of conquest, and I am under no illusions about that.'

'I understand.'

Pineos sighed. 'Do you recall the words Plutarch, the philosopher, said about Alexander and his accomplishments?'

'I do,' Uncle Percy replied. 'He said that *When Alexander saw the breadth of his domain, he wept for there were no more worlds to conquer.*'

'He did say that,' Pineos replied. 'And that is a true story. We had just defeated King Porus, and were looking out over the Hydaspes River, when Alexander began to weep because he knew his days of conquest were over. He was inconsolable and retired to his quarters in a despair that lasted weeks. However, when he emerged, he was a changed man. In his anguish, he had found a goal. You see, it was on that final campaign we heard the story of The Blessed Isle and The Pool of Life. We also gained the artifact known as *The Dahlia Compass*, which is where the story truly begins.'

'And what's The Dahlia Compass?' Uncle Percy asked.

'It is a small ship's compass, enclosed in the finest gold casing,' Pineos replied. 'But although it is made of gold, its true value lies in what it can do. Now, did any of you make a water compass when you were a child?'

'Yeah, I did,' Joe said.

'And how does it work?'

'Err, you attach a cork to a magnetised needle, put it in water, and it points north,' Joe said.

'That's correct,' Pineos said. 'The Dahlia Compass works on a similar principle. However, instead of the needle pointing north, it always points to the Blessed Isle. You see, the water within the compass's golden casing is water from the Pool of Life.'

'And you used this compass to take you to the island?' Uncle Percy asked.

'We did,' Pineos replied. 'Alexander and I faked our own deaths, and we took thirty handpicked men and embarked on the ultimate adventure – *to conquer the last unconquered land*. It was a long journey, but we found it. The island itself was a place of great beauty, but also terrible dangers and we lost a third of our men in the first twenty-four hours to the creatures of the island.'

'What kind of creatures were they?'

'I had not seen their like before. Alexander called them *dragons*, and at the time that was my conclusion, too. I'm not sure now. Anyway, with the Dahlia Compass pointing the way, we traversed the island and eventually found the Pool of Life. There was a large creature guarding it, but we got some water, and we fled to our ship, never to return to the island again.'

'What happened after that?' Uncle Percy asked.

'Every crew member took their share of the water, and started a new life in a different country,' Pineos replied. 'For centuries, Alexander and I travelled the world as free men. To maintain our ties to our old lives, we agreed to meet the other crew members every fifty years at the Parthenon in Athens. As time passed, those who were still alive became fewer and fewer.'

'How?' Uncle Percy asked. 'I mean, if the water makes you immortal, how were they dying?'

'The water does not ensure immortality,' Pineos replied. 'It stops you aging, it stops you dying from natural causes, but you can be killed. I assume, over the years, the rest of the crew were killed in battles or brawls, or because of some other non-natural causes.'

'What happened to Alexander?'

Pineos gave a slow, heavy sigh. 'Sadly, Alexander was killed in a mugging, stabbed in the back like an animal, as he walked home through the Piazza Della Scala in Milan on the 13th June, 1766AD - a random slaying by an unknown assailant. I always remember the date as it was my birthday. Anyway, after I processed his passing and dealt with my grief, I realised it was likely I was the last man alive from that original crew.'

'Then I suppose there's only one more question to be asked,' Uncle Percy said. 'If you believe the way to the Blessed Isle is by using the Dahlia Compass, then what happened to it? Where is it now?'

'That is the one of the great mysteries of this tale,' Pineos said. 'Alexander kept it close to him for many years, but it was stolen from his house in the twelfth century, along with many other items. I don't believe the thief knew what it was, but Alexander never saw it again. Obviously, we searched for it for many years after that, but it eluded us.' His eyes met Uncle Percy's. 'But I never had your powers, Percy Halifax, or your resources. I could never manipulate time, as you do. You have the ability to track it down through the ages. I also hear you excel at finding rare artifacts such as this.'

'We've been fortunate,' Uncle Percy replied. 'Do you have you any thoughts where it might be?'

'Actually, I do,' Pineos replied. 'I believe the compass ended up in the possession of the infamous pirate *Jack Rackham*. I assume you've heard of him?'

'Yes,' Uncle Percy replied. '*Calico* Jack Rackham.'

'The same,' Pineos replied. 'I don't believe Rackham thought it anything other than a valuable golden trinket, but I think he acquired it upon capturing a Dutch merchant ship. I found documents that led me to that conclusion.'

'Which ship?'

'I do not know,' Pineos replied. 'But Jack Rackham was one of the most successful of the pirates of the Golden Age, and it is said he hid his fortune on a Caribbean Island.'

'Which one?'

'No one knows which one, and to my knowledge it has never been found,' Pineos said. 'But I'm convinced the Dahlia Compass lies with that fortune. Anyway, Rackham was captured by the privateer, Jonathan Barnett, and hanged for piracy along with his crew on the 17th November 1720, without ever revealing the island's location. However, the story doesn't end there. Rackham had a wife, a pirate too, *Anne Bonny*, one of the few female pirates at the time. Do you know of her?'

'I've heard the name.'

'Well, I think Anne Bonny is the key to this mystery.'

'You think she had the Dahlia Compass?'

'It's possible.' Pineos replied. 'You see, Anne Bonny was captured along with Jack Rackham. However, she was pregnant, so the courts gave her a stay of execution, and shortly after that, she disappeared from all records.'

'Disappeared?' Uncle Percy asked.

'There's no documentation of her being released,' Pineos replied. 'But there's no confirmation of her being executed, either. In fact, all of the evidence points to the fact she was broken out of jail by Rackham's helmsman, a man known simply as *The Hunter*. Personally, I think she and the helmsman went to collect Rackham's fortune, and then sailed off into the sunset together to start a new life of wealth and privilege. That is all I could find out about the matter.'

'Don't worry,' Joe said. 'We know loads of pirates. I'm sure we can find out more.'

'Do you think so?' Pineos said.

'Deffo,' Joe said. 'One of our best mates is well in with that lot.'

Pineos's gaze panned over the group. 'Then, please, help me, for Marietta's sake.' He reached over to a side table and picked up a small hip flask. Then he stood and approached Uncle Percy. 'I bought this flask in Charlestown, in 1865AD, to celebrate the end of the American Civil War. I believe it's always brought me luck. Please, fill it with water for me... it will be enough to cure her. I'm not asking for Marietta's immortality, just enough to give her a chance at a single lifetime, one of good health and deserved happiness.'

'I understand.' Uncle Percy pocketed the bottle. 'We'll do everything we can.'

'Thank you,' Pineos said. He sucked in a deep breath, as if nervous about delivering his next words. 'My decline will be quick now. I may have a week to live, I may have a month, maybe longer. But I shall happily face my end if I know that little girl has the chance to live.' He gave a resigned smile. 'Find the compass, and you will find the island.' He smiled kindly at Becky and Joe. 'For your parents, Becky and Joe, and for my sweet Marietta.'

'We'll do it, Mister Pineos,' Becky said. 'I promise you we'll get the water she needs.'

'Thank you, child,' Pineos replied. 'Now, is there anything I can do for you - anything at all? I have money, position, influence... just name it and it shall be yours.'

'Thank you, but no,' Uncle Percy said. 'We have all we need.'

Becky watched Joe open his mouth as if to speak, but he stopped himself. Still, she would've put good money on whatever almost emerged had something to do with a Ferrari.

16

WYOMING AND WINNEBAGOS

Becky, Joe, and Uncle Percy bid their farewells to Heath Pineos and Alwyn Thomas before leaving the building, and walking over to the Cadillac. As they did, Uncle Percy took out a notebook and pen and wrote something down.

Becky noticed. 'What're you writing?'

'Nothing really,' Uncle Percy replied. 'Just making notes.'

'What did you think about all that?' Joe asked Becky. 'It's one hell of a story, ain't it? I mean... Alexander the Great... magic compasses... pirate treasure. It's pretty wild stuff.'

'It is wild,' Becky replied. 'The question I want to know though is – *is he telling us the truth?*'

Joe looked surprised. 'What do you mean?'

'I don't know,' Becky said. 'It's just - well, there was something odd about him.'

'What kind of odd?' Joe said. 'Other than him being older than the Colosseum. Hang on, you've not had another one of your freakydeaky visions, have you?'

'No, it's nothing like that,' Becky replied. 'It's just we've been deceived in the past. Remember, Lady Raleigh turned out to be

Mata Hari, and Charles Butterby was a robot. I dunno – I guess I'm a bit more cautious nowadays about whom to trust and who not to.'

'I don't blame you, Becky,' Uncle Percy said.

'What do you think about Pineos?' Becky asked. 'Do you trust him?'

'Yes. I think so,' Uncle Percy replied. 'But I do agree we've been deceived too many times in the past for us to take everything at face value. As it stands, however, I intend to trust him until there's evidence to suggest otherwise.'

'What are the plans now?' Joe asked.

'As Mister Pineos thinks this might be about Anne Bonny and Calico Jack Rackham, then I thought we'd pay Bruce Westbrook a visit. He is, after all, our resident pirate expert.'

'Great,' Joe replied. 'Do you know where he is?'

'I do, actually. He's at his holiday ranch in Wyoming, North America.'

'Cool,' Joe said. 'And when?'

'The Miocene Epoch,' Uncle Percy replied. 'Twenty million years ago.'

Not entirely shocked by this admission, something occurred to Joe. 'Do you actually have enough Gerathnium for these trips? I mean, we're always going places at the drop of a hat, and sometimes they're years back in time. That must use up loads of the stuff.'

'For a number of years now, I've ensured every time machine and portravella is well stocked with Gerathnium to make whatever trip necessary,' Uncle Percy replied. 'Obviously, GITT knows about our ventures and provides me with constant stocks of Gerathnium.'

'Fair enough,' Joe said, as they climbed into the time machine.

As Uncle Percy readied their departure, Becky stared back at the compound. It had been a short trip, but an extraordinary one. She'd seen a lost Leonardo da Vinci painting, encountered Alexander the Great's best friend, and witnessed a fortress equipped with its own private army. And as glittering white light poured from the Cadillac's dashboard, she wondered what she'd see next.

She didn't have to wait long for an answer.

MOMENTS LATER, an emerald prairie met her gaze, as long and wide as the eye could see. Feeding on the greasegrass were thousands of three-toed horses with honey-coloured torsos marked with thin black stripes.

'Crikey,' Uncle Percy exhaled. 'Bruce told me about this place, but I had no idea it would be so spectacular.'

'What sort of animals are they?' Joe asked.

'They're *Hipparions*, Joe,' Uncle Percy replied. 'And they're one of the most successful species of horse to have ever existed. Indeed, they flourished for over twenty-two million years and colonised nearly every continent on the planet. When you think modern humans have existed for around two hundred thousand years, it really puts their evolutionary triumph into perspective.'

'They're amazing,' Becky said. However, glancing left she had an even greater surprise.

A giant motorhome, pristine in its whiteness, was parked beside an aspen tree. Surrounded by stunning flowers of every shade and hue, there was a neon sign attached to its roof that read '*La Westbrook Hacienda.*'

To the motorhome's right was a Hawaiian Tiki bar, constructed from wood panels, and adorned with murals, Polynesian carvings, and countless bottles of alcohol. There was also a jukebox and three 1980s arcade machines: Space Invaders, Ms. Pac-Man and Donkey Kong Jr.

Uncle Percy, Joe, and Becky exited the Cadillac in a stunned silence.

Just then, the motorhome's main door opened and a huge man emerged wearing a Hawaiian shirt, cargo shorts and sandals, his long, brown and grey hair secured in a ponytail.

'YEEEE HAAW,' Bruce Westbrook bellowed, his bearded face crinkled with joy. 'I'LL BE A BABOON'S AUNTY... IF IT AIN'T MY BUDDY, PERCY HALIFAX, AND THE DYNAMICAL DUO. HOWDY TO Y'ALL!'

'Hello, Bruce,' Uncle Percy said, smiling broadly. 'I hope we're not intruding.'

'Never, good buddy. I wouldn't keep givin' ya my coordinates if I thought you could.'

'Hi, Bruce,' Becky said.

'Hey up, Bruce,' Joe added.

'Hiya, kidlets,' Bruce replied. He jumped right down and hugged everyone in turn.

'Your flowers look great,' Becky said.

'As yer know I'm in the floral trade, and this is one of the perks,' Bruce said. 'I've set myself up with the whole kaboodle. There's Apricot Gaillardia, Desert Marigolds, Pansies, Sweet Alyssums, Zinnias and of course, sunflowers. It really brightens up the Winnie B, I reckon.'

'It certainly does, my friend,' Uncle Percy said. 'And she is a magnificent vehicle.'

'She sure is,' Bruce replied. 'She's the Winnebago Adventurer 35F and is as cosy as a momma's hug on a sick day. Yer welcome ter stay fer as long as ya want, but I'm guessin' yer 'ere fer a reason.'

'We are indeed.'

'Then what in the name of Mad Mikey McVie is it?'

'We need some piratey advice,' Joe said.

'Yer do?' Bruce replied. 'Then I'm yer dog, baby. Woof.

Woof.' He approached the tiki bar. 'Let's talk shop over a cold one. What y'all havin'?'

'I'll have a cold one with you,' Joe said eagerly.

Bruce grinned. 'A chilled fruit juice for you then,' he replied to Joe's disappointment. 'Becky – what's your poison?'

'Fruit juice is fine.'

'And, Perce, d'ya fancy a Santa Rita Pale Ale? It's got a heavenly citrus twang and is brewed a stone's throw my florist shop in Tucson.'

'You know, I think I shall, Bruce,' Uncle Percy replied. 'Thank you.'

'Cool beans,' Bruce said. Removing two bottles of beer and juice from a small fridge beneath the countertop, he passed round the drinks. 'Sorry, I ain't got enough seats for y'all, but I don't get many visitors, other than the odd gutsy Hipparion. Now, what piratey advice d'ya need? Can I guess it's 'bout the Fountain of Youth or Pool of Life, or whatever yer callin' it now?'

'You can and it is,' Uncle Percy replied. 'We've had an extraordinary encounter with a quite fascinating chap.'

'Yeah,' Joe said. 'Heath Pineos, and he's over two thousand years old.'

Bruce nearly dropped his beer. '*The* Heath Pineos? The gazillionnaire?'

'That's the bloke,' Joe said. 'He was also the bezzie mate of Alexander the Great.'

Bruce was speechless. 'I dunno what ter say.'

'Then that's in contrast to Mister Pineos - he had plenty to say,' Uncle Percy said. 'Although history knows him better as Hephaestion, Alexander's illustrious general, advisor and closest friend.'

'I'm as shocked as a wet weasel on an electrified fence,' Bruce said.

'As were we,' Uncle Percy replied. 'Mister Pineos claims he

visited the Blessed Isle with Alexander, found the Pool of Life, and he's been drinking its water ever since.'

'Then he knows where it is,' Bruce said. 'What's the problem?'

'Not exactly,' Uncle Percy replied. 'Apparently, there's a magical ship's compass – the Dahlia Compass – that can lead you there. Unfortunately, it disappeared many years ago, and despite his efforts to find it again, he's always failed. He says if we can find the compass, we'll be able to get to the island.'

Bruce fell silent. 'And he thinks its disappearance has somethin' ter do with my old buddies in the eighteenth-century Caribbean?'

'He does indeed. He thinks it may have ended up with Calico Jack Rackham, as part of his treasure haul that was never found.'

'Calico Jack, eh?' Bruce said. 'I heard talk Jack's treasure was never found. Y'reckon this Dahlia Compass was part of tha' treasure?'

'Heath Pineos does,' Uncle Percy replied. 'However, according to his sources the only person who knew where the treasure was located was his wife, Anne Bonny, who may have gone to collect it after Jack's execution.'

'*Irish Annie*, eh?' Bruce said, 'otherwise known as *The Red Shamrock*.'

'Why did they call her that?' Becky asked.

'On account of her fire red hair... and by all accounts her even fierier Irish temper.'

'Have you met her?' Joe asked.

'Nah,' Bruce replied. 'Heard things, though. Quite a woman was our Annie – dangerous, beautiful, and as good with her fists as any pig-bellied swashbuckler.'

Uncle Percy leaned forward. 'Pineos believes Anne Bonny was imprisoned with Rackham, but instead of being executed

was broken out of jail by Calico Jack's helmsman... someone
called *The Hunter*. Have you heard of him?'

Bruce shook his head. 'Not really had much ter do with Jack
or any of his crew.'

'Then do you know anyone that might be able to help us?'

Bruce pondered this for a moment. 'Actually, I just might.'
He chuckled at the memory. 'A few years after Rackham's death,
I met an old buccaneer in a bar in Tortuga. He told me he
sailed with Rackham for a short spell. Yeah, if anyone'll know
'bout any o' this it'll be *Lawless Larry*.'

Joe laughed. 'Lawless Larry?'

'Lawless Larry was literally a law ter himself,' Bruce replied.
'Ah, he was a right dog was old Lawless... with the ladies, the
fighting, and the drinking. And he was always about makin' a
few bucks. In fact, ter give him his due he was one helluva
entrepreneur. After he left the pirating life, he hung up his
cutlass and started his own business. He made a few doubloons
at it, too.'

'What was the business?' Joe asked.

Bruce smiled. 'Well, he figured because so many pirates lost
a hand or a foot in their stock in trade, that he'd make realistic
substitutes to replace the limbs they'd lost, and sell them on.'

Uncle Percy looked amazed. 'He made pirate prosthetics?'

'Indeed, he did,' Bruce said. 'I reckon he figured whatever
he could create for them was better than yer average rusty hook
or peg-leg. Anyway, he'd carve these prosthetics out of the
wood from rubber trees and sell them at a fair old profit. He
even started his own shop.'

Becky couldn't believe her ears. 'A shop?'

'Aye, kiddo,' Bruce replied. 'I only went once, but it was an
experience I'll never forget.'

'What was it called?' Joe asked.

'What else?' Bruce replied. '*Lawless Larry's Lifelike Limbs*!'

17

LAWLESS LARRY

Everyone laughed. 'That could be the greatest name for a shop ever,' Becky said.

'You just wait 'til ya see it,' Bruce replied with a grin. 'He sells every body part it's possible ter lose. He's got more fake eyeballs than a Tiger Shrimp's got legs.'

'And when you say *every* body part?' Joe said.

'I mean *every... body... part*,' Bruce said. 'If a buccaneer loses his Wee Wally Wonky in a cannon accident, ol' Lawless can kit him out with a new one.'

'What a lovely image,' Uncle Percy said. 'And is this noteworthy boutique in Tortuga?'

'Nah,' Bruce replied. 'It's in Port Royal, the biggest pirate city in Jamaica.'

Uncle Percy groaned.

Hearing his dismay, Becky recalled her previous visit to a pirate town. 'It's not as rough as Nassau though, is it?'

'Port Royal makes Nassau look like Addlebury on a Sunday afternoon,' Bruce replied. 'In its heyday, it was known as *the wickedest city in the world*.'

'Terrific,' Becky replied glumly.

'Don't worry, missy,' Bruce said. 'I won't let anythin' happen' to ya.'

'Are you joining us then, Bruce?' Uncle Percy asked.

'Ya don't think I'd miss this hootenanny, do ya?' Bruce replied. 'Besides, yeh'll need someone to introduce ya to Lawless. He ain't overly fond of strangers.'

'That's very kind of you, Bruce,' Uncle Percy said. 'What year do you suggest we go?'

'I'm thinkin' 1724AD,' Bruce replied.

'Could any of the Black Head's crew be in Port Royal?' Joe asked hopefully. 'I'd love to see One-Toe-Tom and the rest of those nutters again.'

'Nah,' Bruce replied. 'Your adventure with the Box of Eternity happened five years before, so they'd be in Merry Olde England spendin' Blackbeard's Treasure on worthy causes.'

Uncle Percy looked at the group. 'Then shall we leave tomorrow morning at ten?'

'Why not now?' Joe replied. 'Get us some piratey clobber and a cutlass each and we'll be sorted. To be fair, I can't wait to see the wickedest city in the world.'

'I bet you can't.' Uncle Percy frowned. 'But no, I think we've seen enough for today. I, for one, would appreciate a good night's sleep before witnessing Port Royal's numerous delights.'

Becky thought Uncle Percy made a good point. After all, in a matter of hours they'd visited a minotaur town, a fortress in the Swiss Alps, and North America in the Miocene Epoch.

'Okay,' Joe said.

'Meanwhile, Bruce, would you care to walk with me?' Uncle Percy said. 'I have a small favour to ask.'

Bruce looked surprised by the question. 'Sure thing, buddy.'

'Why can't you ask in front of us?' Joe said.

'I thought it was obvious,' Uncle Percy replied simply.

'Because I don't want you to hear it.' He flashed Joe a mischievous smile before leaving the tiki bar, tailed by Bruce.

Joe huffed. 'I hate it when he does that.'

Becky watched Uncle Percy and Bruce walk deep into the pasture, before stopping deep in conversation. Uncle Percy pulled out his notebook, tore out a sheet of paper, and passed it to Bruce. Then, still deep in conversation, they returned to the bar.

'Are you gonna tell us what that was all about?' Joe asked Uncle Percy.

'No,' Uncle Percy replied bluntly, leaving no one in any doubt the conversation had ended before it had begun.

THEY SPENT the rest of the afternoon enjoying the splendour of the landscape, and walking amongst the Hipparions, who were both majestic and welcoming. Later, Bruce made them cheeseburgers, and they ate to the kind of banter and laughter that came from being with old and dear friends. They returned to Bowen Hall just as stars appeared like pearls in the lavender sky.

Back in the Time Room, Becky found herself exhausted, and retired to her room for an early night. Unfortunately, she couldn't sleep. Fractured images assaulted her mind - of the day's events, her recent strange visions, but mostly of Maria's face, ravaged by tears, and her thoughts turned to Jacob. Was he really safe and well? Had the Wraith ensured the gunshot wound was treated properly? She prayed they'd both be unharmed from now on.

Becky woke the next morning at 8.00 a.m. to see a familiar outfit hanging from her wardrobe door. It was the same one she'd worn to the Caribbean on her previous visit: tanned leather trousers, white cotton shirt, knitted cap and shin high leather boots. Wasting no time, she showered and dressed before texting Joe to arrange their meeting for breakfast.

Becky and Joe made it to the Time Room at ten precisely, and saw Uncle Percy typing something onto a computer. Unlike their previous trip to the Caribbean, where he looked every bit the well-heeled gentleman, this time he had chosen clothes of the humblest of origins – scuppered leather breeches, a ripped linen shirt and a tatty tricorn hat. He'd even applied dirt and grease to his hair and face as if to stress his poverty.

'Morning,' Uncle Percy said brightly.

'Wow!' Joe said. 'You look like a hobo.'

'Thank you, Joe.'

'I just mean the last time you mixed with pirates you looked really posh.'

'Perhaps I did,' Uncle Percy replied. 'Still, judging by the reputation of some of the characters in Port Royal I thought I'd change my approach. When in Rome and all that.'

'You should do the grunge look more often. It suits you.'

'I'll take that under advisement,' Uncle Percy replied.

'So, where are the weapons?' Joe asked.

'Is that always your first thought?'

'It is if we're going to Port Royal,' Joe replied.

'Then don't worry yourself,' Uncle Percy replied. 'Everyone gets a cutlass.'

'Even Becky?'

'I don't know. Do you want one, Becky?'

'I'm good, thanks,' Becky replied.

'A wise choice.'

'Where's Bruce?' Becky asked.

'He's meeting us there,' Uncle Percy replied.

'And are we takin' a time machine?' Joe said.

'A portravella should suffice,' Uncle Percy said. He walked

over to a desk set upon which were a range of swords and daggers. He picked up a dagger and cutlass and passed them to Joe, who placed them in his belt. Then he raised his sleeve to reveal a wrist portravella, and in a sarcastic tone said, 'Then hold on tight and we'll savour the indubitable delights of the wickedest city in the pirate world.'

Joe gripped Uncle Percy's forearm. 'I can't wait,' he said eagerly.

As she echoed Joe's movement, Becky felt she'd be more than happy to wait... *for a very long time.*

ON ARRIVAL, a repulsive smell filled Becky's nostrils. She could see they'd arrived in a dark narrow alley surrounded by empty rum kegs, broken wooden crates, and bins overflowing with rotten fish and meat carcasses. At the alley's end, three rats gnawed on a dead cat. As she tried to avoid the urge to throw up, a familiar voice met her ears.

'AHOY, ME HEARTIES,' Bruce Westbrook bellowed. 'WEL-COME TO PORT ROYAL.'

'Hello, Bruce,' Uncle Percy said. 'What a charming spot you've found for our arrival.'

'Don't ya like it?' Bruce said. 'I figured no one would spot yer poppin' up behind Sweaty Stan's Meat and Fish Emporium.'

'I'm sure you figured correctly.'

Bruce's eyes widened when he stared at Becky and Joe. 'Hi, kids. I gotta say yer both look the piratey part.'

'Thanks, Bruce,' Becky said. 'But can we get out of this alley, please?'

'Sure, missy,' Bruce said. 'But before we do, I wanna stress some rules. Like I told ya before, Port Royal is a cesspit of vice and depravity – a real hell-hole, worse than Nassau, worse than Tortuga. There are some real bad asses in this town just lookin' fer trouble, so don't look at anyone strange, and don't do anythin' out of turn. It's gonna be a quick visit to see Lawless Larry and then we're outta 'ere. Okay?' His eyes found Joe. 'And you know, kid, that I'm really talkin' to you!'

'I guessed that,' Joe replied. 'I'll behave.'

'Good,' Bruce replied. 'Then let's get this wagon train a rollin'.'

Becky couldn't help but feel anxious as they turned onto a wide cobbled street that looked down over the city. Immediately, she could see it was much larger than Nassau, with a long harbour packed with ships, beside which was a stone fort with a battery of cannons pointed at the ocean. Immediately ahead, she saw a main street of taverns, brothels, silversmiths, pawn-brokers and bakeries.

From near and far, she heard laughter, screams, tuneless singing, and the shouting of obscenities. Pirates were every-where, gathered in groups, many of them standing outside bars drinking tankards of grog, others huddled round tables, gambling with cards and dice. In the distance, a vicious brawl had broken out involving a group of men.

'It's even lovelier than I imagined,' Uncle Percy muttered.

Getting closer to the docks, Becky spied a set of gallows hanging from which were six corpses. Her face drained of colour.

Bruce noticed. 'That's Gallows Point,' he said. 'It's a grue-some place. In fact, that's where Calico Jack was hanged four years ago from this time point. Best not to look, really.'

'Again,' Uncle Percy said. 'Thoroughly charming.'

Bruce turned right down a backstreet. 'Lawless Larry's shop is just down here.'

Grateful to leave the main thoroughfare, Becky saw a door

at the alley's end, above which was a hand-painted sign that read:

Lawless Larry's Lifelike Limbs.

The chime of bells signalled their entrance.

Straightaway, the shop's interior surprised Becky; a large ship's bell hung from the ceiling of a spotlessly clean and tidy room, its air perfumed by a mixture of citrus, vanilla and bleach. Mounted on shelves were dozens of fake limbs, carved crudely and painted in various shades. Considering the name of the shop, the pros-thetics were as lifelike as a three-headed giraffe. There were hands, feet and legs, but also ears, false teeth, individual fingers and toes, and even a range of noses in different shapes and sizes.

She looked over at Joe, who was on the verge of laughing, when she heard movement from behind the counter.

"Allo,' a gravelly voice said. 'What can I do fer ya?'

'Lawless... it's me,' Bruce said. 'Bruce Westbrook - yer Arizonian pal.'

Lawless Larry hobbled forward, shock on his face. He was around seventy years old, with bronzed, heavily lined skin, long, straggly silver hair, and eyes that, although sunken from age, still maintained a youthful glint. 'Bruce?' he said. 'Well, tar and feather me. Get yourself over here and give Lawless a shake of your colonial hand.'

Bruce approached Lawless Larry and shook his hand.

'It's good to see ya, boy,' Lawless said. 'Me eyes don't work as well as they used to, but I can see enough to know you look as happy as a magistrate at a hangin'.'

'Thanks, Lawless, I'm doing well,' Bruce said. 'And how 'bout you?'

'Oh, canna carp,' Lawless said. 'If I did, who'd listen? There's only me and Murray 'ere, and he don't care much as long as I throw him a banana every now and again.' He gave a loud whistle. Promptly, a monkey leapt from the shadows and landed on his shoulder.

'Hi, Murray,' Bruce said to the monkey. 'Now Lawless, I've brought some good people here to see ya, fine, upstanding people. They need to ask you a few questions.'

'Oh, aye?' Lawless said. 'Any chum o' Bruce Westbrook is welcome here.' He gave a broad grin, which revealed a single tooth in his lower gum. As he scanned the group, however, his face dropped. Confusion swept his face.

'H-Henry?' Lawless said with disbelief, squinting. 'But I-I heard you were d-dead?'

Becky saw Lawless's eyes were locked on Uncle Percy.

Uncle Percy was stuck for words. 'I think you're mistaking me for someone else, sir. My name's Percy Halifax.'

Lawless Larry studied Uncle Percy's face for a few seconds more, and his expression changed to one of amazement. 'Blow me down! I'll be an orangutan's auntie – yer the double of me old shipmate, *Henry Hunt*. Same eyes. Same hair. Yer even as tall as a mizzenmast like 'im.'

'Henry Hunt,' Bruce said. 'Is that *The Hunter*?'

'Aye,' Lawless replied.

'But it's him we've come ter ask you about,' Bruce said, astonished.

'It is? Why?'

'That's a long story, but you know him?'

'*Knew him*,' Lawless replied. 'Sadly, I heard his heart packed up in a tavern in Aberystwyth. He's as dead as a doornail, so I'm told. Damn near broke my heart when I heard.'

'When did you last see him?' Bruce asked.

'Must be four years past,' Lawless replied. 'Just after we busted Irish Annie, Jack Rackham's wife, outta them damn dirty cells of Port Royal.'

'*We?*' Bruce said.

'Aye,' Lawless said. 'I helped Henry do it. We blew out the jail wall with a stick of dynamite. Pretty much demolished the whole buildin', too.' He chuckled.

'And what happened ter him and Annie after that?'

'Well, Irish Annie were deep into pregnancy, so they left for Saint Lucia to 'ave the baby there,' Lawless replied. His face creased with sadness. 'I'm 'fraid the rest is a real sad story.'

'Sad? Why?' Bruce asked.

'Irish Annie died shortly after the bairn – a healthy boy – was brought into the world.'

'That is sad,' Bruce said.

'It was,' Lawless replied. 'Henry came back ter see me after she died. He was a broken man. Truth was, he loved Annie, and she loved 'im. And I'll let ya into a secret, too - the blood that flowed through that baby was his, and not Jack Rackham's. The Hunter and Annie had been lovers fer some time. Rackham knew nowt of it, otherwise he would've keelhauled 'em both, baby or not.'

'I'm sure.' Bruce nodded. He hesitated before asking his next question. 'Thing is, Lawless, we're lookin' fer Rackham's loot. D'ya know anything about it?'

Surprised by the question, Lawless's eyes narrowed. 'Is that why you're here? You fixin' to track down Calico Jack's fortune? I never reckoned you fer a treasure hunter, Bruce.'

But it was Uncle Percy that answered. 'We're not,' he said. 'At least we're not interested in it for monetary gain. We're looking for a ship's compass, a special, unique compass. It's essential we get it, and we believe it may be part of Rackham's treasure.'

Lawless looked baffled 'A compass?'

'Yes,' Uncle Percy replied.

'I don't know 'bout no compass,' Lawless said. 'But I know Calico Jack's loot has never been found. It's said he hoarded it on a deserted island known only ter himself. Anyway, from what Hunter told me, Rackham made a map to the island and gave it ter Irish Annie the night before his killin'. I'm thinkin' he wanted her unborn to 'ave his riches. He didna know the baby wasn't his, ya see? Fact was, Irish Annie was a fine actress, and she tricked him into thinkin' it were so he'd give up the whereabouts of his fortune.'

'And what 'appened after that?' Bruce asked.

'As I said their plan were to stay on Saint Lucia 'til the baby was strong enough ter travel, and then get Rackham's treasure and return to London. Sadly, although the baby was tough, Irish Annie weren't. Anyway, after she passed, the Hunter had no stomach for the Caribbean no more, so he took the baby and headed back to Wales, to his family, to raise the child away from a life of piracy.'

'And the treasure?'

'Is still on that island, by my reckonin',' Lawless replied. 'Y'see, the Hunter wasn't interested in wealth for himself. He became a pirate for the freedom o' the life, not for riches.' His face grew sad. 'But I know he didn't want that lifestyle for his boy. I think his plan was ter wait until the boy was of age, and then, using the map, get Rackham's treasure together, as father and son.'

'And what happened to the map?' Uncle Percy asked.

'I canna say,' Lawless said. 'I know Annie gave Henry it before she croaked, but that's all I know. He would've hidden it away from them that would cleave him to the brisket for a shot at Rackham's fortune, but I wouldn't know where. Sadly, he died before the bairn was even a boy, so I'm guessin' any secret hiding place he had died with him.'

Just then, the sound of the chimes rang out as the door opened, followed by heavy footsteps and a powerful stench of cheap alcohol.

Looking over, Becky stared at six pirates, as large as prizefighters, their cutlasses raised. Her heart sank when she recognised the group's leader - a merciless thug hired by Emerson Drake and George Chapman to help find The Box of Eternity. A giant man with a freshly shaven scalp, he had a single hoop earring, and crudely etched tattoos that covered his chest, neck and face. But it was the two razor-sharp iron hooks fixed to his wrists that gave him his name:

Doublehook.

18

FLIGHT, FIGHT AND FEET

'MAYB' THERRE DO BE A GOD, AFT'R ALLLL!' Doublehook bellowed in a voice garbled from a recent intake of rum. 'COZ IT SEEMS ME PRAYERS 'AVE CUM TRUE!' He swallowed a deep breath, causing his gigantic belly to inflate like a hot-air balloon. His eyes found Uncle Percy. 'TELL ME, TIME TRAV'LLER - D'YA RECALL MY PRETTY FACE?'

Although surprised, Uncle Percy remained calm. 'How could I forget, Mister Doublehook? It's delightful to see you again.'

Doublehook returned an unpleasant grin, revealing a distinct lack of teeth. 'Be it so, yeh say? I ain't sure yeh'll be thinkin' tha' after I've spoken me mind. Y'see, you and that bunch of croaky old salts of the Black Head left me impaled on two trees on that accursed Mary Island to die.' He hacked up some phlegm and spat on the floor. 'But I didna die, did I? I didn't die coz I be clever... I be clev'rer than all o' ya.'

'I'm sure you're an unqualified genius,' Uncle Percy said.

'That I doo beee,' Doublehook slurred. 'And I knew one day I'd get vengeance on those that left me ter rot on that island.

Today be tha' day.' He raised his left hook, the tip of which gleamed like a blacksmith's poker. 'D'ya get me point?'

'Jog on back to the pub, *Captain Hooks*,' Joe said. 'You and your tanked-up pirate pals wouldn't stand a chance against us.'

Doublehook glared at Joe. 'The boy's grown in height and mettle, has he? D'ya feeeel like a man now, lad? Coz you ain't!'

'Try me,' Joe replied.

Joe was about to move on Doublehook when Uncle Percy held him back.

'No, thank you, Joe,' Uncle Percy said. 'We've been involved in one brawl in the last forty-eight hours, we are not taking part in another.' He smiled calmly at Doublehook. 'Please, Mister Doublehook, I understand your grievance at being marooned, but in all fairness to us, you worked for both a psychopathic megalomaniac and a notorious serial killer, I'm sure you can appreciate how we felt your character lacked a certain moral fortitude.'

Doublehook clearly had no idea what Uncle Percy had just said. 'Ugh,' he replied.

'You worked for the bad guys,' Uncle Percy said. 'We're the good guys. Do you understand that?'

Doublehook didn't.

'Forget it,' Uncle Percy continued. He waved at the line of pirates. 'Listen, everyone, why don't you all just leave these premises peacefully, and go back to your favourite tavern? I'm sure there's plenty more grog for you to consume before lunchtime.' He gave a kindly smile. 'I say we end our encounter with no one needing one of Lawless Larry's superb appendages, and we all carry on happily with the rest of our day. How does that sound?'

'Argghh, but tha' ain't what I be thinkin',' Doublehook said. 'I'm reckonin' I'd like ter settle my score... with yer blood on me blade. And my crew 'ere agrees with me. Yer see, I'm gonna feed ya to the fish, Halifax. You, the American, and those young 'uns. What d'ya say ter that?'

Uncle Percy sighed. 'Then it seems you leave me no choice but to respond in kind. Still, I want you to know I'm a pacifist by nature, and any consequences you suffer are entirely down to your own obstinacy.'

Doublehook looked as clueless as ever. 'Ugh?'

'It doesn't matter,' Uncle Percy replied. He stared at the line of pirates. 'Now, gentlemen, once again can I suggest you leave now, because if you don't, you'll be running from these premises in roughly sixty seconds' time, experiencing a level of terror you've never felt before.'

Doublehook laughed. 'Terror? These be the toughest buckos on the Spanish Main. They ain't never ran from a fight... and they ain't never lost one either. Ain't that the fact, lads?'

The pirates replied with nods, growls, snarls, and the odd 'Argghh!'

'Good for them,' Uncle Percy replied. 'Then shall we get this display of violence started?'

Becky cast an anxious glance at Uncle Percy. *What was he doing?*

Doublehook gave a wild grin and nodded at his crew. 'Get yer cutlasses ready, me boys. We got us sum killin' ter do.'

'Smashing,' Uncle Percy said. He held up his index finger as if to make one last point. 'But before that I must inform you, Doublehook, I intend to perform a minor miracle on you. Now ordinarily I would never use a phrase like this, nevermind do it, but I intend to kick you in the head... without even using my feet.'

As a look of confusion crossed Doublehook's face, Uncle Percy's reached down and triggered his wrist portravella, which illuminated green.

And then several things happened at once.

With a bloodcurdling scream, Doublehook lunged at Uncle Percy.

Simultaneously, Uncle Percy vanished with a quiet *POP*, leaving Doublehook dazed and bewildered.

Then - *POP* - Uncle Percy materialized at the far wall, and jerked a prosthetic leg from its fixings, before – *POP* - disappearing again.

Becky could barely take it all in.

Eyes wide with disbelief and fear, Doublehook didn't see Uncle Percy rematerialize at his left shoulder.

'I warned you,' Uncle Percy said. Raising the prosthetic leg high, he sent the foot into Doublehook's chin, which connected with a stomach-turning *crack*, sending him soaring backwards and crashing to the floor, unconscious.

Silence cloaked the room.

Wearing a satisfied smile, Uncle Percy turned to Doublehook's crew. 'Now, gentlemen, isn't it time you all fled in abject fear?'

The pirates didn't need telling twice. With a collective high-pitched shriek, they turned quickly, banging into each other as they did, and sprinted for the door.

Moments later, Becky watched them hurtle down the alley as fast as their legs could carry them.

Joe beamed at Uncle Percy. 'That was very cool.'

'Thank you, Joe,' Uncle Percy replied. 'I didn't enjoy it in the slightest, but it was about damage limitation.'

'And what's with the portravella trick?' Joe asked. 'I've not seen one do that before.'

'It's a new feature I've added to their design,' Uncle Percy said. 'From now on, all of my portravellas will come with a *Quantavator* attached. It's a device that offers very short-range time jumps for small distances, so you can vanish and re-materialize for all intents and purposes in real-time. It doesn't need anywhere near the Gerathnium of a standard time jump, hence why it doesn't make the usual loud bang when activated.'

'That could be well handy,' Joe said.

'I think so, too,' Uncle Percy replied. It was then he noticed Lawless Larry's face was as white as a sheet. His next words were delivered at a slow and steady pace. 'Oh, I really should explain, Lawless. I'm a time traveller.' He raised his wrist to show off the portravella. 'This is my time machine. That device allows me to disappear and reappear at will.'

Lawless Larry took a few moments to digest this, before giving a grunt that suggested he'd reached an age where nothing shocked him anymore. 'A time traveller, eh?'

'Yes.'

Lawless looked at Bruce. 'And you, Bruce? Is this what you be, too?'

Bruce nodded. 'Yeah, Lawless. I am.'

'Then pickle my poop deck, this do be an unexpected turn,' Lawless said.

'We'd rather you kept it yourself if you would,' Uncle Percy said.

'Fer sure,' Lawless said. 'Ain't no one else's business.'

'Anyway, thank you so much for your time.' Uncle Percy put his hand in his pocket and pulled out six gold coins and placed them on the counter. 'I hope this covers the cost of any inconvenience to you or your shop.'

'I don't want yer doubloons, Mister Halifax,' Lawless said. 'In fact, I wanna give you summat.' He disappeared through a side door, resurfacing a moment later.

To Becky's surprise, he carried a cutlass.

'I don't know yer plans, Mister Halifax,' Lawless said. 'But as they're summat ter do with Irish Annie and Henry Hunt, I want yer to have this.' He held up the cutlass. 'This be Annie's weapon. Henry gave it ter me before he left fer London. 'Tis a beautiful piece of swordsmanship, and Annie always claimed it brought her luck. It's even got her mark on the hilt – *The Red Shamrock.*' He smiled at Becky. 'I dunno - maybe the girl would like it?' He smiled at Becky.

Before Uncle Percy could reply, Becky spoke up. 'I'll take it,' she said. 'Thank you.'

Lawless passed it over to Becky, who turned it in her hand. It was then she spied the single red three-leaf sprig on the hilt. At once, something stirred in her memory - she couldn't remember where or when, but she was sure she'd seen the symbol before.

'Well, we shall leave you now, Lawless,' Uncle Percy said, turning to Joe. 'Joe, would you help me carry Mister Double-hook onto the street?'

'Argh, leave 'im,' Lawless said. 'Me and Murray will sort out the scurvy dog when he wakes.'

'Then we'll say our goodbyes,' Uncle Percy said.

'It's been mighty fine to meet ya,' Lawless said.

'I'll see ya soon,' Bruce said, shaking Lawless's hand.

'You make sure ya do, my colonial bucko,' Lawless replied.

'Bye, Lawless,' Becky and Joe said at the same time.

'Fare thee well, young 'uns,' Lawless said. He flashed a grin at Becky. 'You take care of that blade, missy. The woman that owned it were a good soul.'

'I shall.'

Then something occurred to Joe. 'Uncle Percy... do you have any more gold coins?'

'Of course. Why?' Uncle Percy replied, giving two coins to Joe.

Joe placed the coins on the counter. 'Is this enough to buy a couple of feet?'

'Er, more than enough, lad,' Lawless replied.

Joe passed over the coins before approaching a wide shelf to the left of the counter. Scanning the vast array of feet, he grinned as he removed a pair painted a vivid shade of pink.

'What are you doing?' Uncle Percy asked.

'I reckon Doublehook needs a new name,' Joe replied.

Less than a minute later, Becky followed the others out of the shop. Still, as she stood in the doorway, she couldn't resist one last look at the unconscious Doublehook, his lethal, barbed hooks having been replaced by two bright pink feet, a look perfect for Joe's new name for him:

Doublefoot.

19

BACK TO THE OLD HOUSE

Laughter filled the air as the group gathered outside the shop.

'Kiddo,' Bruce said to Joe. 'You got a sense of humour as black as my old Nana's last tooth.' He turned to Uncle Percy. 'And that's quite a swing ya got on you, brainbox. You could play clean-up hitter fer the Arizona Diamondbacks.'

'I doubt it, Bruce,' Uncle Percy replied. 'And I took no pleasure in it at all. As you know, I don't condone violence, but he forced me into a corner.'

'He deserved it,' Joe said. 'Anyway, So, what're we doing next?'

'I'm not sure,' Uncle Percy replied. 'I suppose we'll have to undertake some detective work to track *The Hunter* back to Wales.'

'Then best o' luck with that,' Bruce said. 'I'll leave ya to do yer Sherlock Holmes stuff and go my own way.'

'Very well, Bruce,' Uncle Percy replied. 'Will you be returning to your holiday home?'

'Soon,' Bruce replied. 'For now, I fancy findin' a buccaneer bar and attachin' myself to a game o' Bone-Ace. I'm feelin' as lucky as a skunk in a perfumery.'

'Enjoy your gambling, sir,' Uncle Percy said. 'And stay safe.'

'Don't worry 'bout me, brainbox,' Bruce said. 'And if ya need me again, just call.'

'We shall,' Uncle Percy said.

Everyone said goodbye to Bruce, who walked off.

'So, Becks,' Joe said. 'You've finally chosen your sword.'

'I guess so,' Becky replied.

'You're holding a piece of history there,' Uncle Percy said. 'Anne Bonny was the most famous female pirate of them all.'

Rotating the sword in her hand, Becky's gaze fell on the red shamrock again. Suddenly, a memory formed. She had seen the symbol before.

Uncle Percy noticed her face change. 'Are you okay, Becky?'

Becky didn't reply as a thousand ideas assaulted her mind.

'Seriously, Becks, what's up?' Joe asked. 'You're not havin' one of your freaky turns, are you?'

Becky snapped from her daze. 'No.' Her eyes found Uncle Percy's. 'But I think this has got something to do with you.'

'With me?' Uncle Percy said, surprised.

'Yes.'

'I'm not sure I understand what you mean.'

'Didn't you think it was strange Lawless thought you were The Hunter?'

'Cases of mistaken identity are not uncommon,' Uncle Percy said.

'But you once told us you were related to a pirate,' Becky said. 'What was your mum's maiden name again?'

Uncle Percy's face changed as he grasped her point. '*Sarah Ann Hunt.*'

'Exactly,' Becky replied. '*Henry Hunt was your ancestor.* And that tells us where to go next.'

'To my mother's house in Borth,' Uncle Percy said.

'Exactly. Maybe it was once Henry Hunt's house, too... because that's where I think I've seen the symbol.'

Uncle Percy looked stunned. 'Really?'

'Yes,' Becky replied. 'When the Wraith made us go there during *The Empedoclean Trials*, I remember the living room being jam-packed with sea-related objects – an old ship's wheel, models of ships, stuff like that.' She held up the cutlass's hilt and pointed at the red shamrock. 'I'm sure I saw this symbol there... somewhere in that room.'

'You did?' Uncle Percy asked. 'Where?'

'I don't remember exactly,' Becky said. 'But I'm sure I'm right.'

'You've got a *bloody* good memory,' Joe said.

'It was less than a week ago, Joe,' Becky replied simply. She looked at Uncle Percy. 'Do you remember seeing the symbol before? Maybe in the living room?'

'I don't,' Uncle Percy replied. 'Remember, other than being forced there by The Wraith, I hadn't visited that house in nearly thirty years. I don't have a clue what objects are there.'

'Then let's find out,' Joe said.

'Absolutely,' Uncle Percy replied.

As Uncle Percy entered the new coordinates into his portravella, Becky's gaze fell once more on the red shamrock. She was aware this was either an amazing coincidence or something different, something perhaps more sinister. After all, it wouldn't be the first time someone had manipulated their actions for their own nefarious ends.

For now, she preferred to think of it as a coincidence. The alternative was much too worrying to consider.

As HER EYES adjusted from the time jump, Becky felt a sadness within. Their last visit to Borth was arranged by the Wraith to make Uncle Percy relive a tragic moment in his life – one in which his girlfriend, Stephanie Calloway, had informed him he was to be a father. This had happened shortly before she was diagnosed with the illness that would end the life of both her and the baby.

With the sound of the ocean in her ears, Becky stared at the sky and saw countless aeroplane smoke trails, and knew they'd returned to the twenty-first century. She turned right to face a modest-sized stone cottage, quirky and ancient, with yolk-yellow walls, veined with age, a crooked chimney and a black slate roof.

Becky knew that although Uncle Percy never visited the house, he still funded its upkeep and maintenance by local people, as a shrine to a family that had passed on.

Wordlessly, Uncle Percy pushed open a small gate, and advanced up a cobblestoned path to the front door. He fell to his knees, picked up a small white stone, and scooped up the key beneath. 'Being at this house still makes me shiver,' he said quietly.

'Does it shiver your timbers, though?' Joe asked.

Becky shot Joe a stern look.

'What?' Joe said, innocently. 'It's a piratey joke. I mean, look at how we're dressed.'

Uncle Percy gave a sour chuckle. 'Believe me, Joe, my timbers are shivering thoroughly. But you're right, let's get inside before any local people notice we're carrying actual swords.' He inserted the key in the keyhole and turned it.

Uncle Percy entered a narrow hallway, which smelt fresh and crisp as though it had recently been cleaned. Turning right at the end of the hall, he entered the living room.

Following him inside, Becky remembered the room clearly. Maritime paraphernalia was everywhere, paintings and ornaments, photographs and knick-knacks. There was a shelf devoted to glass bottles containing tiny model boats, and a large ship's wheel that hung on the left-hand wall.

Becky scanned every piece closely, but it was when she saw an ancient brass compass that the breath caught in her throat. 'That's it,' she gasped, rushing over and picking up the compass. 'Look.'

Uncle Percy joined her and saw a red shamrock etched clearly into the brass. 'Oh, my word.'

'Is that the Dahlia Compass?' Joe asked, hopefully.

'I doubt it, Joe,' Uncle Percy said. 'It's brass, not gold. In fact, I would say it's an unremarkable eighteenth-century ship's compass.'

'Can you open it up?' Becky asked eagerly, passing it over to him.

Uncle Percy took it, his eyes scanning every detail. Pulling out a penknife, he unfolded a small blade and inserted it into the compass' rear panel.

Becky's heart thumped as she watched him remove the casing, to reveal a single folded piece of paper, brittle and stained brown with age.

'Well, well,' Uncle Percy said. 'What do we have here?'

'Is it Rackham's treasure map?' Joe exhaled.

Without replying, Uncle Percy unfurled the paper to reveal handwriting, penned in an elegant, legible script.

'Read it then,' Joe said excitedly.

Uncle Percy began to read.

MY LOYAL WIFE,

I know the infant that grows within you be not mine. I know you've given yourself to another, and if I had more time for breath, I'd find this treacherous rogue, whoever it may be, and slice him from groin to throat. But time is against me, and by tomorrow's

sunset, I shall be dead. However, this leaves the matter of my
fortune unsettled, and a grand fortune it be.

I have never told another soul where it lies, but I want to offer
you a chance to locate it. Why, you may ask? Because, even though
you should swing for your crimes as I shall, I believe your condition
will allow you to dodge the noose. I also know you to be as cunning
as a fox and believe you will escape your jail cell for freedom.

And it is with this notion in mind, I intend to give you all that is
required to locate my wealth. Because, and this is important, I do
not believe for a moment you shall find it. I think you will devote
your time on this earth searching for it, dwelling over my words in
a lasting effort to unravel the meaning, but you will fail. And it is
that failure that will give me great joy, even as I roast in the bowels
of Hell. The agony of frustration will rot away at you, hopefully
even kill you, and that is a just and true reward for your infidelity
and betrayal.

Seek out the isle
with a sting in its tail.
Where the dragon doth breathe,
yet leaves no fiery trail.
Where the Hog Plum grows,
and a fierce cloud brings rain.
To the ghosts of the slaves,
who broke free from their chains.
And deep in the forest,
'neath bush and 'neath vine.
You'll find their last stand,
their unhallowed shrine.
Their living cut short,
as a warning to all.
That the slave owner's ire
is as fierce as a squall.

And within their shelter,
it's there you shall find.
My wealth lies behind
Emmanuel's sign.
But know in my death,
I'll find sweet delight.
That your first born will die,
without a birth right.
And so with this ode,
I pray you shall be.
In misery for
all eternity.

YOUR FAITHFUL HUSBAND
   Jack

UNCLE PERCY TURNED to Joe. 'There's no obvious X marks the spot, but to answer your earlier question - yes, it's unquestionably Calico Jack Rackham's treasure map.'

20

A GIFT FROM THE HEART

'These pirates do love their stupid rhymes, don't they?' Joe said.

'They do, indeed,' Uncle Percy replied. 'In this case, I'm sure Rackham found it both amusing and would add to his wife's frustration. He was clearly a very bitter man.'

'I think the correct word you're looking for is sick, vindictive scumbag,' Becky said.

'That's three words,' Joe said.

'He deserves more than one,' Becky replied.

'He didn't figure out Anne Bonny was cheating on him with The Hunter, then?' Joe said.

'It seems not,' Uncle Percy replied.

'And what about the poem... any first thoughts?' Becky asked.

'Nothing at the moment,' Uncle Percy replied.

'Can you read it again, please?' Joe asked.

Uncle Percy did. The moment he finished a thoughtful silence swept over them.

'It says the treasure is on an island with a sting in its tail,' Joe said. 'Is there a Wasp Island?'

'Perhaps,' Uncle Percy replied. 'But there are thousands of islands in the world, including inland ones, with many bizarre and exotic names.'

'But it'll be an island in the Caribbean,' Joe said.

'Not necessarily,' Uncle Percy replied. 'These pirates were fine sailors, and many ventured far outside that vicinity.'

'The poem mentions dragons,' Joe said. 'They seem to pop up loads at the moment. Do you think it's got anything to do with the Blessed Isle? Maybe it's the same island.'

'Maybe,' Uncle Percy replied. 'But I doubt it - that would be quite the coincidence.'

'What about the passage regarding slaves?' Becky said. 'That's the key clue, isn't it?'

'I think so,' Uncle Percy said. 'However, I'm not sure how that'll help us just yet. The sad truth was that slavery was absolutely rife in the seventeenth century Caribbean. Indeed, forty percent of enslaved Africans were shipped to the Caribbean Islands to work on the sugar, coffee, or cotton plantations. It was the world's primary marketplace for enslaved labour at the time.'

'That's disgusting,' Becky said.

'Agreed,' Uncle Percy replied. 'And let's not forget many of those slave owners were British, which is forever a stain on our country's history.'

'Definitely,' Joe said.

'The poem suggests some slaves broke free,' Becky said. 'And their so-called owners tracked them down and killed them on the island.'

'It does,' Uncle Percy said.

'What about the bit about *Emmanuel's sign*?' Joe said. 'Does that mean anythin' to you?'

Uncle Percy thought about this. 'Not really, and certainly not in this context. I mean, in Hebrew the name 'Emmanuel'

means 'God is with us', but I'm not sure how that benefits us...
not yet, anyway.'

'But finding out more about the slave story might,' Becky
said.

'I agree,' Uncle Percy replied.

'Then we need Captain Google,' Joe said.

'Perhaps,' Uncle Percy replied. 'We could even use books,
too. Wouldn't that make a refreshing change?'

'Not really,' Joe replied.

'Anyway,' Uncle Percy said, 'we've certainly got resources at
our disposal Anne Bonny wouldn't have had, so shall we return
to Bowen Hall and use them?'

Uncle Percy, Becky and Joe left Borth shortly after that, and
arrived back in the Time Room at eleven.

'I'm a tad peckish,' Uncle Percy said. 'Does anyone fancy
brunch before we start our investigations?'

There was no way in a million years Joe would turn that
offer down.

A LIGHT BREEZE brushed Becky's face as she, Joe, and Uncle
Percy approached the steps that led to Bowen Hall's front door.
It was then they saw three small packages of different sizes
positioned neatly on the top step, each one inscribed with a
handwritten name:

Becky.
Joe.
Mister Halifax.

'What do we have here?' Uncle Percy said.

'I reckon they're pressies,' Joe said, scooping up the packages. He passed them out to the named recipient.

'Hang on,' Becky said. 'Should we open them?'

'Course,' Joe replied.

'But what if they're from the Wraith?' Becky said. 'What if he's playing some sick game?'

Joe was already opening his.

'I don't think Joe cares much,' Uncle Percy said.

Joe tore off the wrapping paper to reveal a small box. Without hesitation, he opened it and his eyes ballooned. Inside the box was a pristine braided leather wrist band, adorned with a series of gold letters that spelled the words, '*Manchester City F.C.*'

'Woooow!' Joe gushed. 'Is that real gold?'

'Almost certainly,' Uncle Percy said.

Joe noticed a slip of paper in the box. 'There's a note, too.' He read it out loud.

TO JOE,

I wanted to get you a little something to say thanks loads for rescuing me. I'd be dead meat if it wasn't for you guys. Anyway, I saw this wristband and figured out you might like it. Personally, I wouldn't be seen dead in it, but I reckon it's right up your street.

Anyway, If there's anything I can do for you, just ask.

Cheers again,

Ben.

'THAT'S WELL NICE OF HIM,' Joe said. 'Open yours, Uncle Percy.'

'I told him not to do this,' Uncle Percy said. Unwrapping his package, he looked down at a wooden box. He opened it and his face creased with shock. 'Oh, my word!'

'He got you booze?' Joe said, staring at the ancient bottle within, which also had a note attached.

'It's a bottle of Croizet Cognac Cuvée Léonie 1858,' Uncle Percy replied, stunned. 'It's the rarest and most valuable bottle of cognac ever made.'

'If he's nicked that from a time trip, he's in big trouble,' Joe said with a grin. 'Anyway, what does your note say?'

Uncle Percy removed it and read.

To Mister Halifax,

I know you told me you didn't want any gift, but you saved my life and I wanted to give you a small token of my thanks. From what my Aunty Helen tells me, you have no interest in money and stuff like that, and even though I know this cognac is quite valuable, I want you to know it wasn't stolen in time. The bottle was actually a present from a rich mate of my dad's when I was born. I think he thought it would be an investment for when I'm older.

The fact is, it means nothing to me. Less than nothing. I hate alcohol, ever since my parents were killed in a drink driving accident. Fact is, I don't want it, and you having it would mean a lot to me.

You didn't have to come back in time to save my life, but you did, and for that I reckon you're a top bloke.

I hope you'll accept it.

Ben

UNCLE PERCY LOOKED TAKEN ABACK. 'I don't know what to say to that.'

'That's well sad about his mum and dad,' Joe said.

'Very,' Becky said.

'I didn't know,' Uncle Percy said.

'You can't give it back to him now,' Joe said to Uncle Percy.

Uncle Percy looked resigned. 'I don't suppose I can.'

'Anyway, Becks,' Joe said. 'What're you waiting for? Open yours.'

Almost reluctantly, Becky unwrapped her package to find an oblong box coated in blue velvet with a silver clasp. Opening it, she gave an involuntary gasp.

The box contained a chain fashioned from a gleaming silver-white metal, attached to which was a pendant in the shape of a winged horse. There was also the obligatory handwritten note.

'Woah,' Joe said. 'Now that looks like it cost a few quid.'

'You're not wrong, Joe,' Uncle Percy said, stunned. 'Unless I'm very much mistaken, it's made from *palladium*, which is amongst the most valuable metals in the world.'

'Read the note, Becks,' Joe said.

Becky did.

DEAR BECKY

I know you said you didn't want anything, but I hope you'll accept this. I've heard how much Pegasus, your winged horse, means to you, and I thought you could wear it as a reminder of her.

I know it's unusual – and maybe a bit weird - for someone you don't know to give you jewellery, but I don't mean to be a weirdo. I just want to express my thanks for you saving my life.

Please don't consider giving it back to me. I've bought it now and it wouldn't suit me if I wore it.

Cheers again,

Ben

'That's well nice of him,' Joe said. 'And I was right about what I said before – I think he might have a crush on you.'

'Oh, shut up!' Becky said.

'It is a beautiful thing,' Uncle Percy said. 'Will you keep it?'

Becky looked conflicted.

'Why would you give it back, Becks?' Joe said. 'It sounds like he's loaded, so the price is no skin off his nose. Plus, he's right - we saved his life.'

Becky looked at it again. It truly was the most gorgeous piece of jewellery. 'I suppose.'

'Then keep it,' Joe said.

'I do like it,' Becky said sincerely.

Joe grinned. 'There you go.'

'Okay,' Becky said. 'I'll keep it... as a tribute to Peggy, of course.' She looped it around her neck and secured the clasp. 'What do you think?'

'It's simply stunning, Becky,' Uncle Percy said.

Just then, a familiar voice met their ears.

'I see you have received your spoils,' Tusk said, approaching them.

'Hey, Tusky,' Joe said. 'Yeah, we did. Did Ben get you something?'

'Aye,' Tusk replied. 'The boy has a generous soul, and I respect a man who upholds his word.'

'He got you some salt and vinegar crisps, then?' Joe asked.

'My spoils are hoarded within the tree house. I shall feast well upon them in the pending days.'

'Good for you.' Joe laughed. 'How many bags did you get?'

'I know not,' Tusk said. 'How many bags doth a box contain?'

'He got you a box?'

'I was given fifty boxes,' Tusk replied. 'They fill your tree-house dwelling from ground to roof. And may Odin be praised for such a wondrous bounty.'

21

THE SHAME OF MAN

Joe was speechless. 'Fifty boxes? Is there any room in there to sleep?'

'Who wishes for slumber when there is such gorging to be done?'

'That's a *no*, then,' Joe said. 'Great!'

'And is there progress in your search for the Isle of the Blessed?'

'We call it the Blessed Isle now,' Joe said. 'And yeah, we think we're onto something.'

'Then you must involve me when you embark on your quest. My axe is ever yours.'

'Don't worry, Tusk,' Uncle Percy said. 'You'll be kept in the loop. Now, would you like to join us for a bite to eat?'

'Why would I consume your food when there are crisps to feast on?' Tusk replied.

'Yeah, eat my bed clear, will you?' Joe said.

'The challenge is set.' And with that, Tusk turned and walked away.

After brunch, Uncle Percy began his research in Bowen

Library, while Becky and Joe went off to spend a few hours with Pegasus and Gump.

Sunlight bathed the fields as Becky cleaned out Pegasus's stable, replaced her drinking water, and re-filled her feed trough. At the same time, Joe rode Gump around the fields as if riding an elephant.

After she'd finished her chores, Becky took Pegasus out for a fly. Unseen by the human eye due to the invisiblator on Pegasus's ankle, they flew over the Cheshire countryside, reaching the pretty market town of Nantwich, before returning to Bowen Hall, careful to avoid any low-flying aircraft, drones and hang gliders.

A short while later, Becky and Joe said goodbye to Pegasus and Gump and were about to head back to the hall when a sphere of light appeared behind the stables. The light grew in size, sizzling and blazing, before exploding with a *bang*. The light vanished to reveal a green and white campervan.

Bertha.

Even now, the sight of her filled Becky with joy. Bertha had been the first of Uncle Percy's time machines she'd seen and was still her favourite by far.

Uncle Percy leapt out of the campervan, a broad smile on his face. 'Ah, you're still here... excellent.'

'You look pleased with yourself,' Becky said. 'Can we assume you know where Rackham's treasure is?'

'I believe so,' Uncle Percy said.

'Where?' Joe asked.

'You were close with your guess of Wasp Island, Joe,' Uncle Percy said. 'I believe it's on a small islet called Scorpion Island, although its more common name is Gasparillo Island in the Republic of Trinidad and Tobago.'

Joe looked suddenly pale. 'Scorpion Island?'

'Yes. It's also known as Centipede Island. I can only assume it's home to an overabundance of centipedes and scorpions.'

'And why d'you think the treasure's there?' Becky asked.

'Everything fits,' Uncle Percy replied. 'To be fair, Rackham gave enough information and more to find his treasure. Anne Bonny, however, didn't have Joe's friend, Captain Google, or access to the books of Bowen Library as I did.'

'Then go on,' Becky said. 'Tell us everything.'

'Gasparillo Island is tiny, only a few hundred metres in length, and entirely covered in forest. For most, it would barely register on a map, but it's a perfect place for a pirate wishing to conceal their ill-gotten gains.'

'Then how do all the clues fit? Joe asked. 'You know, the Dragon stuff and all that.'

'Well, as far as the 'Dragon doth breathe' line goes - Gasparillo Island is one of the Bocas Islands, a chain of islands also known as the *Dragon's Teeth,* and they're named like this because they're located in a stretch of ocean called the Bocas del Dragón or the Dragon's Mouth.'

'And the bit about the *ghost of the slaves?*' Becky asked.

'I found a rare manuscript from 1655 by Richard Ligon called '*A True and Exact History of Trinidad and Tobago,*' Uncle Percy said, 'and it detailed several horrific stories from the Caribbean slave trade. One of these stories involved a dozen slaves – men, women and children – who escaped from their sugar plantation in Diego Martin. The plantation owner, Edward Tewksbury, took a group of men and set off to hunt them down. For weeks, they couldn't find them, but eventually tracked them to Gasparillo Island, where Tewkesbury murdered them one by one in cold blood. Apparently, to conceal their crime they took the bodies away and dumped them in the ocean. In time, the truth was lost, and the story became fable, before being forgotten completely.'

'That's horrible,' Becky said.

'It's merely one of many horrific stories involving the slave trade,' Uncle Percy replied. 'Now, it's doubtful Anne Bonny would've heard of this story. The manuscript was never formally published as a book.'

'Fair enough,' Joe said. 'What're we waiting for? Let's go there now.'

'The coordinates are already in Bertha's chronalometer,' Uncle Percy replied. 'Climb aboard.'

Becky and Joe did.

'Hang on,' Becky said, settling on the passenger seat. 'You said Gasparillo Island was completely covered with forest. How do you know where to materialise? I mean, you don't want to land on top of a tree.'

'And that's precisely why we're taking Bertha,' Uncle Percy replied. 'I thought it best we investigate the island from the water first.' He flicked a switch on the dashboard, and the sound of grinding metal echoed from Bertha's rear, heralding the appearance of two giant propellers. Simultaneously, the campervan rose steadily off the ground, as if elevated by an inflatable cushion.

Becky knew precisely what was going on. Instantly, she recalled cruising down the River Potaro on their search for El Dorado - a feat only possible because Bertha was both a campervan and a *hovercraft*.

22

SCORPION ISLAND

A few moments later, the campervan was afloat on a calm sea, her sizeable air skirt preventing her from sinking to the depths below.

With bright sunshine making the water shimmer, Becky squinted through the passenger window at the smallest island she'd ever seen. Ceiba and crabwood trees, giant ferns, and shrubs covered the bed of limestone rock completely, making the island resemble a giant green cupcake. 'That is one dinky island,' she said.

'It is, Becky,' Uncle Percy said, steering the campervan left to reveal a much larger island behind. 'And that's its big brother, Gaspar Grande, an island with a much more notable history, including its own legend of buried pirate treasure. Anyway, I'll just circle the island to see if there's a spot accessible enough for us to land.'

Joe looked at Gasparillo Island, his face somewhat pale. 'What about these scorpions, then?'

Becky detected an anxiousness in Joe's voice.

'I don't think they'll be an issue, Joe,' Uncle Percy replied.

'They were enough of an issue to name the island after them.'

'Well, there is probably an abundance of them,' Uncle Percy replied. 'But of the two thousand species of scorpion worldwide, only thirty or forty are venomous enough to kill humans, and most in the Caribbean are not fatal at all.'

'What d'you mean *most*?' Joe asked.

A playful glint formed in Becky's eyes. 'You look as white as a ghost. Are you okay?'

'Course I am,' Joe said.

'You're not scared of scorpions, are you?'

Joe hesitated before he replied. 'To be honest, they proper freak me out big style.'

'They do?' Becky asked, surprised. 'But I thought you were the fearless action hero.'

'Not for scorpions,' Joe replied. 'I've had a thing about them since I was about seven, when our teacher, Stinky Starmer, brought one in to show the kids. Weird little things.'

'But you've faced gorgons and krakens and trolls and all kinds of monsters,' Becky said.

'Yeah, and I'd rather face a zombie horde than a single scorpion,' Joe replied. 'They just – I dunno - they give me the creeps.'

Becky laughed.

'It's not funny,' Joe said.

'I know,' Becky replied. 'I just didn't know. Maybe you should stay in the campervan when we get on the island?'

'I'm not doin' that,' Joe replied.

'It's perfectly fine if you do, Joe,' Uncle Percy said. 'No one could or would ever question your courage, or indeed your masculinity.'

'Don't sweat it,' Joe said. Keen to change the subject, he added, 'Anyway, what did the poem say again about the treasure?'

Uncle Percy recalled the poem. 'If memory serves, it said, *'And within their shelter, it's there you shall find my wealth lies behind Emmanuel's sign.'*

'So, we're looking for somewhere the slaves used as a shelter?' Becky said.

'Apparently so,' Uncle Percy replied.

As the campervan reached the northernmost point of the island, Becky saw a fissure in the bedrock concealed by overhanging branches. 'There's a gap there,' she said, pointing.

'Let's take a look,' Uncle Percy replied, guiding them toward the opening.

Slowly, steadily, the campervan edged through the branches into a coal-black tunnel of veined limestone and soft, damp rock with a high natural arch formed from countless years of water erosion. The tunnel fanned into a large sea cave where the water ended and solid ground began.

'It seems like we've found a parking spot,' Uncle Percy said, switching off Bertha's engine and bringing her to a halt.

'It's pitch-black,' Becky said. 'Have you brought some illumino beads?'

'I have a few in my pocket,' Uncle Percy replied. 'But I've also brought another form of illumination... one you may be thankful for Joe.'

'What d'you mean?' Joe asked.

'You'll see,' Uncle Percy said, climbing out.

Becky and Joe trailed him out of the van.

'Go on then?' Joe said. 'What illumination, and why would I be thankful?'

Uncle Percy put his hand into his pocket and withdrew a long cylindrical object. 'This is an ultra-violet flashlight,' he said. 'And it might help with your phobia. Scorpions have beta carboline in their exoskeleton, and so fluoresce when illuminated by ultraviolet light.'

Joe looked clueless. 'Huh?'

'They glow in the dark,' Uncle Percy said simply. 'No one is precisely sure why. It's another one of mother nature's great mysteries. Does that make you feel better?'

'Not at all.'

'Ah, okay,' Uncle Percy said. 'Anyway, let's look, shall we?' He switched on the light, and an eerie, spine-chilling sight met their eyes.

All around, the walls and rocks were covered in scorpions, their contours gleaming a blue-green colour. Some were as big as hands, others were barely visible to the eye. The largest had wide tails, eight legs and slim tweezer-like pincers.

The squeak that left Joe's mouth resembled a car doing an emergency stop.

'Crikey,' Uncle Percy said. 'There are a lot of them.'

'A lot?' Becky said, masking her own alarm. 'There are hundreds of them, maybe thousands.'

'Yes,' Uncle Percy said. 'I believe the big ones are Trinidad thick-tailed scorpions.'

'Are they deadly?'

'Probably not.'

'Probably?'

'Not if they don't sting you.'

'And if they do?'

'Let's not find out,' Uncle Percy replied. He noticed a breach in the wall, beyond which was a sliver of light. 'Anyway, it seems there's an exit, so let's see where it leads?'

Becky and Joe shadowed Uncle Percy's slow, cautious steps; the ultraviolet light brightened the path ahead, ensuring they avoided any scorpions.

Making their way through the gap, they entered a smaller cave, at the end of which was daylight. Emerging into the open air, they found themselves enveloped by thick forest, their ears assaulted by the sounds of insects and birds and the leaves rustling in the breeze. Sunlight barely made it through the blanket of foliage overhead.

'Which way?' Becky asked Uncle Percy.

'I've no idea,' Uncle Percy replied. 'I suppose we just look everywhere. The island's so small we'll have covered every part in ten minutes.'

They pressed on and the trees thinned, with more sunlight breaking through.

Just then, however, Becky had the wind knocked from her lungs.

A human skeleton had been tied to the trunk of a guava tree, its stained, aged bones merging in with the tree's mottled green bark. Straightaway, she saw another one, this time the smaller frame of a child. Her heart melted.

'Oh, dear,' Uncle Percy gasped.

Tears filled Becky's eyes as three more skeletons appeared besides the remnants of a makeshift stove.

'I guess they didn't take the slaves away after all,' Joe said glumly.

'It seems not,' Uncle Percy said.

Looking left, Becky saw a hole in the ground, scantily covered by plant litter. 'There's an opening.' She moved over to it, pushed aside the debris, and peered inside. 'It's an underground cave.'

Uncle Percy stepped forward, raising his ultraviolet light. 'Just brace yourself for more scorpions, Joe.' He switched it on and dropped it below. Then he poked his head inside the hole. 'There are no visible signs of scorpions.'

Joe sighed with relief.

'What is down there, then?' Becky asked hesitantly.

'Let's have some additional light' Uncle Percy pulled out an illumino bead and dropped it. As the bead cracked on the hard ground, light touched everywhere, revealing a rocky incline that led to a large subterranean grotto.

'Well?' Becky asked.

'I'm not going to sugarcoat it,' Uncle Percy said. 'There are more skeletal remains.'

'And treasure?' Joe asked.

'Not that I can see,' Uncle Percy replied. Carefully, he shinnied down the slope into the cavern, followed by Joe and Becky.

Once inside, Becky's heart broke further. Dismembered skeletons were everywhere, alongside crudely whittled spears, knives, bowls, and other items fashioned from the island's resources.

Becky knew at once it was the most depressing place she'd ever seen, one that stank of pain, death and gloom. And yet this small cave, barely more than a hole in the ground, had been a home, a sanctuary, a beacon of freedom to a group of people whose lives would otherwise be ruled by the whims of a cruel slave owner.

She brushed away the tears that escaped her eyes.

Hiding his feelings, Joe remained focussed on the task at hand. 'So, Rackham said that the treasure is behind Emmanuel's sign... what could that mean?'

'I don't know,' Uncle Percy replied.

'Maybe one of the skeletons was called Emmanuel, and he's pointing at something,' Joe suggested.

Then a grim thought struck Becky. 'Maybe this is all part of Rackham's sick, twisted plan?'

'What do you mean?' Joe asked.

Becky hesitated. 'Maybe the treasure isn't here at all. Maybe Rackham wanted Anne Bonny to come here, to see hell on earth, only to find there's no pot of gold at the end of the rainbow? Maybe this is the final, cruel plot-twist in a story from a nasty, jealous sicko?'

'I don't think so, Becky,' Uncle Percy said. 'The chances of her finding Gasparillo Island with her resources were slim. In fact, I would say he's gone out of his way, so she didn't find it.'

'Then if the treasure's here, the Emmanuel's sign must mean something,' Joe said. 'I know it's creepy, but we should investigate.'

As the time crawled by, Becky felt increasingly sickened as she explored the cavern, looking for something, anything that could be a sign. And then something caught her eyes - amidst all the skeletons, she saw something on the far wall: two humerus bones had been arranged in an X pattern beneath a single large skull.

Becky raced over to them. 'It's the Skull and Crossbones. This is it... it has to be. *X marks the spot!*'

Recognition flashed on Uncle Percy's face. 'And we also have the answer to Rackham's riddle.' He chuckled sourly. 'It was the French pirate Emmanuel Wynne who was first credited with designing the skull and crossbones insignia.'

Joe didn't hesitate. Marching over, he examined the wall. 'This isn't rock... it's clay.' Without delay, he ripped away lumps of clay and mud, and threw them aside. In no time at all, a large hole had formed. 'Pass me an illumino bead, please,' he said to Uncle Percy.

Uncle Percy passed one over, and Joe threw it inside. As the bead split, it shed light onto masses of shimmering objects – gold, jewels, silver, and silks, which filled a second, smaller cave.

Joe grinned. 'We're rich again with money we can't have.'

'You know the rules,' Uncle Percy said.

Joe gave a dissatisfied grunt as a reply.

'Don't worry, Joe. On this occasion, I don't intend to just leave it here.'

'You won't?' Joe said.

'No,' Uncle Percy replied. 'I'm going to ask GITT's permission to bring it to the twenty-first century, sell it, and give the profits to food banks, homeless shelters and whatever other charities need funds at the moment. The world is going through a dreadful cost-of-living crisis, and this could help in some minor degree.'

'I heard charity begins at home,' Joe said.

'It does,' Uncle Percy replied. 'It's just your home doesn't need it.'

Joe gave a second, dissatisfied grunt.

'Anyway,' Uncle Percy said. 'I suppose we'd better do what we came here to do and search for the Dahlia Compass. Hopefully, Heath Pineos' information was correct, and this hasn't all been a significant waste of our time...'

23

THE DAHLIA COMPASS

Desperate to get the job done quickly so they could leave, Becky and Joe launched into the task.

As Becky delved amongst the jewels and gems, trinkets and coins, it occurred to her that if GITT agreed to use the treasure for charitable purposes, then it could do a lot of good for struggling families in these difficult times.

It was then, however, her heart flipped. Beneath a silver goblet, she spied a small round golden case about the size of a pocket watch. Reaching down to touch it, she knew at once they'd found *The Dahlia Compass*. The metal shivered lightly, as if containing some strange, otherworldly energy.

'I've found it,' Becky said. Holding it up, her face blushed with a golden tint.

Uncle Percy and Joe rushed over.

'It feels really weird,' Becky said. 'It's like it's alive.'

'Does it open up?' Joe said.

Becky studied it closely and saw a tiny clasp. She opened it to reveal a dish decorated with unusual markings the likes of which she'd never seen before. Inside, a wooden needle pointing north east floated on a shallow layer of water. Transferring the compass to her other hand, she pivoted left and watched the needle reset itself to its former position. 'That's weird,' she said.

'May I, Becky?' Uncle Percy asked, extending his open palm.

Becky passed it over.

Uncle Percy's brow furrowed as he felt the same strange sensation. 'How curious. Holding this stirs a memory, one from our dim and distant past.'

'What memory?' Joe asked.

'Do you remember those two doubloons Bruce Westbrook gave us, the ones that had touched the Box of Eternity?'

'The ones that turned you into a raging psychopath?' Joe said.

'Yes,' Uncle Percy replied.

Joe looked concerned. 'But the compass doesn't do that, does it?'

'Not at all,' Uncle Percy replied. 'I just mean, the doubloons, like the compass, were inanimate objects that seemed to have a life of their own and were desperate to return home. My reading after holding the compass is that the water feels precisely the same way.'

'And what's your point?' Joe asked.

'I don't have one,' Uncle Percy replied. 'I'm just noting a similarity. It's probably nothing.'

Becky thought about this for a moment. 'D'you think this has anything to do with Eden Relics?'

'I don't know what to think, Becky,' Uncle Percy replied.

'Well, whatever,' Joe said. 'We've got the compass now. Can we get off this creepy island now, please?'

No one opposed the idea.

~

It was mid-afternoon when they appeared back in the Time Room, before heading for the kitchens for drinks and an afternoon snack.

Becky stared at the Dahlia Compass, which Uncle Percy had placed in the middle of the kitchen table. Nervous excitement coursed through her. Surely, they'd made the breakthrough needed to find the Blessed Isle, and get what they needed to restore her parents?

'What's next, then?' Joe said, swigging from a cup of apple juice. 'Are we going now?'

Uncle Percy stirred his cup of tea. 'Going where exactly?'

'Well err...'

'That's the problem, Joe,' Uncle Percy replied. 'We simply do not know where to start. Yes, we have the Dahlia Compass, and that should help us when we have a starting point, but currently we don't.' He took a deep breath. 'I mean, what do we really have? Yes, everything points to the Blessed Isle being in the Pacific Ocean, but that's the largest and deepest ocean in the world at over sixty-three million square miles. We have no concrete evidence where to start looking.'

The optimism left Becky's face. 'Oh,' she mumbled.

Uncle Percy noticed. 'But don't feel sad, Becky. Actually, I have one avenue I want to pursue. It's something I've had at the back of my mind for a bit, but we'll have to see if it pays off.'

'What is it?' Becky asked.

'I'd like to investigate before I tell you, but it may give us a more specific part of the Pacific to explore.' Uncle Percy paused. 'It may even give us a specific year to do it.'

'Really?' Becky said. 'How does the year matter?'

'It doesn't,' Uncle Percy said. 'But it might help to solve an eighty-five-year-old mystery.'

'What do you mean?' Becky asked.

'You'll see,' Uncle Percy said mysteriously.

A short while after that, Uncle Percy went off to begin his investigations, leaving Becky and Joe to visit their parents to explain recent events. After that, they did some sword fighting practice to get Becky used to Anne Bonny's cutlass before returning to the hall to cook an evening meal.

All the while, Uncle Percy remained locked in Bowen Library, and Becky didn't see or hear for him until later that night, when she returned to her bedroom to find a note on her dressing table.

DEAR BECKY,

I believe I've had some measure of success and am confident I have found a specific part of the Pacific Ocean that is of particular interest. With that in mind, I feel we can leave tomorrow morning at 9.00 a.m.

And to keep you in the loop, I've decided we shall time travel to the 3rd July 1937. I shall explain my reasons for this tomorrow.

Anyway, I'd like to meet you, Joe and Tusk at the front of the Hall on the main drive. You'll see why when we meet.

As for attire – wear anything you feel comfortable in. Obviously, if you need to arm yourself with your new sword, that is up to you. Personally, I think your mind is a far greater weapon than any you could bring.

Now, although I'm optimistic, we can find the Blessed Isle on this trip, some of my decisions are supposition, deduction and guesswork, so don't be too disappointed if we're unsuccessful on this occasion.

We will achieve our goals; I have every confidence in that.

Sleep well,

UP

.   .   .

As she got ready for bed, Becky thought about the note again and again. Which part of the Pacific Ocean particularly interested Uncle Percy, and why? Even more significantly, however, why was he so keen to travel to 3rd July 1937? She went online and looked up the date, and yet found nothing of any interest, whatsoever. In fact, she couldn't imagine a less interesting day.

Still, she had every faith in Uncle Percy and was more than happy to wait until the next day to find out. What she didn't know was the next day would prove one of the most extraordinary days in her strange and crazy life.

Becky was woken at eight by three sharp raps on her door before it was thrown open.

'Come on,' Joe bellowed. 'Get up... we're going.'

Groggily, Becky glanced at her clock, before looking at Joe, who was wearing jeans, hiking boots, a sweater, and a belt tucked into which was a sword and dagger; a small quiver hung from his shoulder that contained dozens of extendable clip-arrows. 'Not for another hour.' She yawned.

'I know, but we need a big breakfast,' Joe said. 'We don't know how long we'll be gone.'

'I know.'

'Then get ready,' Joe said. 'And don't forget your cutlass.'

'I'm not sure I should take it,' Becky said.

'Why not?' Joe replied. 'Of course, you should. Besides, I got you this.' He threw a leather scabbard onto her bed. 'This should fit.' And with that, he left.

Becky stared at the scabbard. 'I guess I'm taking the sword, then,' she mumbled.

Becky met Joe fifteen minutes later, and they ate a hearty breakfast of sausages, bacon, hash browns, and baked beans before leaving to meet Uncle Percy.

As they opened the front door and stepped outside, Becky saw Uncle Percy, who wore a wide-brimmed hat, a cotton suit, walking boots, and a leather holster that contained a Tempore-volver, a gun that fired harmless pellets that could freeze time when they hit their target. He was standing beside Tusk, who was fully armed with a bow, quiver of arrows, his hammer, and an axe.

It was then, however, she had her first shock of the day.

To Uncle Percy's left was a sleek, elegant convertible car, its glossy black paintwork dazzling in the morning sunlight.

Becky had only seen this car once before in the Time Room, when Uncle Percy was making modifications to what would be his sixth time machine.

Joe looked on the verge of crying. 'We're taking the Bentley!'

'Indeed we are, Joe,' Uncle Percy replied, pride in his voice. 'Brenda is custom made for this trip.'

'I assumed we were taking Bertha because she's a hover-craft?' Becky said.

Uncle Percy smiled. 'Trust me, Brenda is a much better option.'

'Why? Have you made another submarine?'

'You'll see,' Uncle Percy said.

'Can I drive?' Joe asked.

'Obviously not.'

Tusk stared at the car with wonder. 'And this is a time machine?' he said. 'It has the same powers as the wrist bracelets that you wear?'

'Those bracelets are called portravellas, Tusk,' Uncle Percy said. 'And yes, this vehicle will allow us to travel through time in exactly the same way. Now, shall we get the trip underway?'

'Bagsy the front seat,' Joe said quickly.

Uncle Percy laughed. 'Consider it bagsied, Joe. Jump in.'

As Joe leapt onto the front seat, Becky and Tusk climbed into the rear.

Immediately, Becky was gobsmacked by the sheer luxury of the car. It really wasn't like any of Uncle Percy's other time machines. The bright interior exuded lavishness and craftsmanship, with quilted red leather upholstery, high gloss oak veneers, and deep pile carpet.

'This might be the greatest day of my life,' Joe said, settling onto the front seat.

'You're easily pleased.' Uncle Percy chuckled. 'Seat belts on, everyone. Becky, could you help Tusk with his, please?' He turned the engine over and it purred quietly. 'And, Joe, you're chief navigator.' He passed over the Dahlia Compass. 'Keep a tight grip on that. Things are going to get stirring in a moment.'

'I shall,' Joe said. He opened its casing and stared at the needle.

'Have you got that water bottle for Heath Pineos?' Becky asked.

Uncle Percy tapped his coat pocket. 'I have indeed.'

After everyone was buckled up, the Bentley pulled off slowly.

'C'mon, Unc,' Joe said. 'It's a sports car... kick it in the guts.'

Uncle Percy gave a wry smile. 'Your wish is my command. Besides, I need to get to eighty-eight miles per hour before I hit the ramp.'

He slammed his foot on the accelerator and the Bentley took off like a missile.

Joe shouted his delight.

Becky, however, was puzzled by what had just been said. 'Ramp?' she said, leaning forward. 'What do you mean ramp?'

But her eyes provided the answer before Uncle Percy did.

A large, steep ramp over ten feet tall had been constructed on the long driveway.

Uncle Percy steered the Bentley toward it.

'Oh, this is so cool,' Joe said, the wind lashing his hair.

'WHAT IN BALDUR'S NAME IS THIS?' Tusk bellowed.

Ignoring him, Uncle Percy flicked on the chronalometer switch, and a misty light poured from the dashboard.

The Bentley connected with the ramp smoothly, shooting off its end and rocketing into the air.

Tusk's screams merged with a thunderous *BOOM* as Brenda vanished from sight.

24

INTO THE GREEN

Becky's eyes had barely adjusted from the time jump when her stomach tumbled as the car angled downward, before striking water hard, ice-cold spray showering them. Wiping her face, she looked out to see a rambling ocean of murky grey water extend before them on all sides.

Uncle Percy steadied the Bentley, and soon they were skimming across the surface like a pebble.

'You turned a Bentley into a *speedboat*?' Joe said. 'That's awesome!'

'Thank you, Joe,' Uncle Percy said. 'It's an *Aquacar*. Many years ago, a friend of mine, Sid Shufflebottom, a member of the Knights Templar – you both met him once in the Magpie Inn in Addlebury – challenged me to build one. I ended up making dozens for their organisation.'

'It's very cool,' Joe replied.

'And perfect for today's task. Now, which way is the compass sending us?'

Joe looked at the Dahlia Compass. It was then he noticed it vibrating in his grip. 'That's weird.'

'What's weird?' Uncle Percy asked.

'Look at the compass,' Joe said, holding it up. 'It's goin' bonkers now.'

'Astonishing,' Uncle Percy replied. 'It must be excited to be nearly home.'

Joe studied the needle to see it now pointed south west. 'It wants us to go that way.'

As they changed direction, Becky looked at Uncle Percy. 'This is July 3rd 1937, right?'

'It is,' Uncle Percy replied.

'You said you'd explain why that date matters.'

'I did,' Uncle Percy replied. 'The fact is, I may be way off the mark, I may not, but have you heard of Amelia Earhart?'

'Yeah,' Becky said. 'She was a famous pilot?'

'Yes... a remarkable one,' Uncle Percy said. 'She was the first woman to fly solo across the Atlantic Ocean. She broke many flying records and was perhaps the ultimate champion in the advancement of women in aviation. Her greatest ambition, however, was to be the first woman to circumnavigate the globe. Anyway, she set out to achieve this with her navigator, Fred Noonan, on June 1st 1937. Tragically, she disappeared somewhere over the Pacific on July 2nd 1937. Her plane has never been found, her body has never been found, and her disappearance is one of the greatest unsolved mysteries of the twentieth century.'

'And what does this have to do with us?' Joe asked.

'It may have nothing to do with us,' Uncle Percy said. 'But if the Blessed Isle had something to do with her disappearance, it occurred to me this general area may be of interest to us. And looking at the Dahlia Compass's excitable state, then I may be correct.'

'Why didn't her disappearance come up when I checked this date online?' Becky asked.

'Because she went missing yesterday at this time point,' Uncle Percy said. 'I picked the day after her disappearance.'

As the minutes merged into hours, the mood within the car changed. Conversation dwindled, as if the endless ocean, its waves pulsating lightly in a consistent rhythm, hypnotised everyone to silence. They saw no land, no birds, no fish... nothing but water and a dull, grey sky.

In time, Becky felt her eyelids getting heavier as sleep beckoned. It was then she heard Joe's astonished voice. 'What is that?' he panted.

Becky's eyes shot open to see a thick wall of emerald-green fog in the distance.

'I don't know, Joe,' Uncle Percy said. 'I've seen nothing like it before. Have you, Tusk?'

'I have not,' Tusk replied grimly.

Uncle Percy glanced at the compass, which vibrated wildly now. 'Still, the compass appears to be keen to go there... so on we go.'

Becky felt an array of emotions surge through her: fear, hope, and apprehension. What on earth was it?

Uncle Percy steered the Bentley toward the fog, and a moment later it swallowed them.

As the car drove through the thick mist, everyone stayed silent. They all knew they were experiencing something new, bizarre, paranormal. Within a short time, however, the mist dispersed to reveal bright light beyond.

As they emerged on the other side, astounded gasps filled the car.

The seascape had changed entirely. The sky was periwinkle blue, the ocean a shimmering green. But the most astounding thing was the vast tropical island that stretched as far as the eye could see.

Joe swore loudly.

'Crikey,' Uncle Percy said.

'It seems our destination has been reached,' Tusk said.

'Indeed,' Uncle Percy said.

Becky recalled their recent adventure to get the Odin Horn. 'Are we still on earth?' she said, concern in her voice. 'I mean, was that green mist like Cloud Island - a portal to another dimension?'

'I don't think so, Becky,' Uncle Percy said, looking at a dial on the car's dashboard. 'Judging by the chronalometer we're very much still on earth, and precisely *when* we were meant to be.'

Relieved, Becky stared at the island. Coated in sunshine, it was as lush and picturesque as an oil painting, with rocky coves, soaring grey cliffs, and mile upon mile of white sandy beach that bordered an impenetrable forest with trees that speared the sky.

Her attentions, however, was interrupted by Joe's excited voice. 'Hey... it that a whale?'

Becky looked over and saw what appeared to be a large fin break the water's surface about a hundred metres away.

The unseen creature was moving steadily north. Suddenly, its fin turned slowly in their direction as the creature altered its course.

Uncle Percy's face dropped. 'That's not a fin,' he said, both shocked and dumbfounded.

'What is it then?' Becky asked.

'It's a sail.'

Becky could barely believe her ears. 'A sail?'

'Yes. Hold on everyone.' In a flash, Uncle Percy slammed his foot on the accelerator. The car sped off.

Simultaneously, the creature powered after them, its sail – a six feet line of spiked bones covered in skin - sliced the water like a blade.

Horrified, Becky knew the creature was gaining on them.

Just then, water exploded everywhere, and a massive reptile at least sixty feet long leapt from the water before plunging back into the sea.

'T-that was a dinosaur!' Becky gasped.

But Joe was even more specific. 'A *Spinosaurus!*' he said, stunned.

'Correct,' Uncle Percy replied, flooring the accelerator pedal. 'And they can't swim like that... at least they shouldn't be able to.'

25

THE MYSTERY SOLVED

J oe unclipped his seatbelt and extended his Joe-Bow.

'What are you doing?' Becky yelled over the engine's roar.

'Pull the car next to it,' Joe said, pulling out a clip-arrow, which extended to the length of a typical arrow.

'Don't be silly,' Uncle Percy said. 'Put your seatbelt back on now!'

Joe didn't listen. Standing on the seat, balancing precariously, he took aim.

'GET DOWN, YOU MORON!' Becky screamed, grabbing hold of his coat.

'Stop it,' Joe said. Quickly, he aimed just below the Spinosaurus's sail and fired.

The arrow thumped into flesh, but it had no effect. The Spinosaurus powered toward them like a train.

'SIT DOWN BEFORE YOU FALL OUT OF THE CAR!' Uncle Percy shouted. 'YOUR ARROWS ARE JUST GOING TO IRRITATE IT!'

Reluctantly, Joe took the point. 'Fine,' he mumbled, dropping back into his seat.

Becky noticed something up ahead. 'THERE'S ANOTHER ONE!'

A second Spinosaurus's head had risen from the water.

With lightning reflexes, Uncle Percy forced the steering wheel right, barely missing the dinosaur's open jaws.

As they sped away, Becky heard an almighty roar and an explosion of water.

In a maelstrom of movement, the Spinosauri clashed in a ferocious battle, jaws snapping, tails whipping, horrific roars slashing the air.

'GET US ON THAT ISLAND!' Becky yelled.

Uncle Percy wasn't about to argue. Targeting the closest stretch of beach, he steered the Bentley toward it. Soon the water became shallow, and the Bentley's wheels connected with damp sand, which became firmer as they pulled onto the beach, before parking.

Becky's heart pounded like a drum as she looked back at the Spinosaurus battle, which raged on, until suddenly the sea turned red and all around fell still.

'I reckon we have a winner,' Joe said.

'What manner of beasts were they?' Tusk said. 'I have never beheld such things.'

'I wouldn't worry, Tusk,' Uncle Percy replied. 'No one has for – oh, I don't know - ninety million years or so.'

'Then what are they doing on earth in 1937?' Becky asked.

'Good question,' Uncle Percy replied. 'I can only assume the same thing as the Dracorex. I think we've entered a very unusual, inexplicable part of the world.'

'So, this place is like that island in *Jurassic Park*?' Joe said. 'What was it called – *Isla Nublar*?'

'I wouldn't know,' Uncle Percy said. 'I've not seen it.'

'You said they shouldn't swim like that,' Becky said. 'What did you mean by that?'

'I saw a Spinosaurus in the Cenomanian age in North

Africa,' Uncle Percy replied. 'I was on a trip with Ricardo Nero, a friend and fellow OTTER. Anyway, Ricardo was an amateur palaeontologist and was fascinated by that particular species. He told me about their feeding habits, their rituals, and their behaviour. Yes, they were aquatic predators, and they often hunted in water, but it was always freshwater, and they were slow and cumbersome swimmers. That first Spinosaurus was swimming as fast as a Mako Shark.'

As a baffled silence cloaked the car, something caught Joe's eye. 'What's that?' he said, pointing into the distance.

Uncle Percy looked up. Promptly, he turned the engine over and drove along the beach, pulling the car to a halt before a large metallic object that rose upward from the sand like a Cubist sculpture.

His face grave, Uncle Percy exited the car, trailed by the others.

In silence, everyone stood before an airplane wing decked with the characters *NR -16020*.

'I'm guessing that's a bit of Amelia Earhart's plane?' Joe said.

Before Uncle Percy could confirm, he was sprinting further up the beach to what looked like the remnants of a much larger wreckage.

Becky, Joe, and Tusk raced after him.

Within moments, Becky found herself at the twisted wreckage of a fuselage blackened from fire. All around, there were charred fragments of metal, wood, glass, fabric and scorched baggage. A chill scaled her spine. Did Amelia Earhart die here? Would they find her burnt, ravaged corpse some-where in the debris?

At that moment, Becky noticed Uncle Percy leave the wreckage site and walk to the edge of the bordering jungle, where he stood stationary at a particular spot, his head bowed as if in prayer. 'Joe. Tusk,' she yelled. 'Come over here.'

Joe and Tusk heard her, and together they walked over to Uncle Percy.

The moment she reached him, Becky understood why he'd adopted such a pose. A makeshift cross fashioned from two sticks secured with vine had been speared onto a raised mound, together with a leather flight jacket and a single black-and-white photograph of a slender, raven-haired woman in a wedding dress.

'It's Fred Noonan's grave,' Uncle Percy said. 'He must've been killed in the crash. He'd only been married for two months before his disappearance.' He turned his head toward the thick undergrowth and fell silent. 'It also means Amelia Earhart is still alive. At least she was yesterday.'

26

ON THE NOSE

B ecky didn't hesitate. 'Then we have to rescue her,' she
said.

'If the island hasn't got to her first,' Uncle Percy
replied.

'Let's stay positive,' Becky replied. 'How do we go about
finding her?'

'I'm not sure,' Uncle Percy said.

'What would you do if you crash landed on a desert island?'
Joe asked.

Uncle Percy contemplated this. 'I'd focus on the three key
things essential for survival: food, water, and shelter. I'd strip
the plane of anything useful. I'd fashion tools for hunting and
perhaps self-defence. I'd also generate rescue signals, perhaps
by gathering rocks to write a message on the sand.'

'That's a good start,' Becky said. 'And what would you do
first?'

'I'd find a water source,' Uncle Percy replied.

To everyone's surprise it was Tusk who spoke next. 'I shall
find this woman. I believe I've picked up her scent already.
Remain here!' Without another word, he sprang onto the

nearest tree, scuttled up its trunk, before leaping to another, and then another. Soon, he'd been lost to the undergrowth.

'I suppose having a man-squirrel on your team has its benefits,' Uncle Percy said.

'He's located her scent?' Joe said, scrunching up his nose. 'She must reek.'

'Don't be rude, Joe,' Uncle Percy replied. 'Squirrels have excellent senses of smell and vision, which means we're very lucky to have him with us.'

Becky, Joe and Uncle Percy only had to wait ten minutes before Tusk reappeared on an overhanging branch. He jumped off it and landed gracefully to face them.

'I have found her camp,' Tusk said.

'Is she there?' Becky asked.

'Nay,' Tusk said grimly. 'I fear she has been captured.'

'Captured?' Becky said, shocked. 'By who?'

'I know not,' Tusk replied. 'But by men... many men.'

Uncle Percy looked dumbfounded. 'You think there are men on this island?'

'I know it,' Tusk said. 'But you must witness the proof for yourself. Come with me.'

As they advanced through the forest, not one of them said a word.

With each step, Becky's mood darkened. As she stared out at the wall of greenery ahead, she realised nothing about the Blessed Isle made sense. Why couldn't the island be found using modern technology? What was the strange, inexplicable green mist that hid it from the rest of the world? How on earth could dinosaurs exist in the twentieth century?

And then there was the latest bombshell: what exactly were humans doing on the island and who were they?

Before long, Tusk led the group into a shaded glade with a shallow rainwater pool bordered by a stretch of scorched grass. A ring of layered dry stones had been constructed beside the water, at the centre of which was a firepit filled with ash and dust. Vestiges of the plane crash were scattered about – a first aid kit, a pen-knife, a box of matches, a woollen blanket, and a bottle. A shelter had been constructed from branches, sticks, and a canopy of huge ferns secured with vines.

Tusk walked over to the far side of the camp and gestured at a large area of muddy ground, impressed with countless sets of footprints. 'Upwards of six, perchance eight men were here, and though this woman fought valiantly, she was taken in that direction.' He pointed east.

'How do you know she fought valiantly?' Uncle Percy asked.

Saying nothing, Tusk approached a patch of scrub and pushed it aside to reveal a male corpse, the nearby leaves stained with blood. The corpse wore a felt hat, a silk undershirt, a quilted robe, and heavy leather boots. A spear, whittled from a tree branch, protruded from his chest.

Becky gasped with horror.

Joe surveyed the corpse. 'That's really weird clothing.'

'It's a soldier's outfit, Joe,' Uncle Percy said. 'He's a Mongolian warrior from the thirteenth century. I've seen them before first hand when I visited China in 1266AD.'

'You're telling me he's over seven hundred years old?' Joe said.

'I think so,' Uncle Percy said. He paused as something occurred to him. 'Do you remember I once said Kublai Khan, ruler of the Mongol Empire, lost many soldiers in the Dragon's Triangle during a failed invasion of Japan. I think this could be one of those soldiers.'

Becky looked stunned. 'And you think they ended up here, and drank water from the Pool of Life to stay alive?'

'Anything's conceivable on this island,' Uncle Percy replied. 'Literally... anything.'

'So... we're near Japan?' Joe asked.

'Not at all,' Uncle Percy said. 'We're over three thousand

miles away. That's another bizarre twist in this story. This island appears to be moving, which, of course, should be impossible.'

'Dinosaurs and seven-hundred-year-old humans existing together should be impossible,' Joe said. 'That doesn't mean it's not true.'

'Fair point,' Uncle Percy said.

'But what really matters isn't that the island's moved,' Becky said, 'but that alongside mutated dinosaurs, we might face a medieval army?'

Uncle Percy sighed. 'Who knows what we're facing?'

'Then can we go now, please?' Becky said. 'I'd rather face whatever we have to face without a dead bloke with a spear in his chest quite so close.'

'Fair point,' Uncle Percy said.

Becky remained at the group's rear as they pushed further into the island. Her mood didn't improve one bit. All around, the trees aged – they grew taller, their trunks thickened and their roots grew fatter, gripping the earth like tentacles. The wind picked up and thrashed the leaves above into a riotous frenzy, drowning out the sounds of any animals, birds, or insects that inhabited the area.

With each step, Becky felt her anxiety rise. Despite the breeze, she struggled to breathe and her lungs felt like paper straws. It was then she saw Tusk come to an abrupt halt, his head tilting upward as he sucked in air through his nostrils.

Joe noticed. 'What is it, Tusk?'

'I smell blood,' Tusk replied. 'But tis not the blood of man.'

Becky's spine froze. Suddenly, she heard movement from her left. Pulling free her cutlass, she glanced at Joe, whose face had turned to stone.

'Follow me,' Tusk said. Warily, he pushed through a thick canopy of leaves.

The group emerged into a scene of utter devastation in

every direction – churned earth, trees ripped from the ground, branches shattered and strewn all around.

It resembled a war zone.

As her gaze panned right, Becky's heart stopped.

A Tyrannosaurus Rex lay dead on the ground, its lifeless jaws dangling open, exposing wide, flat teeth with ridges quite unlike any Tyrannosaur she'd seen before in real life or in a museum.

However, the Tyrannosaur was not the most shocking thing about the scene.

A colossal dinosaur, the size of a school bus, stood beside the T. Rex, its small head angled down as if inspecting the corpse.

And Becky recognised the species of dinosaur immediately. With its arched back lined with enormous diamond-shaped plates, short front limbs, long hind limbs, and its four-spiked tail, the Stegosaurus had always been one of her favourite herbivorous dinosaurs.

But this wasn't a herbivore at all.

To her horror and disbelief, Becky watched the Stegosaurus's sharp, serrated teeth tear flesh from the Tyrannosaur's underbelly before swallowing it and returning to the open wound for more.

Neither Uncle Percy, Becky, Joe, nor Tusk moved a muscle.

Just then, the Stegosaurus registered their presence and ceased eating. It raised its small head and turned it toward the group. Instantly, its charcoal-black eyes locked on them like lasers. Then it gave a soft, low growl, which gradually swelled in volume in a crescendo of stomach-turning sound.

And then, slowly, it moved away from the T. Rex...

27

GRIEF IN THE UNDERGROWTH

The Stegosaurus took a single step forward, and then another. Blood dripped from its mouth, splashing the leaf-strewn earth. Tilting its head down, its eyes still locked on the group, it charged. Picking up speed like a train, its huge feet pounded the ground, making the air shudder like an earthquake.

Becky froze with fear.

At speed, Uncle Percy withdrew his Temporevolver and fired.

In a burst of blinding light, the pellet hit the Stegosaurus, but nothing happened.

Simultaneously, Joe pulled his Joe-bow from his backpack, squeezed its grip and extended it, before pulling out a clip-arrow. In a swift movement, he secured it to the bowstring and fired.

The arrow split the air.

The Stegosaurus barely decelerated as the arrow punctured its eyeball, piercing its brain, and killing it instantly. Crumbling to the ground, its massive form skidded to a halt barely inches from Joe's feet.

All went silent.

Tusk stared up at Joe with awe. 'You are truly Thor's heir, boy,' he breathed. 'With that lone shot, you have proved yourself Ullr's equal with the bow.'

'Er, ta,' Joe replied.

'T-thank you, Joe,' Uncle Percy said. 'You've just saved our lives. A temporevolver pellet was nowhere near powerful enough to work on a raging Stegosaurus.'

Her head spiralling, Becky glared at Uncle Percy. 'What is going on here... on this island?' she asked, desperate for an answer that made sense of everything. 'I mean, I've seen Stegosauruses before – they eat leaves and ferns and green things. They *do not* eat Tyrannosaurs.'

'No, they don't,' Uncle Percy replied. 'And neither can they run like that... they're slow, cumbersome creatures -' But then something had caught his eye, and he walked over to the dead T. Rex. Kneeling down, he studied its open mouth with an astonished expression on his face.

'What is it?' Joe asked.

'*This* Tyrannosaurus Rex is a herbivore,' Uncle Percy replied. He pointed into its open mouth. 'Look, the teeth are blunt and flat, like all herbivores. They evolved like that to strip, mash and grind tough vegetation.'

'Then I'll ask my question again,' Becky said. 'What is with this island? How can it be like this? I mean, everything's topsy-turvy and back to front.'

'I can't answer that, Becky,' Uncle Percy replied. 'All I know is the evolutionary development of these creatures is different to everything palaeontology has ever taught us about them, or anything I've seen in my many years of time travel. In fact, not only is it different, it's illogical, unscientific, even nonsensical. I can't explain why at the moment, but I'll try to find answers at some point in the future. For now, however, I just want to achieve our goals and leave this place as soon as humanly -'

Before he could finish his sentence, a soft whine resonated from the adjacent bushes.

Without hesitation, Joe withdrew another arrow.

The whine echoed again.

Gripping his sword tightly, Uncle Percy shifted the bush to reveal a small dinosaur staring back at them and shivering. With mottled reddish-brown skin, it stood five feet tall with small, crooked arms and muscular hind legs.

Becky knew straightaway it was the dead Tyrannosaurus's child.

Joe lowered his bow. 'Hello,' he said softly. 'Was that your mother? I'm sorry.' He stepped forward.

The young T. Rex flinched and stepped backward.

'I don't mean to scare you,' Joe said. 'You're safe now. Nothing can hurt you.'

Watching this, tears filled Becky's eyes.

'Is it male or female?' Joe asked Uncle Percy.

'I believe it's a male.'

'Then he's coming with us.'

Uncle Percy looked perplexed. 'Joe... he's a Tyrannosaurus Rex, and no more than twelve months old. He won't follow us like a puppy. It's not in his nature.'

But Joe didn't waver. 'Who knows what's in his nature growing up here?' he said. 'Besides, his mother is dead and he'll be dead, too, without our help. I'll carry him if I have to.' He smiled at the T. Rex. 'You're coming with us, mate. We can protect you.'

The T. Rex looked over at his mother and whined again. Tramping over to her, he nudged her lifeless body with his nose.

Joe followed him over. 'I'm sorry, but you have to come with us. You won't survive if you stay.'

The T. Rex sat down beside its mother and let out a heart-wrenching moan.

Joe's eyes dampened. 'Please... come with us.'

Slowly, Uncle Percy approached Joe. 'We have to go,' he said softly. 'But, listen to me, after all of this is over, I'll return here, to this island...' He gestured at the young T. Rex. 'And I'll get him.'

'You will?'

'I will. I promise.'

'He can come and live with us at Bowen Hall?'

'He can,' Uncle Percy said. He cast Joe a gentle smile. 'To be honest with you, I've always wanted a vegetarian Tyrannosaurus Rex.'

Joe returned a smile. 'You're the best.' His eyes found the young T. Rex. 'Now, you stay here... mourn all you have to. We'll come back as soon as we can and take you somewhere safe.'

Uncle Percy nodded at Tusk. 'Lead the way, sir,' he said.

Joe looked at the young T. Rex. 'I'll see you soon,' he said resolutely. 'I promise.'

Becky approached Joe, doing her best to conceal her own sorrow. 'That was a nice thing you did there,' she said. 'I'm proud of you.' She placed her hand tenderly on his shoulder. 'And the T. Rex will be safe until Uncle Percy gets him. He's never once let down an animal in need, not once. You know that.'

Joe nodded. 'I know.'

Becky stared at Joe's dejected face and opened her arms before drawing him into a tender hug. After some time, she said, 'Now, let's go... we've got a job to do.'

As they left the T. Rex to its grief, Becky slipped her hand into Joe's and gripped it tightly. She wanted to tell him how much she admired him, how his inherent kindness and decency moved her, how he was every bit Will Shakelock's equal in heart and body, mind and soul.

She wanted to tell him that, but she couldn't.

She knew that if she had, Joe would've branded her a soppy sausage and teased her about it until the end of time.

28

TAKEN

The further they advanced, the more the foliage blocked the sunlight until they could barely see their hands in front of their faces. After ten minutes, however, the jungle ended, and they surfaced into a wide, beautiful savannah of grass, sand and scrub that stretched on for miles in all directions.

Staring at the new vista, Becky's mind spun as she pondered the diverse mix of birds and animals that inhabited the landscape, creatures that simply shouldn't exist at the same time, many acting and interacting in unexpected ways. Overhead, a flock of Archaeopteryx soared in formation, weaving the air in twisting patterns; on her left, a group of mammoths grazed happily on bluestem grass, sharing the pasture with a herd of brontosauruses. And then beyond all this, an extinct volcano rose from the earth like a vast sandcastle.

'This is all quite astonishing,' Uncle Percy said simply. 'My gob is well and truly smacked.'

'It's flippin' bonkers is what it is,' Joe replied. 'And one day you can figure out why it's like this, but for now - which way do we go, Tusky?'

Tusk gestured at the volcano. 'The woman was taken that way.'

'Then let's get going,' Joe said. 'And hopefully those mammoths won't get bored of eating grass and make us their next yummy snack.'

As they set off, Becky knew Joe's joke masked a highly relevant point. They really did not know which creatures were dangerous and which were not.

The Blessed Isle was just as Uncle Percy said – '*illogical, unscientific... nonsensical.*'

They had walked unthreatened for a further ten minutes, a warm breeze brushing their faces, when Tusk stopped abruptly. Dropping to the ground, he pressed his long ears against the earth. 'Animals are coming,' he said. 'Large animals... much heavier than horses.'

From somewhere ahead, they heard a horn's blast.

Fear scaled Becky's spine. She saw Uncle Percy pull out a pair of amnoculars, a device more powerful than standard binoculars, and hold them to his eyes. As he looked out, he exhaled a single, panic-filled word, '*Crikey!*'

'What is it?' Joe said.

But Uncle Percy didn't hear the question. 'Unless I'm mistaken, Tusk, we'll be captured shortly,' he said, his delivery as rapid as machine gun fire. 'There's no point fighting, there's too many of them, and – well, they have support. I suggest you head back to the jungle, and come to our aid at some point in the future if and when you can.'

Without even questioning, Tusk turned about and scurried off.

Like a mirage forming before their eyes, tiny dots appeared on the horizon, increasing in number and growing bigger all the time as they advanced.

As the image came into focus, Becky saw ten soldiers on horseback charging toward them.

It was then she gasped with astonishment.

The soldiers weren't riding horses at all. Instead, they were sitting atop huge creatures with short legs, thick reddish-brown fur, and massive heads, their snouts crowned by long, curled horns.

'They're riding woolly rhinoceroses,' Joe said, amazed.

But the shocks didn't stop there: to the left of the riders were eight dracorexes, which ran alongside them obediently like a pack of trained hounds on a fox hunt.

'Becky, Joe. Turn on your transvocalisors,' Uncle Percy said.

At that point, the dracorexes broke away from the riders and zipped toward Uncle Percy, Joe and Becky, forming a wide circle, ensuring they could not escape.

Becky watched the manoeuvre with horror and disbelief.

Slowly, the dracorexes parted and one particular soldier led the others inside the circle.

The soldier brought his rhino to a halt, and dismounted, trailed by two other soldiers, who marched behind him as he walked over.

As the soldier approached, Becky gulped at his sheer size.

At approaching seven feet tall with a muscular build, the soldier resembled a tank. He had a flowing mane of dark hair, a thin oil-black beard peppered with flecks of grey, a flat nose, and protruding cheekbones. His outfit was identical to the one they'd seen on the corpse earlier, except for a scarlet sash which he wore around his neck. 'You are with the American female?' he said, his voice deep and booming.

'We are, yes,' Uncle Percy replied. 'Where is she? Is she alive?'

'She is safe,' the soldier replied. Suddenly, his gaze locked on Becky. 'I see you have another woman with you.'

'We have a *girl* with us,' Uncle Percy said, a threat in his voice which the soldier failed to detect.

'Countless years have passed since I viewed a woman,' the

soldier said, staring at Becky with an ugly expression on his face. 'And now I have seen two in as many sunsets.' He walked up to Becky. 'My name is Jingim. I am First General of the King's Watch. I am an important man in the city of Tian... second only to his majesty, the King.'

'Er, good for you,' Becky replied. 'Can you take us to the American woman, please?'

The soldier ignored the question. 'Your appearance pleases me.' And without asking, he went to stroke Becky's face.

Before Becky had the chance to slap the hand away, someone else did it for her.

'You don't just touch someone else, mate!' Joe fired, his hands balling into fists. 'Have you never heard of consent?'

Jingim turned on Joe, his eyes wild. 'You dare strike me, boy?'

Even though Jingim was much taller and broader, Joe didn't flinch.

'If you touch my sister... yeah,' Joe replied. 'I wouldn't think twice about it.'

'Leave it, Joe,' Becky said, fearing escalation.

'We don't want trouble, Jingim,' Uncle Percy said quickly. 'We're just searching for our friend.'

'But trouble has found you,' Jingim growled. He nodded at the two guards. 'Beat the boy like a dog.'

Promptly, the soldiers moved to Joe's rear and seized his arms.

But Joe was too fast. Slipping from their grip, he whirled round and punched the first guard squarely in the face, sending him to the ground.

Before the second guard could react, Joe had pitched a powerful uppercut to his chin, and he, too, collapsed. Within seconds, both guards were out cold.

Barely able to process this, Jingim's face blazed with fury. He clapped his hands loudly and gave a piercing whistle.

Promptly, four dracorexes sprinted over to Joe, their razor-sharp teeth bared. They surrounded him, growling fiercely.

Uncle Percy raised his arms in a gesture of submission. 'No, please, Jingim. We surrender.'

An ugly smile rounded Jingim's mouth. 'That is wise, silver hair.' He glared at Joe. 'Your warrior spirit is admirable, boy. It may serve you well in *The Stadium of Assian*. You may even perform well enough to taste the sacred water and survive... but I doubt it.'

Becky glanced at Uncle Percy, who looked suddenly concerned.

'You now belong to the King of Tian, and he will decide what is to be done with you,' Jingim said. 'TAKE THEIR WEAPONS!'

Within seconds, soldiers set upon Becky, Joe and Uncle Percy, taking their swords, daggers, backpacks, even Uncle Percy's temporevolver, and hurling them to the ground.

Satisfied they were disarmed, Jingim mounted his woolly rhino and sucked in a deep breath. 'TO TIAN!' he bellowed.

The group set off in the volcano's direction.

Surrounded by dracorex, Becky knew there was no chance of escape, but then neither did she want that. They still had a job to do, and there was no way she'd leave until it was done.

In no time at all, the volcano rose before them, rugged and ridged against a bright blue sky, its low slopes forming a crater that stretched as far as the eyes could see. Ahead, an arched tunnel had been cut into the solid rock, offering a glimpse of the light beyond.

Entering the tunnel, the bizarre assembly of humans, dracorexes and woolly rhinoceroses were swallowed by blackness.

When they emerged into daylight, Becky gasped. The vast crater, over a mile in length, housed a fortified city on the right-hand side, and an enormous body of water on the other, quite unlike any she had seen before.

The water had the appearance of liquid gold, and its rippling surface shimmered as though it were a living, breathing entity. Instantly, an inner calm filled her, and she felt like a newborn gazing at the world with fresh eyes.

In that moment, she knew it was a spiritual, otherworldly, even holy place, and for the briefest of moments felt a deep familiarity as though she'd been here before.

'I reckon that might be the Pool of Life, don't you?' Joe said sarcastically.

'D'ya think?' Becky replied.

'It's like summat from a dream,' Joe said.

'I only wish I had dreams as beautiful as that,' Becky replied.

As Jingim steered the group to the right, Becky stared at the city walls and felt a sense of Déjà vu. With its tall posts, whittled to a point, and its imposing gate, it reminded her of Caradan, the minotaur town. Glancing at Uncle Percy, she saw his expression had changed to one she couldn't quite read.

As Becky's gaze returned to the fortified wall, something alarmed her. The posts weren't made from wood at all, but from colossal bones that once belonged presumably to local sauropods.

'Behold the city of *Tian*,' Jingim announced. 'The eternal city – its immortal presence fed by the enchanted water of *Lake Xi Shi*. It may be your home, too, if you survive the challenge.'

'What challenge?' Uncle Percy asked quickly.

'In time, you shall see,' Jingim replied mysteriously.

As the group approached, the huge gates opened.

Entering the city, Becky once again saw parallels with the town of Caradan in terms of its design and architecture, although most of the buildings, both residential and civic, were much smaller in height and width, suited more for humans than minotaurs. There were, however, two structures that stood out from the others. The first was a giant stone building, much larger and grander than the rest, which she assumed was the King's Palace. The second was a gigantic amphitheatre made of wood and sandstone, and set upon a hill at the far edge of the city.

Jingim guided his rhino to the front of the King's palace before climbing down and approaching Uncle Percy, Becky, and Joe. 'The King shall see you now... follow me!' he said, before turning toward the front door, which was opened by two armed guards.

As Becky, Joe, and Uncle Percy followed him inside, they found themselves in a large entrance hall filled with various statues, ceramics, oil paintings, tapestries, furniture, and wall hangings.

Jingim approached a door at the far end of the hall. 'Wait here.' He disappeared through it.

His gaze scanning the hall, Uncle Percy looked astonished. 'This is all remarkable,' he said. 'This room is a treasure trove of history. It contains artifacts created thousands of years apart, and from countless civilisations, including Japan, Greece, Italy, Egypt, France, Persia, China, even Britain.'

'Er, who cares?' Joe said. 'We're prisoners again, and other than Becky's freaky brain we ain't got any weapons - we could be in trouble here.'

'We're not in trouble,' Uncle Percy said. 'I'm on top of it.'

'Yeah, right,' Joe said sarcastically. 'What was that Jingim said about us surviving a challenge?'

'I don't know,' Uncle Percy said. 'He didn't exactly elaborate.'

Before the discussion could continue, Jingim appeared. 'You will now enter the throne room, where you shall await the King's presence.' He ushered them inside.

Entering, Becky saw six guards line the walls, their faces

impassive and stern. Her unease grew as she considered what the next ten minutes had in store. Would this be a sympathetic or a malevolent king? What was the challenge Jingim had mentioned? Staring ahead, she was fleetingly blinded by the dazzling sunlight that streamed in, colouring the marble floor with a golden tinge. As her eyes adjusted, however, she saw something astonishing – a giant throne, much too big for any one person, had been shaped from various dinosaur skulls.

Jingim approached the throne and stood beside it. 'PRIS-ONERS... BOW YOUR HEAD IN REVERENCE OF THE KING!'

Becky, Joe and Uncle Percy complied.

Her gaze fixed on the floor, Becky heard a series of slow, thunderous footsteps that shook the ground, together with deep, protracted breaths that arose from powerful lungs.

As the seconds crawled by, a sense of dread filled her as she contemplated a single question: What creature was heavy enough to make such loud footsteps?

'YOU MAY NOW BEHOLD THE KING,' Jingim shouted.

Looking up, Becky felt sucker-punched. Suddenly, every-thing made sense.

A giant minotaur was sitting on the throne. Instantly, she recalled the events at the Hall of Knowledge in Caradan – the stories told by Erikka and the Keepers of the Sacred Word, and more significantly the tale of Herathon, the minotaurean sailor, who had been the first to land on the Blessed Isle.

Becky knew she was staring at *Kallibane*, the traitorous minotaur who had tried to murder Herathon and been marooned here. Somehow, he had survived and prospered, building a city that emulated the minotaurean town in which he once lived.

And thanks to the water from The Pool of Life, he'd survived here for over five thousand years.

29

THE KING'S SPEECH

'I am King Kallibane,' the minotaur said in a gravelly tone, his every word delivered with a lazy swagger. 'But the question that intrigues me is... who are you?'

Containing his surprise, Uncle Percy bowed. 'I am Percy Halifax, King Kallibane. This is my nephew and niece, Becky and Joe Mellor. We are travellers from Britain, and are honoured to be in your presence.'

Kallibane ignored the compliment. 'Britain? I have heard of this place. Many ships from your country have landed on these shores in the last five hundred years. None of your people remain alive to this day.'

'I see,' Uncle Percy said.

'Tell me,' Kallibane said. 'What brings you to my city?'

'We're looking for our friend, an American woman – Amelia Earhart,' Uncle Percy replied. 'We believe she's here with you.'

'She is my guest here, yes.'

'We've come to take her home.'

Kallibane exhaled a long, slow breath. 'And what if she does not wish to leave?' he said. 'What if she considers Tian her home now?'

Uncle Percy looked surprised by the question. 'Then if she tells us that in person, we'll leave happy in the knowledge it's what she wants.'

Kallibane's black eyes narrowed as they locked onto Uncle Percy. 'You intrigue me, human.'

Uncle Percy looked unsure of how to reply. 'I do? Why?'

'Does my appearance not strike fear into you?' Kallibane said.

'No, your majesty,' Uncle Percy replied. 'It does not.'

'Then you are the first of your kind to feel that way,' Kallibane replied. He gestured at Becky and Joe. 'And judging from the expressions of your young ones, I do not scare them, either. What do you believe that tells me?'

'It tells you we've met minotaurs before,' Uncle Percy replied.

'It does,' Kallibane replied. 'And have you?'

'We have, your majesty.'

'And I can only conclude these encounters have been fair and agreeable.'

'Very much so,' Uncle Percy replied. 'One of our best friends is a minotaur.'

Kallibane hesitated. 'Over the last five millennia, countless humans have stood before me – humans from all realms of the earth, representing many civilisations and cultures. Not one of them has mentioned my species before, other than in the dominion of fantasy, legend, and myth.'

'We've been fortunate enough to meet many minotaurs and minotauras,' Uncle Percy replied. 'They're amongst the most noble and virtuous beings on the planet.'

Kallibane spent some time dwelling on this answer. 'And do you believe me noble... virtuous?'

Becky detected a barbed edge to Kallibane's voice that made her feel anxious.

'I'm certain you are, your majesty,' Uncle Percy said.

'Consider my word a fact, Percy Halifax - *I am not*,' Kallibane replied, his tone both chilling and absolute. 'I am far from noble or virtuous. Now, tell me - where did you first happen upon my kind?'

'We first met a minotaur on the island of Crete,' Uncle Percy said, 'and then more recently we visited the minotaur town of Caradan.'

Shock flashed in Kallibane's eyes. 'I have not heard that name for an age,' he said, his nostrils flaring. 'You have entered Caradan?'

'We have.'

'And did the drums of Caradan sound for you?'

'They did, your majesty. We were very honoured.'

Kallibane exhaled slowly. 'Caradan must prize you for them to bestow such a tribute.'

'As I said, I have a great respect and liking for your kind,' Uncle Percy replied.

If Uncle Percy thought the compliment would please Kallibane he was wrong.

He was very wrong.

Kallibane's eyes darkened. 'Your generous words about my brethren are misguided,' he growled. 'Foolish, even.' He stood up to his full height, unveiling a physique more muscular and daunting than any minotaur they'd seen before. 'The truth, human, is that I loathe my species. I would wipe every one of them from this earth if I could - minotaurs, minotauras, calfans.' He paced slowly. 'To my eternal pride, I am an ancestor of the minotaur, Kraven - the one they claimed stole The Spear of Fate, the one they blamed for sending Atlantis to the ocean's depths. Unlike you, my bloodline meant the community of Caradan never treated me or my kin fairly. They never gave us honour or respect. Because of this, when I was a calfan, my father found the tallest tree in the jungle and hanged himself from the highest branch.'

Uncle Percy knew instantly he'd made a mistake. 'I'm very sorry.'

'Your words are meaningless to me,' Kallibane replied. 'I grew up an outcast in Caradan, a pariah, and was considered a worthless stain. When I was of age, I was desperate to leave the town and the island. I wanted to find a new home in the wider world. I joined the crew of Herathon, their revered seafarer, but I found no more respect from him than I did from the community, perhaps less. One day, after landing on these shores and loading the ship with its enchanted water, I mutinied, to kill him, so I could seize his ship and find a new home, away from minotaurean rule, but he bested me. As a punishment, he forsook me to this island to be food for the creatures that lived here. He should've slain me for my crime. I begged it to be that way, but he wouldn't even offer me that swift mercy. No, he left me here alone, and with nothing but the breath in my lungs. And it is here, on this island, that I found the sanctuary I sought, a new home, and it is here I truly learned to live.'

'I understand,' Uncle Percy said.

'Do you, human?' Kallibane replied. 'Can you imagine being left here with no food, no companionship, in a land where hungry dragons roam, soar and swim in such numbers that you can never feel secure, even in slumber?'

'I can't, no,' Uncle Percy replied.

'No... you cannot,' Kallibane replied. 'I could've allowed the island to destroy me, but I refused to take that path. I was determined to survive... and survive I did. Each day something tried to kill me, and each day I defeated it, until all the creatures on the island feared me and gave me their allegiance. Fed by the water, I grew stronger, mightier... I became more powerful than Herathon, mightier than Thoth, more formidable than any minotaur before me. I became one with the island, and it became one with me. Over time, humans landed on my beaches, bringing their weapons, their knowledge, their greed. Every time, I fought them, conquered them, and they became my subjects. I built a city – this glorious city of Tian – and I allowed some who were worthy to stay, but there was always a problem.'

'And that problem was?'

'The island has limited resources,' Kallibane said. 'Therefore, I ruled only one thousand could inhabit my city at any one time. I decreed any human who wished to live here, to enjoy an eternal life fuelled by the water from my golden lake, had to prove their worth, and if they could not... they *perished*. For this purpose, I built an arena – *The Stadium of Assian* – where contestants fight to ensure only the strongest remain to protect my city.'

'And by fight, you mean to the death?'

'Is there a fairer way to control the population?' Kallibane replied. 'Surely, only through inflicting death can you appreciate the blessings of an everlasting life?'

The words sent a chill through Becky.

'I see,' Uncle Percy said.

'Do you, human?' Kallibane stared in turn at Becky, Joe, and Uncle Percy. 'Because it seems your arrival is timely. You have arrived on a special day – a historic day – for tonight the Stadium of Assian will be opened, and the people will gather for a grand celebration. And as part of this celebration, I intend for there to be games.' His eyes found Joe. 'Jingim tells me you are a fierce warrior... perhaps you would like compete in the arena? Surely, immortality is the greatest reward a mortal can receive?'

'No, he wouldn't,' Uncle Percy said before Joe could even respond.

And for the first time, Kallibane raised his voice slightly. 'I asked the boy!'

'No thanks,' Joe replied. 'I'm not interested.'

'That saddens me.' Kallibane turned to Uncle Percy. 'Then, Percy Halifax, friend of minotaurs, adopted citizen of Caradan. Would you care to test yourself in the Stadium?'

'Thank you, but no,' Uncle Percy replied. 'We're not here for rewards. We do not wish to stay and use your resources. We do not wish for immortality. All we want to do is talk to Amelia Earhart, and then leave peacefully with her, if that's what she wishes.'

Kallibane fell silent. 'But I cannot allow that,' he said, his voice darkening with each syllable. 'I said this was a historic day, a day of celebration, and it is.' He sucked in a deep breath. 'Tonight, for the first time in my long life, I intend to marry, and I shall give Amelia Earhart the honour of becoming my wife!'

30

THE OMEGA MAN

Becky wasn't sure at first that she'd heard correctly. *King Kallibane was going to marry Amelia Earhart?* The thought was preposterous, repellent, absurd. She could also tell from Kallibane's tone that Amelia had no say in it whatsoever.

Uncle Percy concealed his disgust. 'And has she agreed to this?'

'It is a great privilege for her,' Kallibane replied. 'Just as you should think yourself fortunate when you enter the arena this night.'

Uncle Percy's face dropped. 'But –'

'–Did you truly believe you had a choice?' Kallibane replied in a mocking tone. 'Unlike Caradan, the drums of Tian never sounded for you. You are trespassers here, and you have come to steal from me, to rip my intended bride from her new home.'

But Joe had heard enough. 'You're nuts!'

'Joe... be quiet,' Uncle Percy said.

'What for?' Joe replied. 'He's already decided we're fighting in his stupid stadium.' He glared at Kallibane. 'Seriously, you weirdo... you plan on getting married to a human? You're seventeen feet tall with a bull's head? I've got a feelin' she might not fancy you, mate.'

Kallibane looked astonished, as though no one had ever spoken to him like this before. 'SEAL THIS BOY'S MOUTH!'

'Enough, Joe!' Uncle Percy said.

'JINGIM,' Kallibane roared. 'TAKE THE CAPTIVES TO THE CELLS AND PREPARE THEM FOR THE ARENA!'

With an ugly sneer, Jingim seized Uncle Percy's arm and shoved him forcefully toward the door, as Becky and Joe were trailed out by four guards.

Once outside, Becky turned to Uncle Percy. 'I hope you've got some brilliant Uncle Percy-esque like plan to get us out of this mess, because if you don't, then we're in serious trouble.'

Uncle Percy didn't hear her. Trying to hide his movements from the guards, he was rooting in his jacket pocket, searching for something. A second later, a confused look appeared on his face.

'What are you doing?' Becky asked. 'What's going on?'

'I'll tell you in a bit,' Uncle Percy whispered.

'Tell me what?' Becky replied.

'Don't worry about it,' Uncle Percy said, his mind clearly on something else.

'But I am worried, and I'm getting more worried by the second,' Becky said. 'Do you or do you not have a brilliant plan to get us out of this mess?'

'I thought I did,' Uncle Percy replied. 'I'm not sure now.'

'Then I'm even more worried than I was a minute ago.'

'What you frettin' over, Becks?' Joe said. 'Old Tusky is out there somewhere. He'll sort summat out.'

'He'd better do it soon, then,' Becky replied. 'Because we're heading into *The Hunger Games* in a few hours.'

'That squirrel ain't let us down yet,' Joe said.

'It only takes one time,' Becky muttered.

Before long, the Stadium of Assian filled the skyline, daunting and impressive.

Jingim led them to a rectangular sandstone building. 'Follow me,' he ordered, before disappearing inside.

Entering the jail, Becky gave a deep sigh. She'd been in far too many places like this than was healthy for a teenage girl. Scanning the dark, dank space, she saw countless cells fronted by rusted iron grilles, all of which appeared empty. She presumed it had been some time since other humans had landed on the island.

Jingim approached a short, broad Japanese man with a waist length ponytail and crudely inked tattoos adorning his chest and neck. 'Gaoler,' he said. 'These three need your hospitality until their appearance in the arena later.'

With a sharp nod, the gaoler stared frostily at Becky, Joe, and Uncle Percy before lumbering off, a heavy set of iron keys jangling from his waistband. With Jingim and the guards to their rear, they were led to the furthest cell.

The gaoler thrust a key into its lock, turned it, and flung open the door. 'In!' he snarled. After everyone had entered, he slammed the door shut and locked it again.

Immediately, Becky surveyed the large cell, noticing a clay bowl of untouched soup, an amphora jug filled with water, and several low beds constructed from wooden planks and compressed hay. As her gaze drifted to the corner, she spied a lone female sitting there, her head tucked between her legs, and shivering despite the oppressive heat.

Uncle Percy noticed her, too. 'Amelia,' he said softly. 'Amelia Earhart?'

It took a few seconds before Amelia responded. 'H-hello?' she replied, her voice small and brittle.

Becky's heart broke. She'd seen numerous photographs of Amelia Earhart in books, magazines and online articles, and she'd always appeared stoic, self-confident and poised. This woman, however, looked a shadow of her former self.

Wearing a collarless suede flight jacket, torn at the seams, a mud-stained cotton shirt and wide pants, Amelia Earhart's face was a mask of cuts and bruises, and her wheat blonde hair was caked in blood and dirt.

'Hello, Amelia,' Uncle Percy said with a kindly smile. 'It's a true honour to meet you.'

'W-who is that?'

'I'm Percy Halifax,' Uncle Percy said. 'This is Becky and Joe Mellor.'

'How do you know who I am?' Amelia said. Suddenly, her voice teemed with hope. 'Are you with the U.S. Navy?'

'Not exactly, but I'm a friend,' Uncle Percy replied. 'And we intend to get you out of this situation.'

Hope flickered in Amelia's eyes. 'You do?'

'That is our intention,' Uncle Percy replied.

'How?'

'I don't know yet,' Uncle Percy replied. 'But we've been in much tougher spots than this and always survived, and with a smashing story to tell - haven't we, kids?'

'Yeah,' Joe said. 'Always.'

'Not sure about smashing, but everything he's said is true,' Becky added.

'Tougher spots than this?' Amelia said with disbelief. 'We're on an island swarmin' with actual dinosaurs, in a city ruled by a minotaur king that claims to be immortal, and who insists is gonna marry me tonight.' She gave a sour chuckle. 'How does a spot get tougher than this, Mister Halifax?'

'Trust me,' Uncle Percy said. 'This is par for the course for us three.'

Amelia Earhart thought on this for a second. 'Who exactly are you, sir? And how do you know who I am?'

'Okay,' Uncle Percy said. 'Although this might sound farfetched, crazy even, I'm going to be honest with you.'

'Nothing you say could approach the craziness I've seen in the last twenty-four hours.'

'I bet,' Uncle Percy replied. 'Then the truth is, we're time travellers, and we're from the twenty-first century.'

Even after all she'd just said, Amelia still looked stunned. 'Please, sir, don't play tricks on me.'

'I'm really not,' Uncle Percy replied. 'We are time travellers, and that's also how we know precisely who you are.'

'You travel in time... like the time traveller in H.G. Wells' novel, *The Time Machine*?'

'Exactly like that,' Uncle Percy replied. 'H.G. Wells' fictional concept was realised.'

Amelia fell silent. 'And is this common in the twenty-first century?'

'Not at all,' Uncle Percy said. 'I am a member of a secret organisation with a few hundred well vetted members. It's important for world security that we maintain our anonymity.'

Again, Amelia paused. 'I see,' she replied. 'Normally, I would accuse you of being a liar, a drunk or a fantasist, but as I said before, after all I've witnessed recently, I'm more than prepared to believe you, Mister Halifax.'

'You should,' Uncle Percy said. 'It's all true.'

'You never explained how you knew who I was?'

'That is a long story,' Uncle Percy replied. 'But the reality is your disappearance always mystified the world - no one was sure what happened. Obviously, your plane was never found and there were plenty of other unusual factors in play that meant that conspiracy theorists had a field day with your story. However, the key point is you, as a woman and an aviator, became one of the most famous and iconic figures of the twentieth century.'

'I did?' Amelia replied.

'Absolutely,' Uncle Percy replied. 'And I think it's fair to say you become a role model to young girls and women across the world at what can be achieved if you put your mind to it. Isn't that correct, Becky?'

'Yes, it is, Ms. Earhart,' Becky said.

'Please, child, call me Amelia.'

'Okay, Amelia... but Uncle Percy's right.'

'Holy moly,' Amelia said, a flicker of pride in her voice. Her face changed as something occurred to her. 'Then it is a shame that I'll die here then.'

'No, you won't,' Uncle Percy said, surprised. 'Why on earth would you say that?'

'Well, sir, if you rescued me, if I was to survive,' Amelia said, 'then the world would not have had the eighty-plus years of doubt as to my whereabouts. Therefore, it seems that you won't rescue me, and that I must die on this rock, because I have no intention of living as the wife of a monster.'

'I can understand your reasoning, but that's not necessarily true,' Uncle Percy said. 'Just because you don't return to public life doesn't mean you don't return to the world at large. Becky, Joe and myself have saved the lives of various people in one timeline, only to place them successfully, perhaps with new identities, in another. We could do this for you.'

'This sure is confusing, Mister Halifax.'

'I understand that,' Uncle Percy said. 'But I promise you - we have every intention of rescuing you and getting all of us safely off this island.'

Finally, Amelia found a hopeful smile. 'Then I shall put my faith in your word, sir.'

'You should. And –'

Footsteps approaching the cell cut short Uncle Percy's words.

A moment later, Jingim, the gaoler, and two armed guards appeared at the bars.

'American woman,' Jingim said. 'Come with me.'

Fear creased Amelia's face. 'What? Why?'

'You must prepare for your wedding!'

'No,' Amelia replied. 'I'm not going anywhere.'

'COME HERE!' Jingim roared.

'NO,' Amelia shouted back.

The gaoler opened the door, and Jingim stepped inside. To Becky's horror, he was holding a braided leather bullwhip.

'Do not make me use this,' Jingim said, raising the whip into the light. 'I shall do what I must to get your cooperation.'

Horrified, Amelia looked at Uncle Percy. 'Mister Halifax?'

'Amelia,' Uncle Percy said calmly. 'Don't cause a fuss. We don't want them to hurt you. Just go with Jingim and remember all we've discussed.'

'Yes, sir.' Amelia paused, before saying quietly, 'My life is in your hands, Mister Halifax.' Slowly, she followed Jingim out of the cell, which was instantly locked.

'And that's a safe place for it to be,' Uncle Percy replied just loud enough for Amelia to hear it as she was escorted away.

The moment they were out of earshot, Becky turned to Uncle Percy and said, 'You seem confident you won't let her down – is there any reason for that?'

'I am confident,' Uncle Percy said. 'Joe's right – Tusk is out there somewhere. Plus, I didn't lie, we do have a knack of surviving these things with all our limbs intact.'

'Only just, though,' Becky mumbled.

'Why don't we just break out now?' Joe said. 'Becky can use her freakydeaky powers on the lock, and we'll be out of here in no time.'

'And what will happen to Amelia, then?' Uncle Percy said. 'No... for the moment, we'll just stay put. As I said earlier, I am on top of all of this, so don't worry. Furthermore, there's something strange going on that we need to consider.'

'What do you mean *strange*?' Becky asked.

Uncle Percy reached into his pocket and pulled out a small gadget that resembled a calculator. 'Jingim and his cronies may have taken our weapons, but they didn't take this.'

Becky recognised the device at once as a *pagidizor* – a paging device for time travellers that sends a distress flare through time to request aid from GITT's Tracker division. 'You've got a pagidizor?'

'I have.'

Hope gleamed in Becky's eyes. 'Then use it,' she said. 'Contact the Trackers... they can come and rescue us.'

'It's not synchronised to any Tracker unit,' Uncle Percy replied.

'Then who is it synchronised with?'

'That's not important,' Uncle Percy replied. 'And neither is it the issue... this is.' He pressed a button on the pagidizor. Promptly, his thumb vanished from sight. Quickly, he moved it away, and it took a solid form again.

Becky's eyes widened. She recognised the occurrence at once – it had happened to her before when she witnessed her own death as a child. 'The Omega Effect happens when you trigger it?'

'It does,' Uncle Percy replied. 'I first tried pressing it after we left the palace - I thought we could do with a well-timed rescue - but the same thing happened. Bottom line is that the Omega Effect prevents it from working as it should.'

'What does that mean?' Joe asked.

'I don't know yet,' Uncle Percy said. 'But as you're aware, the Omega Effect occurs when a time traveller tries to change events that, for want of a better word, *fate* insists cannot be changed. Subsequently, as the Omega Effect has occurred whatever happens here in the immediate future needs to unravel as it will. Fate decrees it, and there's nothing we can do about that.'

'Great,' Becky replied sarcastically.

'Even if it means we're meant to die in that stadium, eaten by a carnivorous diplodocus?' Joe said.

Uncle Percy sighed. 'Don't be so pessimistic, Joe.'

'I'm not,' Joe said. 'But it is true though, isn't it? Fate could insist *we* die here, that our deaths must happen in that stadium, and that's why the Omega Effect won't allow your rescue.'

Uncle Percy looked awkward. 'In theory... it's not untrue.'

31

ARENA

This admission didn't make Becky feel any better at all. Still, she knew it was futile worrying about it. There were so many variables in play, any speculation was pointless.

As the minutes bled into hours, Becky felt ever more claustrophobic, and her anxiety grew. Still, no matter how bad she felt, she knew Amelia Earhart must've felt so much worse. After all, since yesterday she'd been involved in a plane crash, lost her close friend, discovered an island filled with mutant dinosaurs, and was being forced to marry a monster.

It didn't get more insane than that.

Before Becky knew it, the last warm breath of day had yielded to a cool, moonlit evening.

It was then that Jingim appeared at the cell door. 'The stadium is being prepared,' he said, 'and when you hear the drums sound, you will be escorted there, presented with weapons, and you will have the chance to earn your survival.' His eyes found Becky. 'Girl... I have used my sway with the king, and he has agreed you do not need to fight this night if you agree to my offer.'

'What offer?' Becky asked.

'You shall become my willing bride.'

Barely able to comprehend what had been said, Becky stared at Jingim as if he'd grown a second head. 'Are you bonkers?'

Joe was even less polite. 'You *bloody* freak!' he said. 'Jog on, you weirdo!'

Jingim's gaze didn't leave Becky. 'I am giving you your one and only chance to live!'

Uncle Percy glared at Jingim. 'What is the matter with you? BE ON YOUR WAY!'

Jingim ignored Uncle Percy. 'Wed me or die, girl.'

Becky maintained her composure. 'I'd rather be torn apart, limb from limb, by a thousand starving dinosaurs than marry you.'

Jingim looked dumbfounded, as if it was the last thing he expected to hear.

'YOU HAVE YOUR ANSWER!' Uncle Percy bellowed. 'LEAVE!'

Joe scooped up the bowl of Amelia's untouched soup. 'Oh, and before you go...' he said. 'Here... *marry this!*' He threw the bowl's contents through the bars, drenching Jingim from head to toe in thick, brown soup.

For a moment, Jingim's face conveyed bewilderment, but fury instantly replaced this. His hand shot for his sword, but as he pulled it from its scabbard, he stopped himself. 'I SHOULD ENTER YOUR CELL AND SLAY YOU ALL WHERE YOU STAND!' He wiped the soup from his face. 'But why deny the crowd their amusement?' He filled his lungs with air. 'I had no plans for combat tonight, but that has now changed. The three of you shall now face me in the arena, and I have been the victor in upwards of forty death matches. Trust me, you shall all be dead within the hour.' With that, he stomped out.

'What a scumbag,' Joe said.

'Definitely,' Uncle Percy said. 'And don't worry, no one will die tonight.'

Becky only wished she shared Uncle Percy's confidence.

IT WAS ONLY a matter of minutes before they heard more footsteps. Six guards and two dracorexes appeared alongside the gaoler who chuckled in an ugly manner.

'Oooh, you've sealed your fate,' the gaoler hissed, unlocking the cell door. 'Jingim is enraged, and even brings *Terrakus* to the arena this night.'

'Who or what is Terrakus?' Uncle Percy asked.

'*Terrakus is death!*' the gaoler replied simply.

'Why do people like you always say overly dramatic things?' Uncle Percy said.

The gaoler opened the door, and together Becky, Joe, and Uncle Percy exited the cell.

Becky's heart sank as they were shepherded to a large wooden door. Glancing at Uncle Percy, she saw he held the pagidizor in his right hand, which briefly became invisible when he tried to trigger it.

The Omega Effect was still in force.

The gaoler approached the door and heaved it open to reveal a slope that led to a tunnel lit by torches, their flames barely dancing in the airless space.

As the group advanced toward the tunnel's end, they heard a crescendo of sound - the clamour of a baying crowd eager to be entertained.

'Do you still think you're on top of everything?' Becky asked Uncle Percy.

'Certainly,' Uncle Percy replied, forcing a half-smile. 'I'm sure the Omega Effect will lift any second, allowing us to be rescued in a timely fashion.'

Becky glanced at Joe, but could tell from his expression he wasn't expecting a rescue. *He was readying himself for a fight.*

As the group emerged from the tunnel, a deafening sound of a large crowd met their ears. From all sides, cheers and jeers, shouts and taunts rained down on them like mortar fire.

Her head spiralling, Becky scanned the packed amphitheatre. All around, people were crammed onto stone benches that overlooked a vast circular, sandy arena. Giant blazing torches that sent threads of smoke twirling to the heavens illuminated all of it. On the south side of the arena was a giant wooden door secured by six armed guards and four dracorex.

Directly opposite, Becky saw a raised platform with a throne in its centre, sitting upon which was King Kallibane and beside him, Amelia Earhart, who wore a flowing white dress and a crown of powder blue flowers; her hands were bound by thick rope, and there were fresh bruises on her face.

Becky felt her blood boil.

Just then, a man approached the arena's centre and raised his arms high. Dressed in a long blue robe, a golden breastplate decked with precious stones, and a headdress made from silver feathers, he waited for the crowd to fall silent. 'CITIZENS OF TIAN!' the man yelled. 'As your high priest, I welcome you on this historic day – the wedding of our revered ruler, King Kallibane! Soon, I shall perform the wedding ceremony for our king and his joyful bride, but before that the Stadium of Assian will host a contest of combat.' He drew a breath. 'Look around you, absorb the games that have been fought here over the ages, and appreciate all this space provides us: The Stadium of Assian is where we solve our differences, where we ensure our city survives, for with the death the arena brings, so too does it bring life – life for those of us that remain, an eternal life granted us by our goodly king and the water of Lake Xi Shi.' He raised his arms. 'So I ask you, citizens of Tian... RAISE YOUR

VOICES HIGH AND SALUTE THE STADIUM AND THE KING!'

The crowd cheered loudly.

The High Priest pointed at Becky, Joe and Uncle Percy. 'Today, we have three new souls wishing to face the challenge - visitors that have insulted our First General of the King's Watch, the mighty Jingim, who has now chosen himself to lead them to their deaths.' He gestured to the gates. 'SO, CITIZENS OF TIAN! I GIVE YOU, THE MASTER OF THE ARENA, JINGIM... AND HIS LOYAL PET – *TERRAKUS!*'

Two guards opened the gates, revealing a pitch-black tunnel behind. Slowly, from out of the gloom, an armour-clad Jingim appeared, wielding a lance fashioned from a single, long bone.

To Becky's astonishment, he was sitting astride a colossal dinosaur which he steered into the arena, using heavy leather reins. With its three horns, huge frill capping its massive skull, and curved beak, she recognised the species of dinosaur immediately.

After all – they had one at Bowen Hall.

With a cruel smile, Jingim yanked the reins hard, and Terrakus opened her mouth to reveal curved, sabre-like canine teeth, before delivering a thunderous roar.

It was then Becky knew that, unlike Gump, this Triceratops was very much a carnivore.

32

CLASH OF THE TITANS

Jingim punched the air with his lance, acknowledging the crowd's ovation as he paraded Terrakus around the ring's perimeter.

A guard approached Becky, Joe and Uncle Percy and passed them each a sword.

Gripping the sword tightly, Becky looked at its blade, then looked up at Terrakus and knew they had no chance whatsoever. 'Now would be a great time for that rescue,' she said to Uncle Percy.

'I agree.' Uncle Percy said, holding up the pagidizor, and pressing a green button. His thumb faded from sight. 'Unfortunately, fate doesn't appear to agree with us.' He returned the pagidizor to his pocket. 'Still, I have one more card up my sleeve.' He thrust his hand in his pocket and pulled out something shiny.

Just before Becky could make out the object, she felt a hand push her into the arena, as a guard echoed the action with Joe and Uncle Percy.

The High Priest raised his arms again. 'CITIZENS OF TIAN... LET COMBAT COMMENCE!'

As the High Priest ran to safety, the crowd exploded with sound.

His eyes wild, Jingim yanked the reins and guided the Triceratops toward Becky, Uncle Percy, and Joe. Then he screamed, slamming his massive legs against the Triceratops ribs.

Terrakus charged.

'SPLIT UP!' Uncle Percy yelled.

Following his lead, Becky veered to the left, Joe to the right.

Uncle Percy raised his car keys to his mouth and shouted, 'BRENDA! JOIN US!' Immediately, a sizzling orb of electricity appeared to his left, quickly expanding in size, before – *SNAPPP!* – it exploded, ragged fingers of light igniting the air. The light vanished, heralding Brenda's sudden appearance.

Uncle Percy sprinted over to the Bentley, flung open the driver's door, and leapt in.

The crowd's bloodthirsty shrieks morphed into disbelieving gasps.

Jingim couldn't believe his eyes, and drew Terrakus to a halt as he tried to make sense of the situation.

Powering up the Bentley, Uncle Percy slammed his foot on the accelerator.

The car sped off in Becky's direction.

Steering Brenda alongside Becky, Uncle Percy yelled, 'GET IN!'

Becky didn't need asking twice. Throwing the rear door open, she leapt onto the backseat, banging her head on the way. 'LET'S GET JOE, AND GET OUT OF HERE!' she screamed, pointing at Joe, who was on the other side of the arena.

Uncle Percy spun the wheel, and the Bentley powered off again.

They had barely made it two metres when – *BOOOOM* – Terrakus slammed into the car, knocking it off its trajectory, sending it spinning across the arena in a cloud of sand and dust.

Uncle Percy struggled to maintain control of the wheel. Through the cloud, he spotted Joe who was sprinting toward them. 'OPEN THE DOOR, BECKY!'

Becky did, and a moment later, Joe jumped in.

'LET'S GOOOOO!' Becky bellowed.

'Absolutely,' Uncle Percy replied, reaching for the dashboard. 'We'll return for Amelia later!' He struck a key on the dashboard when –

Two giant horns punctured the driver's door, missing Uncle Percy by inches, before piercing the chronalometer, which exploded in a flash of sparks and smoke.

Fear filled Becky as she stared at Terrakus's head pressed against the car door. 'G- GET US OUT OF HERE!'

With the car shuddering madly, Uncle Percy studied the dashboard. 'I CAN'T,' he yelled back. 'THE CHRONALOMETER'S DAMAGED!'

'WHAT?' Becky yelled.

Suddenly, the car inched upward as Terrakus tried to lift it off the ground.

As they tipped at an angle, Becky and Joe slammed into each other.

'DO SOMETHING!' Becky yelled at Uncle Percy.

Hastily, Uncle Percy triggered the pagidizor. However, as had happened before, his hand vanished.

Even over the bedlam, Becky heard heavy thumps on the roof above. She glimpsed a small figure leap through the air and land deftly on the triceratops's back.

Joe saw it, too. 'IT'S TUSKY!'

Jingim's eyes enlarged when he saw the squirrel before him.

'You wish to harm my friends,' Tusk said to Jingim. 'That I cannot allow!' And with a mighty swing, smashed his hammer against Jingim's helmet.

With a shattering *CLUUUNK*, Jingim lost all consciousness, and slid off the triceratops. As he plummeted down to the ground, Tusk caught his spear.

In a lightning-fast movement, Tusk spun the spear around, aimed the spearhead down, and thrust it through Terrakus's heart, killing her instantly.

The Bentley crashed to the ground.

Silence enveloped the stadium.

Dazed, Becky stared out of the window at the dead triceratops and the unconscious Jingim.

'Is everyone okay?' Uncle Percy asked.

'Yeah,' Joe said.

'I'm fine,' Becky said.

'What do we do now?' Joe asked.

'I'm not exactly sure,' Uncle Percy said. 'Let's hope Kallibane puts this down as our victory for the three of us, and lets us live. Anyway, it seems we have a squirrel to thank.'

With Terrakus's carcass pressed against the driver's door, Uncle Percy climbed out the passenger door and dusted himself down.

Becky and Joe clambered out of the car, as Tusk appeared.

'I knew you wouldn't let us down, mate,' Joe said, patting Tusk on the shoulder.

'Thanks again, Tusk,' Becky said.

'It seems like you're always saving our bacon, Tusk,' Uncle Percy said. 'Thank you.'

'Your thanks are not needed,' Tusk replied.

It was then they heard three loud *bangs* somewhere beyond the arena, followed by a low, continuous thrumming sound.

'What's that?' Joe said, looking up.

Becky thought she recognised the sound as it grew in volume. 'It sounds like -'

Uncle Percy's expression darkened as he interrupted her. '- *Helicopters.*'

Becky's gaze was drawn west, as three jet-black helicopters appeared over the stadium's ramparts, lights blinking, their whirring blades blurred against the evening sky.

'Is this your rescue team?' Becky asked Uncle Percy, suddenly hopeful.

'No, Becky,' Uncle Percy replied grimly. 'No... it isn't.'

The helicopters hovered over the stadium.

'THEN WHAT'S HAPPENING?' Becky shouted over the rising noise.

Before Uncle Percy could reply, however, the thunderous rattle of gunfire filled the air.

33

GUNSMOKE

The crowd's initial confusion was replaced by terror, as bullets struck humans and dracorexes alike. Soon, countless people were hurtling frantically to the exits, many stumbling over in the panic and landing beside the injured and the dead.

It was bedlam.

Carnage.

'IN THE CAR NOW!' Uncle Percy yelled. 'IT'S BULLETPROOF.'

Joe and Tusk didn't hesitate and leapt inside the Bentley.

Becky, however, had frozen. Through the chaos, she saw Kallibane had vanished, leaving Amelia Earhart on her own, crouching behind the throne, bullets puncturing the surrounding ground.

'BECKY!' Joe bellowed. 'WHAT'RE YOU DOIN'?'

'I'LL BE BACK,' Becky shouted back.

Joe couldn't believe it. 'WHAT?'

But Becky had gone. Sprinting across the arena, she ignored the bullets, and kept her gaze locked solely on Amelia Earhart.

Within twenty seconds, she had reached her. 'AMELIA,' she yelled. 'COME WITH ME!'

Amelia looked up, scared and bewildered. 'I-is this your rescue?'

'No,' Becky replied. 'But come on.' She held out her hand, which Amelia grasped.

Becky heaved Amelia to her feet, and then together they dashed back to the Bentley.

Joe threw open the door, and Amelia clambered in followed by Becky, who was panting wildly.

'Well done, Becky,' Uncle Percy said.

Joe squeezed Becky's arm. 'That was gutsy, sis. Nice one.'

'Are you okay, Amelia?' Uncle Percy asked.

'Yes,' Amelia replied. Just then, her eyes locked on Tusk, and her face dropped.

'Oh, yeah,' Joe said. 'Amelia Earhart meet Tusk. He's a talking viking squirrel.'

'Hail, woman,' Tusk said.

'H-hello,' Amelia said, her expression suggesting nothing much shocked her anymore.

'So, what is all this?' Becky asked Uncle Percy.

'It's Heath Pineos,' Uncle Percy replied. 'I knew he was bad. I never expected this.'

The gunfire stopped.

Becky watched as the helicopters landed in a vast sand cloud. Within seconds, dozens of armed men in black jump-suits leapt out.

'Can you fix the chronalometer?' Becky asked Uncle Percy.

'No,' Uncle Percy replied. 'But everything's fine.'

'It just isn't,' Becky said flatly.

'Trust me,' Uncle Percy replied. 'Let's see what Mister Pineos has to say for himself.'

Moments later, Becky, Joe, Uncle Percy, Tusk and Amelia Earhart stood in line, watching a group of people approach.

Heath Pineos led the way, a smug, self-satisfied smile on his face, trailed by Mayara Lenya, Alwyn Thomas and a number of bodyguards.

'Hello again, Mister Halifax,' Pineos said. 'I'm pleased you weren't killed in the crossfire.'

Uncle Percy nodded at the bodies nearby. 'And yet many were,' he said coolly, restraining his anger.

'So I see,' Pineos replied. 'And who exactly were they? There were no humans on the island when I was last here.'

'Do you really care who they were?'

Pineos shook his head. 'I honestly couldn't care less,' he replied. 'But it seems they've built a remarkable town here. I suppose it belongs to me, now, which pleases me. I always like to expand my property portfolio.'

'We'll see about that,' Uncle Percy said in a curious tone.

'We shall, indeed,' Pineos replied. Just then, he noticed Tusk and his look of astonishment lingered for an uncomfortable length of time.

'If you gaze at me longer, I shall take your eyeballs,' Tusk growled.

'T-the squirrel speaks?' Pineos laughed.

Tusk's grip tightened on his hammer. 'Let me slay him now!'

'No, Tusk,' Uncle Percy replied, as two guards turned their guns on Tusk.

Pineos raised his hand to calm the situation. 'I apologise. I have no excuse except I've never witnessed your kind before, but please, forgive me.' He turned back to Uncle Percy. 'Anyway, it seems I owe you a great debt of gratitude. Thank you for leading us here. It has been a very long time since I last stepped foot on this soil.' He smiled at Becky and Joe. 'The three of you are every bit as remarkable as I hoped. Obviously, you found the Dahlia Compass.'

'Yep,' Joe said bitterly. 'Here... have it.' He hurled the compass at Pineos's head.

Pineos, however, caught it. 'I don't think we need it now, do you?' he said, dropping it on the ground. His attentions turned to Amelia Earhart. 'And Ms. Earhart? This is where you ended up? I just knew as soon as Mister Thomas informed me of the date and spatial coordinates of the island that somehow you'd be involved. It's very nice to meet you.'

'I don't feel the same way, sir,' Amelia said. 'You appear to be a sociopath.'

'Not at all,' Pineos replied. 'Just a survivor... like you.'

Uncle Percy cast Alwyn Thomas a frosty stare. 'Can I assume it was you that organised for a chrono-tracer to be placed on us, Alwyn?'

Becky recalled a chrono-tracer was a device for tracking time machines through time and space.

'It's cast into the base of the bottle that Mister Pineos gave you,' Thomas replied with an indifferent shrug. 'I'd say I was sorry for the betrayal, Perce, but I ain't. Fact is, I told you I'd always been broke, but Mister Pineos has made me a very rich man. He also showed me how to keep me assets away from GITT's prying eyes. Me and him make a great team.'

'I hope it's worth it,' Uncle Percy replied. 'Because you'll get your comeuppance.'

'Then I'll get my comeuppance with a few quid in the bank,' Thomas replied, smirking.

Uncle Percy turned back to Pineos. 'You know, many things repulse me about you, Mister Pineos, but the fact you'd invent a story about a dying grandchild to get your own way – well, that takes a true fiend.'

'Marietta's not real then?' Joe said.

'No, Joe, she's not,' Uncle Percy replied.

Joe glared at Pineos. 'You're sick in the head, mate.'

'I've seen and done too much to be overemotional about such things,' Pineos said.

'Oh, I know very well what you've done,' Uncle Percy said.

Before Pineos could pursue this, however, a devastating roar sounded from the far tunnel.

Becky looked over as a massive figure charged into the stadium.

'INVADERRRRRSSSSS,'   Kallibane   bellowed. 'PREPAAARE FOR DEATH!'

Becky had never seen a more formidable sight. Dressed in gleaming silver armour, Kallibane wielded a spiked wooden club in one hand and a double-headed axe in the other.

He ran toward them, the ground trembling beneath his feet.

To Becky's astonishment, Pineos remained composed, calm even. Turning to one of his men, he extended his hand and took hold of a bolt-action rifle. About a metre in length, the rifle had a long barrel, a telescopic sight and a six-bullet magazine.

It looked considerably older than all the other guns on display.

Coolly, Pineos raised the rifle and controlled his breath. He lined up his shot.

Then – *CRACK* - he fired.

In a perfect shot, the bullet pierced Kallibane's helmet, and a puff of red coloured the air.

Kallibane was dead before his body hit the ground.

Pineos, however, didn't stop there. Marching toward Kallibane, he reloaded and fired again and again, every bullet slamming into the minotaur's body.

Standing over Kallibane's corpse, Pineos gave a nod of satisfaction before returning to the group. 'I've been dreaming of doing that for over two thousand years... and it was every bit as satisfying as I'd hoped.' He smiled at Uncle Percy. 'I would say the island is most definitely mine now, don't you think?'

Uncle Percy could barely find the words. 'Your bullets were made from orichalcum?'

'They were,' Pineos said. 'And that was all thanks to you.

After all, it was you that confirmed orichalcum was the only metal that could kill a minotaur. Of course, orichalcum is a rare substance, but I have been collecting Atlantean relics for five hundred years and had more than enough orichalcum to create six bullets for this gun.' He held up the rifle. 'It's a weapon with quite a colourful history for destruction. Surely, you recognise it?'

Looking at the weapon, Uncle Percy's face dropped. 'How did you get it?' he gasped. 'I thought it was locked away in a Federal building in Maryland.'

Pineos nodded at Alwyn Thomas. 'The time traveller's ability to appear when and where they choose is a huge benefit when committing burglary,' he said. 'Mr Thomas acquired it for me for a fee. I do like to collect mementos of historical significance, and Lee Harvey Oswald's rifle, the one that assassinated President John F Kennedy, was always high on my things to own list.'

Uncle Percy stared at Pineos with disgust. 'Of course, it was,' he said. 'Speaking of assassinations, did you keep a memento after you murdered your friend?'

'What do you mean?' Pineos asked, surprised.

'Oh, Heath,' Uncle Percy said. 'I've been onto you for some time.'

Pineos angled his head, intrigued. 'How so?'

'You told us Alexander was stabbed in a mugging at the Piazza Della Scala in Milan on the 13th June, 1766AD,' Uncle Percy said. 'I made a note of the date and place after we first met, then I asked a friend of mine, Bruce Westbrook, to travel back to see if that was indeed what happened. It turns out that yes, Alexander was killed there that night. However, his attacker wasn't the unidentified thug you claimed, just two very old friends walking home from a restaurant.' He inhaled a breath. 'Becky, Joe, it turns out Mister Pineos stabbed his best friend, his so-called brother, and someone he'd known for over two thousand years. You are looking at the man who murdered Alexander the Great!'

34

FEAR, FATE AND FRIENDS

Pineos's mouth arched into an ugly smile. 'I'm afraid that's true,' he said. 'I was running out of water, and Alexander was the only one left from the original crew who had any. Yes, it was regrettable Alexander had to go. I loved him and still miss him to this day, but I was just continuing the plan he created many years earlier.'

'What do you mean?' Uncle Percy asked.

'Don't think Alexander was an innocent victim in all of this,' Pineos replied. 'It was his idea to track down every one of the crew, kill them, and take their water so he and I could continue to live. And that is what we did.'

'And was it worth committing all that murder just to stay alive?'

'Of course,' Pineos replied. 'Let's not forget the worst part of living, of life in general, is the fear over its end. For many years, so many more than anyone else, I never considered the notion of death. Murder was just a way to ensure my life continued, that I never had to contemplate my end. How could that not be worth it?'

Uncle Percy paused. 'I've encountered many people in my

life,' he said. 'But you're possibly the most pathetic excuse for a human being I've ever met.'

Pineos smirked. 'Really?'

'Really,' Uncle Percy replied. 'You murdered someone you claim to have loved. At least, I believe Emerson Drake was incapable of love. You say you loved Alexander, yet killed him with no guilt or remorse so you could live a few extra years.'

'Any guilt I felt taking Alexander's life was tempered by the fact it would've only been a matter of time before he took mine. I just got there first.'

'The fact you think like that supports my case,' Uncle Percy said.

'Uncle Percy's right,' Becky said. 'You're a sad, miserable waste of space... a nobody.'

'A total loser,' Joe added.

Rage flared in Pineos's eyes. 'And yet I own all of you,' he hissed.

'Own us?' Uncle Percy replied, stunned by the comment. 'You don't own us!'

'I think I do,' Pineos said. 'In fact, there's nothing now that I don't or won't own if I so choose. I have an everlasting supply of enchanted water - just imagine what someone would pay for a single bottle of that? A billion? Five billion? I really could name my price... and I intend to. Thanks to Mister Thomas, I can travel in time. Therefore, I can own the past and the future. You see, there really is nothing I don't own, and that includes you.'

'But you don't own us,' Uncle Percy repeated. 'You could *never* own us.'

'You need water for John and Catherine Mellor, don't you?' Pineos nodded at the Bentley, the dead Triceratops still stuck in its bodywork. 'Looking at the state of your time machine, you also need transport to the twenty-first century. Well, I'm the only one that can offer those things. Therefore, it's safe to say I very much own you.'

Uncle Percy smiled. 'That's where we disagree,' he said, a surprising confidence in his voice. 'The thing is, I've planned for this moment.'

Becky glanced at Uncle Percy and her heart leapt. *He knew this was going to happen?*

'Once it was confirmed that you killed Alexander,' Uncle Percy said. 'I knew you were a man without morals or virtue or any human decency whatsoever. This was compounded when I researched your family and realised Marietta didn't exist. Subsequently, I examined your '*lucky*' bottle closely and discovered the chrono-tracer within. This, however, is where it gets interesting. I tried to remove the chrono-tracer, but I couldn't. The Omega Effect occurred, which was highly peculiar. In fact, I'd not seen it happen like that before. The Omega Effect only occurs when a traveller attempts to influence the past, not when they are operating in the present. Subsequently, the only conclusion I could reach was that fate wanted the chrono-tracer to remain in the bottle, and therefore allow you to trail our movements to the Blessed Isle. Logically, therefore, it meant I knew this moment would come, and I could prepare for it... which I did.' He raised the pagidizor into the light.

'What's that?' Pineos asked.

Immediately, Thomas's face changed.

'It's a pagidizor,' Uncle Percy said. 'And the strange thing is that for a great deal of time on this island, the Omega Effect has stopped me using it.'

Panicking, Thomas pointed to a guard. 'Train a gun on him,' he barked.

The guard obeyed.

'Give me the pagidizor, Percy!' Thomas said.

'As you wish, Alwyn.' Uncle Percy pressed the pagidizor's tip, and with a soft *click*, it flashed green. 'Ooops,' he said. 'Do you still want it?'

Becky's eyes widened. *The Omega Effect had lifted.*

At that moment, about two hundred metres away, three large, glittering orbs appeared, growing in size.

'Oooh, look at the pretty lights,' Uncle Percy said. 'It seems the cavalry is here. You see, Mister Pineos, I know you have guns, but there's a weapon more powerful than any firearm: *friendship.*'

With a resounding *bang*, the orbs exploded in a glittering spectacle of light, which then dissipated to reveal Edgar, Vilja and four other minotaurs.

Joe cast Pineos a rude hand gesture. 'Ha. You're in trouble now!'

'He is, Joe,' Uncle Percy said. 'Particularly as he's recently killed a minotaur.'

The six minotaurs strode toward the group.

Fear and panic coloured Pineos's eyes. 'SHOOOT THEMM-MM!' he screamed.

The guards turned their guns on the minotaurs and opened fire.

Even through the onslaught, however, Becky didn't feel an ounce of concern. Pineos had specified he only made six orichalcum bullets, and he'd used them on Kallibane. More-over, she knew how useless conventional bullets were against minotaur skin. She'd seen it first hand on the island of Kera, a few years before.

Becky watched as bullets bombarded the minotaurs, but not one of them looked fazed in the slightest. In fact, she saw Edgar and Vilja giggling throughout as though enjoying a cold shower.

The guards stopped firing, each one both dumbfounded and horrified at what would come next.

And with good reason.

While Edgar and Vilja continued their advance, the other four minotaurs charged off toward the guards, and before long were relishing a very one-sided brawl, as they threw, thumped and thrashed every guard they could get their massive hands on.

It was clear Tusk didn't want the minotaurs to have all the fun, either. With a roar, he lifted his hammer high and dashed off into the thick of the fight.

Pineos saw his men had no chance. Turning quickly, he sprinted off to the nearest helicopter.

But Joe wasn't about to let him get away. He set off after him like an athlete.

Pineos was fast, but not fast enough.

With a mighty dive, Joe pulled Pineos down in a ferocious rugby tackle, sending him crashing to the ground.

Watching this, Maraya Lenya pulled a small pistol from her pocket and aimed at Joe.

But Becky was on it. Focussing hard on Lenya's hand, she felt her telekinesis take hold. And with a tiny nod, she urged the hand upwards and forced the index finger to pull the trigger.

Six shots shattered the air until – *click* - the pistol was out of ammunition.

Staring at the empty gun, Lenya froze with shock and disbelief.

Becky grinned. 'What can I say?' she said. 'I've got skills.'

Meanwhile, Joe heaved Pineos up and slammed a fist into his face.

Pineos's body grew limp as all consciousness left him.

In a single punch, the fight was over.

Edgar approached Uncle Percy. 'Greetings again, Perce, my most excellent friend. We came as soon as we received your distress message, and we brought some friends. I hope our timing was agreeable.'

'Your timing was perfect, Edgar,' Uncle Percy said.

'Humans with guns, I see,' Edgar said. 'Such a silly pursuit.'

'It really is,' Uncle Percy replied. 'Thank you for coming, Vilja.'

'Not at all, Percy,' Vilja said. 'The pleasure is ours.' She stared out at the stadium. 'And where are we?'

'This is the Blessed Isle,' Uncle Percy said.

Vilja gasped. 'The Blessed Isle - you found it?'

'We did.'

'Is it as magic and dangerous as Herathon -' But before she could finish her sentence, she noticed Kallibane's body. Taking slow, uncertain steps, she approached it. 'I - I don't understand.'

'It's Kallibane,' Uncle Percy said, joining her. 'The crew member that was left here with Herathon. He was alive for over five thousand years.'

'Who killed him?' Vilja said.

Uncle Percy nodded at Pineos's unconscious body. 'He did.'

'And his punishment will be?' Vilja asked.

'He'll stay here,' Uncle Percy said. 'They can all stay. I'll empty the helicopters of both Gerathnium and fuel, and they can truly enjoy the fruits of the island for all eternity.'

Thomas approached Uncle Percy, his face pale. 'I'm really sorry, Perce.' He was trembling. 'I made a mistake.'

'You did, Alwyn,' Uncle Percy replied. 'And I told you that you'd get your comeuppance.'

'You can't leave me here.'

'I think I can,' Uncle Percy replied. 'You wanted riches. Look around. You're now living in the most valuable real estate known to humankind. Enjoy your long life.' He turned away.

'You can't do this to me,' Thomas said, spinning Uncle Percy around by the shoulder.

'I loathe violence, Alwyn,' Uncle Percy said. 'But my family could've been killed in that helicopter massacre, and I hold you responsible for that.' And with that, he pitched a shattering punch at Thomas's chin, who crumbled unconscious to the ground.

Becky's mouth tumbled open.

Joe punched the air. 'That's what I'm talking about.'

Uncle Percy winced as he rubbed his fist. 'This thumping malarky hurts far too much for my liking.'

'But you feel better for it,' Joe said.

'On this occasion, I don't feel worse.'

As the minotaurs finished thrashing the guards, Becky surveyed the surrounding chaos. 'What happens now, then?'

Uncle Percy turned to Edgar. 'Could I borrow your portravella, please, my friend?'

'Of course,' Edgar said, slipping the portravella off his wrist.

'I'll be back in two ticks and half a jiffy.' Uncle Percy keyed in some coordinates and within a few seconds, he disappeared. A moment later, he reappeared again, but this time he looked completely different. Dressed in a tunic, loose fitting wool trousers, and a cloak fastened at the shoulder by a brooch, he resembled a medieval commoner. He also held several bottles, and another object - *The Odin Horn*.

'Why are you wearing that outfit?' Joe asked.

'I've been to the ninth century on a research mission,' Uncle Percy said.

'And you've brought the Odin Horn?' Becky asked.

'I have.' Uncle Percy smiled at Tusk, who had just re-joined them. 'I think it's high time we lifted a serpent's curse from a certain Viking warrior, don't you?'

35

KING VIKING

Tusk's whiskers twitched anxiously. 'You do, Percy Halifax?'

'I do, my friend.'

'What if the magic cannot be reversed? What if I am doomed to stay in this form forever?'

'Don't worry, Tusky,' Joe said. 'It's obviously magical water. Look at all that's happened on this island.'

Tusk sucked in a nervous breath. 'Then, Odin willing, now is the occasion for my rebirth. I am ready.'

'Excellent,' Uncle Percy said. 'Let me just ensure Pineos and his cronies really do stay here to enjoy the island's splendours with no opportunity to leave.'

Over the next ten minutes, Uncle Percy disabled the helicopters of their time travelling capabilities and emptied them of fuel. After disarming the guards, they allowed Pineos, Thomas, Lenya and the guards to leave without further incident to start their new lives on the island.

Then Uncle Percy, Becky, Joe, Amelia Earhart, Edgar, Vilja and the other minotaurs left the stadium and walked over to the Pool of Life.

Night was falling fast now, the full moon making the water flicker like golden teardrops.

Becky had never seen a more picturesque sight, and despite all the recent horror and violence, the sickening scenes caused by Heath Pineos and his men, she felt a deep serenity as if in the presence of a higher power.

With all eyes fixed on him, Uncle Percy approached the water's edge and filled the Odin Horn before turning to Tusk.

Becky had never seen Tusk so nervous before.

'Are you ready, my friend?' Uncle Percy said.

Tusk nodded. 'Aye.'

Uncle Percy tipped the horn over Tusk's head, the water causing his fur to shimmer lightly with a strange, ethereal glow.

Her heart pounding, Becky whispered a silent prayer.

Drenched from top to bottom, Tusk stared out at the water. Then, to everyone's surprise, he leapt in headfirst, vanishing beneath the surface in a flurry of ripples and swells.

Becky glanced at Joe, who looked nervously on when Tusk didn't reappear.

Five seconds passed.

Ten seconds.

Twenty seconds.

But then, strands of long, silvery blond hair broke the surface, as the chiselled, handsome face of a man emerged, followed by a tall, toned muscular body moulded from a life-time of combat and working the land.

Wearing the robes of a Viking chieftain, Tusk smiled as he surveyed the dumbfounded group. 'It seems the curse is lifted,' he said quietly, as if struggling to believe it himself.

'Too right it is, Tusky.' Joe beamed.

'Tusk is no more, Joe. From now on, I am Ragnar again... Ragnar Lothbrok.'

'Then, hiya, Ragnar,' Joe said.

'Hail, Joe.' Ragnar pulled Joe into a powerful hug before

turning to Becky. 'And Becky... I can finally see you with my own eyes.'

'Hello, Ragnar,' Becky said.

Ragnar placed his hand on Uncle Percy's shoulder. 'How can I ever repay my debt to you, my friend?'

'Don't be silly,' Uncle Percy said. 'I'm just pleased you're back to normal.'

Ragnar smiled. 'I forgot the feeling of being tall... and without fur.'

Everyone laughed.

'I'll take you to Lagertha soon,' Uncle Percy said. 'Let me just sort out a few other things first.' He approached Edgar, Vilja, and the minotaurs. 'My friends... we thank you all for our rescue. We would have surely been ended without you.'

'Tush and Frapplepotts,' Edgar replied. 'It was the very least Vilja and I could do.' He gestured at the other minotaurs. 'And I'm sure my brothers here enjoyed the exercise.'

The four minotaurs nodded their agreement.

'We'll always be there for you, Percy Halifax, whatever the request,' Vilja said. 'You, Becky and Joe are like blood to us.'

'And you to us, Vilja,' Uncle Percy replied.

They spent the next few minutes exchanging hugs and well-wishes, after which Edgar, Vilja and the minotaurs returned to Caradan.

After watching them leave, Uncle Percy approached Amelia. 'Amelia... this is the point you have to make some decisions.'

'I understand, Mister Halifax,' Amelia said. 'And although I have had little time to think about it – well, it's clear to me I can't go back to my old life. There would just be too many questions I couldn't answer, that would be impossible to answer. So... with that in mind, I was thinking about something you said to me in the jail cell – that you could place me in a different timeline. Is that possible?'

'It is, indeed,' Uncle Percy replied. 'I can give you a whole new identity, give you all the necessary documents you'd need to start again, and give you enough funds to make your start comfortable, wherever it is you wish to begin again.'

Amelia thought about this. 'I can see no other way. Also, if my disappearance and subsequent celebrity can influence future generations of women to strive and succeed, I would have it no other way.'

'I understand,' Uncle Percy said.

'Then it is decided. I shall be put in a new time, a new place, with a new identity.'

'Are you sure?'

Amelia nodded. 'I have no children,' she said. 'My marriage had deep faults, and I'm sure George would be much better off without me. Yes, I think I would like to start again. I certainly have other ambitions, and I'd like to focus on them.'

'Very well.'

'Now, I assume I would need a new name - could I pick that for myself?'

'Of course.'

'I once met a woman called Irene Craigmile, and she left quite an impression on me,' Amelia said. 'Perhaps I could take her name and start again?'

'I can make that happen,' Uncle Percy said.

'Thank you, Mister Halifax.' Amelia extended her hand, and they shook.

Amelia exhaled. 'I've always relished the thrill of travelling... but this – this is one trip I never imagined I could embark upon.'

'I understand.'

'But at least I'm sure it'll be somewhere without carnivorous dinosaurs and lovelorn minotaurs.'

Uncle Percy chuckled. 'I'm sure,' he said. 'Then this is how it'll work. I'll take you to my home, Bowen Hall. You're a similar size to Becky, and I have a place called the Fitting Room that contains many, many clothes from many eras. All the while, you can think about where and when you'd like to live, and we can kit you out from there. How does that sound?'

'That sounds mighty fine, sir,' Amelia said. 'But I've already decided where and when I'd like to live.'

'You have?'

'I have,' Amelia said. 'I always thought that 1950 will be such an exciting, eventful year – being clean midway through the century, and all that. Would I be able to live in 1950?'

'I think that's an excellent choice,' Uncle Percy said. 'The nineteen fifties was a fascinating decade on so many levels, with many wonderful developments in popular culture, science and economics. And where would you like to live in 1950?'

'In 1932, I landed in Ireland on my first solo flight across the Atlantic,' Amelia replied. 'I ended up staying the night with a lovely family in Donegal. To be frank, I plumb fell in love with the entire country, and have always meant to return, but I never did. Could I live there?'

'Absolutely,' Uncle Percy said. 'Ireland is a beautiful part of the world, and I know a lady time traveller that retired there in that very time period, so, yes, it most certainly can be arranged.'

For the first time, optimism flashed in Amelia's eyes. 'Gosh... how exciting.'

'Then if you'd like to say your goodbyes,' Uncle Percy said. 'I'll take you now.'

Amelia beamed. 'Very well. Becky... Joe... it's been lovely to meet you both, and quite a ride, although no one would ever believe a word of it if I ever had the courage to share our story.'

'No, they wouldn't,' Becky said. 'Good luck, Amelia.'

'And good luck to you and your family, Becky.'

Becky and Amelia hugged.

'And thank you, Joe,' Amelia said.

'Enjoy Ireland,' Joe said.

'I mean to.' Amelia smiled at Ragnar. 'Many thanks, Ragnar, and if I may say you look much more handsome as a man than a squirrel.'

Ragnar laughed. 'I thank you, Amelia. And may the fortune of Njǫrd be ever with you.'

Uncle Percy stepped forward. 'Now, just touch my person, Amelia, and we'll get going.'

Nervously, Amelia reached out and held Uncle Percy's arm as he keyed digits into the portravella.

A moment later, fingers of electrical charge coiled up Uncle Percy's arm, before wrapping him and Amelia in a blinding bubble of light.

'Oh, my!' Amelia gasped.

And with a loud *bang*, Amelia Earhart left to start a new life.

36

NO WAY, IT'S NORWAY!

When Uncle Percy returned a few seconds later, he looked completely different. With a clean-shaven face, he wore his signature outfit –linen jacket, shorts, waistcoat, shirt and tie. 'I'm back,' he said.

'We can see,' Joe said.

'And how's Amelia?' Becky asked.

'She's fine. Actually, she's more than fine. I think she's excited about starting her life afresh. I've arranged for her to live in a cottage on the outskirts of Galway Bay, with some spectacular views over the Atlantic Ocean.'

'And has she met your friend, the retired traveller?' Becky asked.

'She has, and they hit it off like a house on fire,' Uncle Percy replied. 'Pepper Shaftsbury is a few years older than Amelia, but she's young at heart and will help her settle in just fine. I've also given Amelia a pagidizor in case she needs me for any reason. Yes, I think Amelia will be happy with her new life.'

'Good.'

'Now, let me get some more water and we'll leave.' Uncle Percy took the bottles and filled them before turning to Ragnar.

'Anyway, Ragnar, I said before I'd been on a research mission. Well, that mission was to your home town in ninth-century Norway.'

'You visited my homestead?' Ragnar said. 'Did you see my Lagertha?'

'I did,' Uncle Percy replied. 'Only from a distance, but I talked to some of the townsfolk, so I know her situation. She never remarried, and still grieves you as a fallen warrior. She and your children have been waiting for the last year, hoping one day you'd return home to them.' He smiled. 'Shall we make that day today?'

Ragnar gave a nervous nod. 'Aye.'

'Right, everyone,' Uncle Percy said. 'Take one last look at the Blessed Isle. I don't understand how the island has become what it has, but I intend to find out at some point in the future.' A curious tone marked his voice. 'In fact, I think I have an idea.'

'You do?' Joe said, surprised. 'What?'

'I'm not getting into that now,' Uncle Percy said. 'Still, I don't have any immediate plans to return, so enjoy the view one last time. After all, it's not every day you see a golden lake.'

Becky took a final, lingering look at the Pool of Life. Yes, it was beautiful, and she'd never seen a stranger or more enchanted place, but she had no desire to return. They'd achieved what they came for, and now was the time to move on, reunite Ragnar with his family, and, hopefully, return her parents to their normal states. 'Let's go,' she said.

'Absolutely.' Uncle Percy inputted new coordinates onto his portravella.

As everyone touched Uncle Percy, something occurred to Joe. 'Hey... what about the Bentley?' he said. 'Will you return and get her later?'

'No,' Uncle Percy replied. 'Heath Pineos enjoys mementos. He can have one to remind him of us.'

'Damn,' Joe said. 'I was hoping to learn to drive in it.'

A shattering *boom* drowned out Uncle Percy's response.

AS A NEW LANDSCAPE formed before her, Becky felt a cool breeze brush her skin. Surveying the immediate vicinity, she saw an expanse of green fields which led to a snow-capped mountain range in the distance. Glancing over at Ragnar, she saw tears fill his eyes, which were trained to their right.

'I am home,' Ragnar said, his voice trembling.

Tracking his gaze, Becky saw a longhouse with smoke drifting upward from a vent in the ceiling. The longhouse was the largest of a small cluster of buildings, surrounding which were a chicken coop, and numerous fenced pens that contained cattle, pigs, sheep and goats.

Just then, a woman with long, braided blonde hair emerged from the longhouse carrying a bucket of feed. Approaching the coop, she threw in food for the chickens within.

Ragnar was trembling now. 'My Lagertha,' he said in a whisper.

'I think you're long overdue your reunion, my friend,' Uncle Percy said.

'You have taught me so much, Percy Halifax, and know this - my sword or counsel is always yours should you require it. My bond to you is as strong as Viking steel.'

'Thank you, Ragnar,' Uncle Percy said. 'That means a lot.'

Ragnar looked at Becky and Joe. 'Now you liberate your kinfolk,' he said. 'I know it shall work as the water worked on me.'

'We will,' Becky said. 'And good luck.'

'Cheers, Ragnar,' Joe said. 'I'll drop off some crisps when we're in this timeline again.'

Ragnar laughed. 'Aye. You must.' He extended his arms and invited Becky and Joe in for a final hug. 'And may the luck of the *Hamingja* accompany you throughout your life.' And with those words, he set off toward the farm.

Becky felt a pang of sorrow as Ragnar Lothbrok walked away. Would they ever see him again? She really had no idea. But the one thing she knew was the chances of meeting another talking squirrel with a fondness for television soap operas, pork pies, and Ed Sheeran were highly unlikely.

37

ALL'S WELL THAT ENDS...

'I'm gonna miss that crazy squirrel,' Joe said.

'We all shall, Joe,' Uncle Percy said. 'But it's best for everyone if the Squirrel Man of Addlebury doesn't make a reappearance.'

'Fair point,' Joe said. 'And at least I get the tree-house back for myself.'

'You've got five tonnes of crisps to eat before then,' Becky said.

Uncle Percy chuckled. 'That's true. Now, shall we take the Odin Horn and this water and get your parents back?'

'Deffo,' Joe said.

Becky was on edge as she took Uncle Percy's arm. She couldn't feel the wind, she couldn't taste the clean air, her every sense was somewhere else. And she barely registered the thunderous *boom* that returned them to the twenty-first century.

A MOMENT LATER, they materialised in John and Catherine's bedroom at Bowen Hall.

A thick seam of sunlight illuminated an oak wood floor covered with Persian rugs, upon which was a four-poster bed, and matching mahogany bedside cabinets. A vase brimming with fresh Stephanie Roses had been placed on a Victorian dresser, colouring the air with a honeyed fragrance.

Becky couldn't see any of it. Her gaze was locked solely on the two statues at the window.

'What will we do if it doesn't work?' Joe said quietly.

'Then we start the research stage again,' Uncle Percy replied. 'We do whatever it takes and we never stop until it's done. However, after all we've seen I don't feel a shred of doubt that it will work.'

'Me neither,' Joe said.

'Well... here we go.' Uncle Percy uncapped the first bottle and poured water into the Odin Horn. Then he approached John and poured some of the water over him, before moving over to Catherine and repeating the action.

Her anxiety rising, Becky closed her eyes and said a silent a prayer.

They didn't have to wait long for a result.

The moment the water struck John's statue and trickled down, a dull glow spread through the stone, which dissolved like thawing ice, its hard outer shell being replaced by the living, breathing form of the man beneath.

Becky's heart was in her mouth.

It was working.

Becky glanced at her mother to see the same thing was happening.

As the last of the stone melted away, John Mellor crumpled to his knees, gasping for breath and shivering madly.

'DAAAD!' Becky yelled, dropping to his side and cradling him in her arms.

Simultaneously, Catherine Mellor also collapsed, but was caught by Joe before she hit the floor. 'MUUUM!' he cried, as she clawed for breath, desperately filling her lungs with air like a newborn baby.

Tears spilled down Becky's face. 'Dad... you're okay. It worked. You're back.'

His face porcelain white, Mr. Mellor coughed again and again, before finally finding his words. 'I'm alright, Becky,' he rasped. 'I'm fine.' He stared at his wife. 'Cathy... are you okay?'

'Y-yes,' Catherine spluttered.

'T-The Pool of Life – y-you found it?' Mr. Mellor said.

'You knew about that?' Becky replied.

Mr. Mellor gave a half-smile and kissed her forehead 'You told us about it... you beautiful girl.'

'Y-you heard us?'

'We heard it all, Becky,' Mr. Mellor said. 'Every time you and Joe visited us... we heard you, we heard everything you said.'

Becky couldn't find a reply. She stared at her mother and the tears began again. 'Mum!' She scrambled over to Mrs. Mellor and embraced her, as Joe went to hug his father.

'I'm okay, Becky,' Mrs. Mellor said. 'Thanks to the three of you.'

Joe held his father tightly. 'I'm glad you're back, Dad.'

'Me too, son,' Mr. Mellor said. 'And, once again, thanks to you, too, Percy... for everything.'

'You are very welcome, John,' Uncle Percy said.

'Now where's Tusk?' Mr. Mellor said. 'I'm desperate to meet him.'

'He's returned to the Viking age,' Joe said. 'The water made him human, too.'

'Ah, well that's good, I suppose, although I would've liked to have met a talking squirrel.' Mr. Mellor forced himself to his feet. 'Listen... I don't know what you've all been through, but –'
Suddenly, he stopped mid-sentence, and his face became blank

as if he'd lost all cognitive function. Stumbling forward, he crashed to the floor.

Becky screamed. 'DAAAAD!!!'

Simultaneously, Mrs. Mellor lost consciousnesses and fell, landing hard beside her husband.

Joe froze.

Momentarily dazed, Uncle Percy snapped out of it and withdrew his pagidizor. Swiftly, he tapped something onto its dial and it flashed green.

Instantly, two small balls of light materialised beside the dresser, expanding outward. *BANG* – the light exploded to reveal a bearded Asian man who wore a white coat and carried a leather bag; to his left was a middle-aged woman with a severe face, her hair coiled in a neat bun.

Becky recognised them both at once: *Doctor Aziz* and *Nurse Appleby*.

'Ahmed, Emily, thanks for coming,' Uncle Percy said. 'John and Catherine came out of the curse, but they've fainted.'

Without hesitating, Doctor Aziz and Emily sprang into action.

Her mind spiralling, Becky watched anxiously as the doctor and nurse examined their patients.

A minute passed. Finally, Doctor Aziz looked up and said, 'Okay, Percy, kids, we're taking them with us. Now... they're fine. That's the most important thing to remember. We prepared for an eventuality like this and we have a treatment room set up at our GITT facility in the Lake District, so try not to worry. We'll be in touch soon.' And with that, he triggered his portravella.

Barely able to breathe, Becky watched as her mum, dad, doctor and nurse were enveloped in a sphere of light and – *BOOM* – they vanished.

Silence.

'W-what happened?' Becky said, tears filling her eyes again.

'Don't worry, Becky,' Uncle Percy said. 'I didn't know how

their bodies would react to emerging from the curse, so I had Ahmed and Emily on call. Now, in terms of medical professionals, they're the very best, so your parents are in excellent hands.' He flashed Becky a kindly smile. 'Now I'm going to the Lake District, but I'll return as soon as I have some news. Okay?'

'We want to come,' Joe insisted.

'Not on this occasion, Joe,' Uncle Percy replied. 'Please, I know you're worried, scared even, but everything will be fine. Just have something to eat, try to stay positive, and I'll return as soon as I know more.' He triggered his portravella and a few moments later he'd gone.

Becky felt nauseous. All the joy, the optimism, the hope she'd had vanished in a heartbeat, and she couldn't help but wonder if the Wraith knew all this would happen.

And that this was what he'd planned all along.

38

LOVE AND LOATHING

Becky and Joe barely said anything to each other and remained in their parents' bedroom for the next hour. When Uncle Percy hadn't returned, they went to the kitchen to make themselves a drink.

One hour became two, which bled into three. Outside, a mild dusk fell all around, with the first smattering of stars peppering the clear evening sky.

It was seven in the evening when Becky and Joe heard the loud *snap* of an arriving portravella from the entrance hall. As quick as a shot, they sprinted there to see Uncle Percy smiling back at them.

'I'm sorry I was so long,' he said. 'Are you both okay?'

Becky wasn't interested in small-talk. 'Are Mum and Dad awake?'

'They are,' Uncle Percy replied. 'But they're poorly, and tired and need to rest.'

'Can we see them?'

'You may,' Uncle Percy replied. 'But only for a short while. Doctor Aziz wants to keep them at the hospital for a while, just to ensure there aren't any other side effects.'

'Fair enough,' Becky said. 'But can we go now?'

'We can, indeed.' Uncle Percy extended his hand. 'Hold on.'

Moments later, they left Bowen Hall.

MATERIALISING IN A HOSPITAL WAITING ROOM, Becky looked round to see a floral-patterned sofa, two chairs, a coffee machine, and a stack of paper cups.

'Now, before we see them,' Uncle Percy said. 'Remember, they're not well, and we don't want to over excite them.'

'Absolutely,' Becky said impatiently.

Uncle Percy pushed open a door and led the way into an adjoining room.

Becky entered a plush room. Mr. And Mrs. Mellor were lying in two single beds, approximately a metre a part, and both were attached to a variety of high-tech apparatus.

Although pale, Mr. Mellor's eyes ignited when he saw Becky and Joe. 'Ah, we have visitors.'

Mrs. Mellor looked equally unwell. 'Hello, you two,' she said, pushing herself up onto her elbows.

'Please, don't sit up,' Becky said, struggling to contain her tears.

'Don't be upset, Becky,' Mrs. Mellor said. 'We're being well looked after.'

'We may look rough, but we're feeling good,' Mr. Mellor said. 'Trust me, this is much better than being frozen solid, like a massive garden gnome.'

'And we'll be out soon,' Mrs. Mellor said.

'Just don't get into any more crazy adventures until we're back,' Mr. Mellor said. 'I want to come on the next one.'

'We can't promise that, Dad,' Joe said. 'We don't find these adventures. They find us.'

Mr. Mellor managed a smile. 'I'm sure.'

'Listen, we'll leave you now,' Becky said. 'I suppose - well, I suppose we just wanted to see you and tell you how much we love you.'

'We know that,' Mrs. Mellor replied. 'And we love you, too... so very much.'

'More than anything,' Mr. Mellor said. 'And don't worry, we'll be back soon.'

Joe approached his father, picked up his hand, and kissed it. 'I love you, Dad.'

'More than Man City?'

Joe laughed. 'Yeah. Even more than City.' He turned to his mother. 'Love you, Mum.'

'I love you, too, Joe,' Mrs. Mellor said.

'We'll come back tomorrow,' Becky said, before looking at Uncle Percy. 'That's okay, isn't it?'

'Of course, it is, Becky,' Uncle Percy replied. 'And the next time we'll bring flowers.'

'Good.' Becky gave both her mother and father a final kiss. 'You two get better now – we'll be back before you know it.' Then she left the room.

Joe and Uncle Percy bade their farewells, and then joined Becky in the waiting room as they prepared for the return trip to Bowen Hall.

'Do you feel better now, Becky?' Uncle Percy asked, activating his portravella.

'Absolutely,' Becky replied. 'They're in the best place.'

The instant they appeared in the entrance hall of Bowen Hall, however, Becky's positive mood morphed into fear. Two chairs had been positioned on the grand staircase, sitting on which were Jacob and Maria, their hands tied behind their backs, their mouths bound by gags. A man stood to their rear, his hands gripping a pistol that was pointed at Jacob's head.

Becky recognised Heinrich Müller immediately.

'I've been waiting for you,' Müller said. 'I see the Mellors have made a full recovery.'

Uncle Percy contained his anger. 'And how did you see that?'

'We see everything,' Müller replied.

'I'm sure.' Uncle Percy gestured at Jacob, whose leg was bandaged. 'You shot my friend.'

'He's lucky I did not shoot him in the head.'

'Trust me – you're lucky you didn't shoot him in the head,' Uncle Percy replied. 'And I will not forget what you've done, Müller. I promise you that.'

Müller snorted. 'Idle threats. Now, where are the water and the Odin Horn? That was the deal.'

Uncle Percy left the entrance hall, reappearing moments later, carrying a bottle and the horn.

His gun trained on Uncle Percy, Müller walked over and took the bottle. 'How do I know this is genuine?'

'Because you have my word. Now, leave... but remember we *shall* meet again.'

'I look forward to it.' Müller smirked as he activated his portravella. Seconds later, he vanished.

Becky, Uncle Percy, and Joe raced over to Maria and Jacob.

Uncle Percy untied Maria as Becky did the same for Jacob.

'Ohhh, siiir,' Maria cried, tears leaking down her face. She tried to say something else, but it came out as an incoherent noise.

'You're safe now.' Uncle Percy hugged Maria to his chest. 'How's your leg, Jacob?'

'It's not the first time Nazi scum has shot me in the leg,' Jacob replied. 'It's barely a flesh wound.'

'I'm still getting someone to look at it,' Uncle Percy said.

'It really isn't necessary, sir.'

'It really is.'

Jacob sighed. 'I am so sorry.'

Uncle Percy looked puzzled. 'Sorry... why?'

'Because, again, that masked monster has used us as hostages to get his own way. You had to give him the water.'

'I couldn't care less about that,' Uncle Percy said. 'All that matters is you're safe.'

'We are now,' Jacob replied.

Maria hugged Becky desperately. 'My child, is it true your parents are returned to us?'

Becky nodded. 'Yes.'

'Where are they?'

'They're at a hospital in the Lake District,' Becky replied. 'They're poorly, but they're going to be fine.'

'I am so pleased for you.'

'It's worked out well,' Becky said. 'But I'm sorry for what's happened to you.'

'Pah!' Maria said, sniffing loudly. 'One day that beast will get his punishment.'

'He certainly will,' Uncle Percy said. 'Now, let's us make you a cup of tea, and I'll get Doctor Aziz to look at Jacob's leg.'

'No, sir,' Jacob said. 'It is fine.'

'I'll believe it when Doctor Aziz tells me that's the case,' Uncle Percy said. He curled his arm round Jacob's shoulder and helped him off the chair. 'Joe, would you help Maria to the kitchen, please? She may be unsteady on her feet.'

'Sure,' Joe replied, moving to Maria's side and helping her stand up.

'Becky, would you care to wait here for a minute?' Uncle Percy said. 'After Joe and I return I have a nice surprise for you both.'

'Er, okay,' Becky replied.

As Becky watched them leave, she considered her own feelings. On one hand, she was delighted her parents were back to normal, that they'd saved Amelia Earhart, had returned Tusk to his former life, and regained Maria and Jacob. On the other, she knew they'd given the Wraith two magical artifacts – a bottle of enchanted water and the Odin Horn. And although she didn't know how he planned to use them, she knew nothing good could come of it.

She wasn't wrong.

39

A PROMISE FULFILLED

U ncle Percy and Joe returned a few minutes later.
'What's this surprise, then?' Becky asked Uncle
Percy.

'If you care to follow me, I'll show you,' Uncle Percy said, setting off toward the front door.

Becky and Joe trailed Uncle Percy out of the hall and turned left onto the porch. Soon, they passed the Time Room building and were heading toward the north bank of Bowen Lake.

As they neared the stables, Becky's heart fluttered when she saw Pegasus lying on the ground, her wings extended as she basked in the summer sun. Gump, the Triceratops, stood beside her, chomping happily on hunks of grass.

It was what she saw next, however, that gave Becky a wonderful surprise.

A smaller theropod dinosaur stood upright in Gump's shadow - *a young Tyrannosaurus Rex.*

Joe saw it, too. 'You did it,' he said to Uncle Percy. 'You brought him here.'

'I said I would,' Uncle Percy said with a smile. 'I got him when I brought back Amelia Earhart. You could see he would fit in instantly, and has made two very good friends. Peggy, in particular, has really taken him under her wing, so to speak.' He chuckled. 'Anyway, they all seem very happy together, so that's another positive to come out of all of this.'

Joe approached the Tyrannosaur. 'Hiya, mate. Welcome to Bowen Hall.'

The T. Rex seemed to recognise Joe and pushed his nose playfully against Joe's chest.

'I think you've got a new bezzy mate,' Becky said, grinning.

'Zammo will be gutted,' Joe said.

'Now, Joe,' Uncle Percy said. 'As it was you that insisted on his coming here, then I think it should be you that has the honour of naming him. Any thoughts?'

'Er, I don't know,' Joe said.

'You could name him *Shakelock*, after your hero,' Becky suggested.

'He doesn't exactly look like a *Shakelock*, does he?' Joe replied. 'He doesn't look like a Will, either.' He paused as a name formed in his mind. 'But he does look like a *Wilbert*.' He chuckled. 'Yeah, that'll do.' He patted the T. Rex's head. 'Hiya, Wilbert.'

'A lovely name for a lovely dinosaur,' Uncle Percy said. 'Wilbert, it is.'

Wilbert gave a contented moan, as if in full agreement.

Uncle Percy disappeared into the nearest stable and re-emerged carrying a gleaming metallic object. 'And when I collected Wilbert, Becky, I also got this,' he said. 'If it is a lucky sword, as Lawless Larry believes, then you may need it in the future.'

Becky took hold of Anne Bonny's cutlass. 'I didn't expect to see it again. Thanks.'

'You're very welcome,' Uncle Percy replied. 'Anyway, I suppose all's well that ends well.'

'I guess so,' Becky replied.

'Definitely,' Joe said.

But then, just as Becky watched a beaming Joe rip up some grass and feed it to Wilbert, another image formed in her head – a horrific image she'd last seen in a recent dream.

Standing on a muddy path in an ancient Eastern-European village, she was staring at a corpse, its eyes wide open to expose blood-red eyeballs. However, that wasn't the thing that troubled her. No, what worried her was the more she thought about it, the more she knew it wasn't a dream at all.

It was one of her future visions, and that meant it wouldn't be long before that vision became a reality.

40

THE CUCKOO'S CALLING

Over the next week, Becky and Joe managed their time effectively, visiting their parents daily, spending time with Wilbert, Gump and Peggy, and still finding time to attend school.

Becky had no more visions; Jacob's leg was on the mend; and everything appeared to return to normal. That was until the next Saturday morning.

Becky and Joe were sitting on the tree-house veranda, enjoying a glass of apple juice and staring out at the forest. The tips of the trees swayed in the warm breeze, their leaves rustling like crêpe paper. Suddenly, a shrill bleep echoed from inside the treehouse.

Entering the lounge, Becky and Joe saw the hologramophone receiver.

INCOMING HOLOGRAMOPHONIC MESSAGE.
   Recipient: Becky and Joe
   Sender: Percy Halifax
   Location: The Morning Room

. . .

JOE PRESSED a button on the hologramophone, which launched three lasers into the air, forming a life-sized, three-dimensional image of Uncle Percy.

Although he was smiling, Becky saw something in Uncle Percy's eyes that told her all was not well.

'Good morning, Becky, Joe,' Uncle Percy said.

'Morning. What's the matter?' Becky asked, concerned.

'Yeah,' Joe said. 'You never call us here.'

'This is true,' Uncle Percy replied. 'The fact of the matter is that I made you a promise some time ago, and it's only right I make good on that promise, whether or not I want to.'

'Okay, now we're worried,' Becky said honestly.

'Don't be,' Uncle Percy replied. 'This is my problem, not yours.'

'What's it about?' Joe asked.

'Do you recall that before we went to get the Odin Horn, a traveller came to Bowen Hall that wished to speak to me privately?'

Becky remembered it well. Shala Abdul, an Indian time traveller appeared just after they'd said goodbye to Hans Keller, wanting to see Uncle Percy about a personal matter. It was an exchange that left him perturbed, but one he wasn't prepared to tell Becky and Joe about at the time. 'Yes,' she said. 'You promised to tell us about it when our parents were restored.'

'Exactly,' Uncle Percy replied. 'Anyway, that time is now. Would you care to join me in the morning room?'

'We'll be there in five minutes,' Becky said.

'I'll see you soon,' Uncle Percy said, and with that he ended the transmission.

Becky and Joe exchanged an ominous glance.

'Do you get the same feeling about this as I do?' Becky asked.

'What?' Joe replied 'That this is a *big* deal?'

'I was thinking a *huge deal!*' Becky replied.

A short while later, Becky and Joe sprinted back to the hall. Entering the morning room, they were surprised to see Felicity Butterworth sitting on the couch. She looked every bit as confused and concerned as they were.

'Hi, guys,' Felicity said. 'Good to see you both.'

'Hiya, Felicity,' Becky said, walking over and embracing her. 'How's your poorly friend?'

'She's much better, thank you,' Felicity replied. 'I hear your parents are back. I'm so pleased for you all.'

'Thanks,' Becky said.

'Hi, Felicity Steel Fist,' Joe said, hugging her, too.

'Hi, Joe Straight Arrow.'

'So, where's Uncle Percy?' Becky asked.

'He's just popped out,' Felicity replied. 'He'll be back soon.' She hesitated. 'I must say this is all rather mysterious.'

'Do you know what this is all about?' Becky asked.

'I don't have a clue,' Felicity replied. 'I really don't. He just asked me to meet him here and said it was important.'

'It's got something to do with a time traveller called Shala Abdul,' Joe said. 'Just before we went to get the Odin Horn, she came here and told him something important, but we don't know what. I'm guessin' you don't know either?'

'I don't,' Felicity replied simply. 'I know Shala visited him, but he didn't tell me what it was about. In fact, he was very guarded about it, which isn't like him at all. He's usually an open book.'

'Yeah,' Becky replied. 'He was weird after it happened.'

'Really weird,' Joe said.

At that moment, Uncle Percy entered the room. 'Ah, I thought I heard talking,' he said, forcing a smile.

'What's this all about, then?' Joe asked abruptly.

'Patient as ever, eh, Joe?'

'Sorry,' Joe replied. 'But we're all dying to know what's goin' on.'

'I understand,' Uncle Percy said. He took a few seconds to gather his thoughts. 'The thing is, I recently learned of something troubling, something about my family, and I needed time to process it. It's very personal, and very painful.' He exhaled.

'You're worrying me now, Percy,' Felicity said.

'Me, too,' Becky added. 'What's this all about?'

'I'm not sure where to start?' Uncle Percy said. 'Okay... you all know Shala Abdul came to see me within the last few weeks. Well, after the Wraith claimed to be my brother, Myron, she thought she'd take it on herself to do some detective work into my family's past. With this in mind, she did something I would never have thought to do, never had the courage to do.'

'What was that?' Joe asked.

'She travelled back in time to my mother's hospital room on the night of Myron's birth,' Uncle Percy said. 'She set up a nano-camera fitted with a hologramophonic recorder to capture all that transpired in that room while my mother was in hospital. Anyway, after my mother was released, Shala examined the footage, and she was stunned by what she saw. It was that footage she came here to show me, and that I shall now show you. Prepare yourself for a shock.'

Becky's stomach churned as Uncle Percy walked to a hologramophone and hit the play button.

Immediately, three lasers fused to generate a three-dimensional image of a private hospital room. A clock fixed to the wall read 11.56 p.m. A woman was fast asleep in a single bed, and beside her was a cot that contained a sleeping newborn baby.

'That's my mother, and my brother,' Uncle Percy said, his voice quivering slightly. 'He was only eight hours old at this point.'

Just then, the door opened, and a man stepped silently in,

carrying a package wrapped in a towel. The man was tall and lean, with raven-black hair and sallow, gaunt features.

Becky gasped. Even in the dimness, she'd recognise Emerson Drake anywhere.

His expression detached, Emerson Drake approached the cot and placed his bundle inside, before scooping up the sleeping baby. Then he carried the real Myron Halifax to the door and left.

As the hologramophone clicked off, Becky felt sick to her core.

'So let me get this straight,' Joe said. 'The Myron Halifax you knew, the one who became the Wraith, was planted there by Emerson Drake.'

'That's correct,' Uncle Percy said.

'Then who is the baby that Drake left?' Becky said. 'Who did he belong to originally?'

'I don't know.'

'And the Wraith isn't actually your brother at all?' Joe said.

'I've never met my real brother,' Uncle Percy said sadly. 'My parents never raised their true son.'

'That's awful,' Felicity said, her eyes dampening.

'It's sickening,' Becky said.

'That's Emerson Drake for you,' Uncle Percy said. 'Furthermore, when I investigated this situation more closely, I realised there were little clues throughout this house that pointed to what he'd done.'

'What sort of clues?' Becky asked.

'Well, for instance, my so-called brother's passion for his Hubert Herr Cuckoo clock.'

Instantly, Becky recalled the antique cuckoo clock in Myron Halifax's bedroom.

'How's that a clue?' Joe said.

'We all know what cuckoos do, don't we?' Uncle Percy said.

Becky understood immediately what he meant. 'They lay

their eggs in the nests of other birds,' she said, 'so someone else can raise their young.'

'Indeed. And that's precisely what's happened here,' Uncle Percy said, his voice unsteady. 'Emerson Drake planted a baby for someone else to raise – my poor, poor parents.'

Silence cloaked the room.

'He was a true monster,' Felicity said quietly.

'He was an evil freak of nature,' Joe said. 'I'm glad he's dead.'

'But why did Drake do it?' Becky asked.

'That I don't know,' Uncle Percy replied. 'All I can assume is that he hid a baby in my family, so he could control him in later life, perhaps to get to me.'

When Becky spoke next, it was in a small, brittle voice. 'And what do you think Drake did with your - your real brother?'

Uncle Percy swallowed a slow, pensive breath. 'I don't know. But that's obviously what matters most to me.'

'And what are you going to do, Percy?' Felicity asked.

'I'm not sure,' Uncle Percy replied. 'I really don't know how or where to start, but what I know is I have every intention of using all of my resources, my skills, my intellect to find my true brother, the real Myron Halifax. I don't know what will happen if I do, I don't know what form that journey will take, but I have to try at least.'

'And we'll help you,' Becky said resolutely.

'Definitely,' Joe said.

'We'll do everything we can,' Felicity said.

Uncle Percy gave a sad but determined smile. 'I never doubted any of you for a second.'

EPILOGUE

THE DARKNESS RETURNS

The Führerbunker, Berlin. 1954

I n an explosion of light witnessed by nobody, Heinrich
Müller appeared in a narrow corridor. Deep below the
ground, he stared at a heavy door that led to a room he
now knew as *The Greenhouse* – a sophisticated laboratory
constructed to mature '*hyperclones*', perfect anatomical replicas
of humans grown in record time.

Grudgingly, Müller inhaled the stale air. He disliked being
down here, in Adolf Hitler's Führerbunker, it held too many
bad memories of the end of the Second World War – memories
of horror, disgust and perhaps most of all... *failure*.

Staring down at the two objects in his hand – a bottle of
water and the Odin Horn – he wondered if they really could
achieve what the Wraith believed they could. But then, after all
the things he'd seen the Wraith accomplish, he knew better
than to doubt him.

And he never would.

Müller rapped twice on the door, which opened to reveal a

tall, well-built man in a snow-white suit, his head covered entirely by a dazzling golden mask.

'Herr Müller,' the Wraith said, staring at the horn and water. 'I see you were successful.'

'Of course, sir.'

There was a trace of nervous excitement in the Wraith's voice. 'Good. Come in.'

Müller entered see to a large white cylinder, over seven feet in length, in the room's centre. A vast network of wires connected it to a myriad of machines, computers, and devices. He also knew within it lay the most important hyperclone in history: *Emerson Drake.*

Suddenly, Müller's eyes were drawn to a female in the corner of the room bound to a chair by rope. She was shivering madly, her head covered with a burlap sack.

'As you can see, Heinrich, we have company,' the Wraith said in a chilling tone. He walked over to the woman and ripped off the sack.

A small, elderly Indian woman, her mouth sealed by silver-grey tape, peered at the brightly lit room through tear-ravaged eyes.

'Heinrich Müller meet Shala Abdul,' the Wraith said. 'Shala has recently stuck her nose into my business and has now found herself part of my future plans. Are you excited, Shala?'

Shala Abdul gave a terrified squeak.

'I'll take that as a *yes*,' the Wraith said. 'I'm afraid you really have no one else to blame. Bowen Hall has been under my watch for a very long time - remember, I used to live there, and I installed comprehensive, not to mention discreet surveillance a long time ago. And although you showing Percy Halifax the hologramophonic recording forced my hand, it was always my intention he found out about *my* origins. I also plan for him to find out about his real brother when the time is right. That will happen soon enough, in the form of a diverting game I've designed. Anyway, such matters are for the future.'

The Wraith approached a computer and hit a key. At once, a sharp *buzzing sound* scratched the air and an emerald light blinked wildly. The cylinder's outer casing slid open to reveal the naked man within.

Crippled with terror, Shala Abdul released a silent scream from behind her gag as she recognised Emerson Drake.

Ignoring her, the Wraith walked over to Müller and took the water and the horn. 'For now, Shala,' he said serenely, 'I invite you to witness a miracle – a true marvel born of science, innovation, and, I suppose, *magic.*' Unscrewing the bottle's cap, he poured its contents into the Odin Horn before walking over to the cylinder. Then he emptied the horn into a connecting tube, and soon water was flowing throughout the chamber, feeding Drake's lifeless body.

The hint of a smile formed on Müller's mouth.

'The truth is, Shala,' the Wraith purred, 'the end of the world you know is approaching, and from its ashes, a new earth shall be born. And that world will need a leader, an architect, an *allfather* – that world will need Emerson Drake.'

At that moment, the lights above flickered, and the cylinder trembled violently. Drake's body convulsed in ferocious spasms, his every muscle jerking and jolting as if injected by a colossal energy source. Then, as quickly as the convulsions started, they stopped.

All became as still as the grave.

And Emerson Drake's eyes opened.

The End

IF YOU ENJOYED the book I'd appreciate an Amazon review or star rating. They really help me. Thank you so much.

Carl

THE TIME HUNTERS will return in 'The Time Hunters and the Silent Child.'

IF YOU WOULD LIKE to receive the Carl Ashmore Newsletter then please SUBSCRIBE at www.carlashmore.com

A RECOMMENDATION

I would like to take this opportunity to recommend a middle-grade fantasy adventure book series I love. Written by my good friend and writing ally, Keith Robinson, it's the wonderful series: Island of Fog. Perfect for adults and children alike, if you like The Time Hunters books, I'm certain you'll enjoy these.

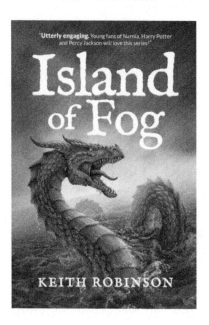

Made in the USA
Monee, IL
10 May 2023

33412283R00163